THE CRAZY DOCTOR

THE

ARIE VAN DER LUGT

translated from the Dutch by Alfred van Ameyden van Duym

CRAZY

DOCTOR

 RANDOM HOUSE   NEW YORK

THE CRAZY DOCTOR

1

A short distance from the village, in the center of the dark brown clay, lies the farm belonging to Christ-in-the-Wilderness, low upon the soil and lost on the wide plain. His is a humble farm, a long, white-plastered house with a thatched roof and a pigsty behind it. Abandoned there under the broad sky, it doesn't even really deserve the name of farm, so poor and shabby does it look in the grayness. But Christ-in-the-Wilderness, that uncouth farmer of grim mien, steps outside into the daylight. He bends his giant frame beneath the low door and clumps out to the farmyard. His wooden shoes clatter over the narrow doorstep that shines red-brown in the rain, and then the noise fades away as he crosses the threshing floor around the back to the pigsty, broken-down and seedy like everything else belonging to Christ-in-the-Wilderness, who is not numbered among the rich farmers of the region.

This is the abiding order of things here on the island: solid, rich farmers, their plump wives and insolent, screaming kids, and on the other hand, hungry farm hands with shaky cabins, hollow-eyed wives and spindly-legged youngsters. No one but farm hands here, in the eyes of the rich gentlemen farmers. But Christ-in-the-Wilderness, that strange, silent giant, doesn't believe it, because his heart is more proud than that of Arend de Griepert who's worth half a million, or Jan van Vliet who probably has about the same amount in his safe.

Christ-in-the-Wilderness! What a name for that towering man. It's not his real name, of course; none of the humble farm hands carries a "van" to his name like the big farmers do. Janus van Lent is called Trul and Jochem Sloor, Fatty. But why has Aai Bladder carried his nickname intact throughout his lifetime? Isn't he a farm hand? No, Christ-in-the-Wilderness he's called, because of his bushy beard and his disturbing bright eyes. . . . But that is too far-fetched. Who can explain where all these nicknames came from? They are there, that's all; they have developed in the course of time, become a part of the farm hands' heritage, and like everything else on the island, the people have adhered to them with the tenacity of a centuries-old tradition. The peasant works and thinks and dresses just as he did in his grandfather's time. He is ignorant of all the events that fashion the world beyond the island. The clock is about half a century behind; time seems to have stopped. It is a restful place.

Take Dr. Walrave, that small gentleman with the silver beard and top hat. He lived next door to the dominie in his tasteful house with the blue shutters and the geraniums in front of the windows. For as long as the farmers had known him he remained the same fine aristocrat. Only his beard changed color and his hair disappeared with the passing years. Perhaps, too, he walked a little more stoop-shouldered toward the end, and the old folk remembered that twice he'd had a new horse hitched to his tilbury. But otherwise there was no change worth mentioning during his fifty years of practice. Each morning he visited his most serious patients in his little carriage, in the same sequence, with the same regularity. He helped little souls into the world with a solemn, severe countenance, scarcely mumbling a word into his beard. He assisted souls out of the world in the same spirit, notifying the priest in time when they were Catholic, or the dominie when they were otherwise. Thus he performed his duty for half a century, in silent, undisturbed dignity, until one morning he was found dead in his carriage on the broad polder under the low sky. No one gave him a send-off, except perhaps his old mare, Vos, who stood trembling on the road bank, her faithful head bowed toward the earth. Moisture hung over the wet fields and absolute silence prevailed all around.

The two Briools discovered him in the fog, and the twin cobblers almost died of fright. They had set out early that morning, as they did every week, with a blue bag over their shoulders to collect farmers' shoes in need of repair. Kris—always the leader because he'd been born an hour earlier—old Kris led the way as he had done for three-quarters of a century, and behind him shuffled Teun, patiently chewing his quid.

"Well, what have we got here!" cried Kris. "Now what's that!" And he stopped, looking near-sightedly into the gray haze.

Teun lifted his pointed face like an evil old bird and stood still too. "Have a swig, Kris?" he asked meekly, and took from his pocket the flask of Schiedam that they faithfully took turns carrying until one of them got thirsty. But Kris shook his head and pointed ahead to the misty figure looming out of the grayness. Then Teun said, "Kris, isn't that Vos, the doctor's horse?"

"Yes, that's her all right!" said Kris. "That's Vos for sure!" Fraternally they continued ahead on their shaky legs, peering with each step into the fog. It was eerie, the motionless, somber stance of the horse in the stillness. When they came to Vos, the faithful beast lifted her head for a moment and looked at them pleadingly.

"That's funny," Kris said tremulously, "mighty funny. An empty carriage and no doctor in it. It's crazy, so far from the village with no farm nearby!"

"Maybe the doctor went behind a tree for a moment," Teun smirked nervously.

Kris gave him a reproachful look. There wasn't a tree to be seen, and it was very disrespectful to think something like that of the doctor. They shuffled around the little carriage a couple of times until Kris, with a queasy stomach, stepped hesitatingly onto the footboard. Teun gave him a boost and shot backwards in fright when Kris leaped from the box with a shout of anguish. They shuffled over to the road bank and sat trembling in the wet grass.

After they took a few tentative swigs from the gin flask, Teun turned his bird's profile to the tilbury and asked, "Is he there?"

"Below," whispered Kris, "with his legs almost up to his chin, his eyes wide open and his top hat in tatters!"

They were speechless with horror. Somewhere far away a cow mooed, and a small steamer bellowed hoarsely from the Dirty Hole. The strident cry sounded subdued across the dike and made the silence even more eerie.

Vos scratched her hind leg over the cobblestones, and with that sign the little Briools stood up, wiped off their wet pants and shuffled into the polder to look for help.

"It ain't right," philosophized Kris, his face assuming a righteous air. "It certainly ain't right, the way the doctor's lying. The man belongs on the coach box and not underneath it, and that's the truth!"

They shuffled along the road, bending their thin bodies into the breeze that was gradually dissipating the gray shreds of mist. They were no longer so aware that their trousers seats were so wet or that their shoes had taken in water. Contrary to their usual habit, they walked on side by side, because they had to solve their problems together. It was very bad, the way the doctor lay there in his coach. "Maybe he fainted," opined Kris, "or had a nervous attack!"

But Teun held out for murderous assault. Otherwise the doctor might have stayed home, he thought, but murderers don't dare come into a village when the constable lives so close to the doctor, and the new constable, he was a shrewd one.

So the Briool oldsters talked together on the long walk across the polder, where the disappearing mist bared the desolate emptiness of the flat fields. At the farm of Geert Molenaar they stopped and peered through the high spiked fence at the farm dog, who was barking furiously at them. Hesitatingly Kris lifted the knocker, but the dog began to yap more violently, baring his gleaming teeth, and they didn't dare to open the gate. They stood in front of the driveway entrance, shouting until Geert stuck his red head around the edge of the barn door.

"Nothing to repair!" he yelled, and back he went behind the inaccessible door.

Nonplussed, the Briool oldsters looked at each other and peered again through the picket fence at the dog, who pulled furiously at his chain. "Stay here!" ordered Kris. "He'll keep barking and then his master'll come back." They stood there shivering and rubbing their hands, and when the Cerberus had barked himself hoarse, the barn door clattered open. Geert appeared in the doorway in all his broadness. What kind of deviltry was this, to tease the dog from behind the fence? Down, Hector! The Briools were probably soused again! It was a pity, so early in the morning! And if they didn't get out of here quickly, he'd set the beast after them!

"Get away, you drunks, away from my yard!"

Finally Kris, sweating from the strain and anxiety, managed to get a word in. "The doctor!" he shouted. "The doctor's fainted! Over there!"

"Over there!" Teun ventured loudly, and busily stamping their feet and motioning with their arms, they managed to rouse Geert Molenaar's curiosity.

That one gave Hector a kick and clumped in his white wooden shoes to the gate. The oldsters were ready to jubilate, but Geert looked mad. He couldn't even understand half of it. "What're you talking about? What's the matter with the doctor? Now, hurry up. I've still got a lot to do!"

"Yes Sir! 'Course Sir! The doctor, over there! He's lying on the bottom of his coach—must be a nervous attack—and his eyes are wide open!" Kris gasped.

"And his hat's in tatters!" Teun added. "It might be a murder, so far from home!"

Geert Molenaar thought that over for awhile; then he mumbled a curse and ran to his threshing floor. "Siem! Hitch up the Brown One!" he roared into the stable. "Something's happened to the doctor!" His wife and maid came curiously. What was going on? "Nothing! Tend to your work! Those souses tell me the doctor's fainted, but I think they're drunk again!"

"No, Sir! Certainly not, Sir!" the oldsters bleated from behind the fence. "He's lying on the bottom of the carriage, and that's the truth."

With a loud noise, the milk cart came rattling around the corner of the stable and Siem stood on the driving box, big and hefty like his father, but with a grinning face and a mop of blond hair under his cap. The Brown One, sleek and fat, snorted in his harness and stopped, stamping impatiently, in front of the gate that Geert Molenaar swung open. "Giddyap! Get in the back, you, and if the doctor hasn't fainted I'll drag you through the cesspool!"

The oldsters meekly allowed themselves to be lifted by his strong hands and were plunked down on their wet behinds. Their spindly legs dangled over the loading flap, and they had to hang onto each other, so strongly did the Brown One pull when Geert jumped up on the driving box next to his son. What wild men they were, those Molenaars! With a dizzy speed the cart rushed off into the polder, back to the bend in the road, where the oldsters had left the doctor more than half an hour before. Geert sat on the box, and Siem clicked his tongue and lashed his whip over the gleaming hindquarters of the Brown One. The shivering Briools clung to each other, and then both fell back into the cart. "Now we're lying just like the doctor," Kris thought fleetingly, but before he could grin about it, Brown drew foaming to a standstill, and they found the doctor's coach just as they had left it.

Peering through his fingers, Teun dared to look for a moment at the doctor, but it was such a frightening sight, the old man crouching there motionless and staring at the low sky, that he closed his eyes with a feeble cry.

But Kris was braver. He stood up trembling in the milk gig and looked with great curiosity at Geert Molenaar, who jumped on the box of the carriage and began to tap and feel the body of Dr. Walrave. "Dead as a doornail!" he concluded. "If this wasn't a stroke, I'm no farmer!" Siem nodded gruffly. Father ought to know, but to him it was a miserable sight, the way the little doctor was looking at death with wonder in his eyes. He thought of the rabbit that he had recently killed with a blow of his flail. That little animal had looked at him just as pitifully.

"And his hat in tatters!" sighed Kris. "It's a shame, such a beautiful silk hat! What're we going to do now, Sir?"

Yes—what to do now? . . . Thoughtfully Geert Molenaar scratched under his cap. There was a lot of work to do on the farm, and the village was quite a distance. Of course, there would be a great hubbub when he came riding in with the dead doctor. The constable would be there and the priest and . . .

"You know what to do, Siem? Ride like greased lightning to the village and take the Briools along. Tell the whole story to the constable and be back before afternoon."

Siem nodded stiffly; he knew his father's word was law. But the oldsters protested, arguing that they didn't have the time, they had to call on farmers about their shoes. . . .

"What? No time?" roared Geert Molenaar balefully, as if they had done away with the doctor. "No time? A couple of miserable souses have no time? What about my own time? Me, an important farmer, taken away from my work by a couple of boozers? Get on with you! Hurry up!"

And not waiting for an answer, used to giving orders, he grabbed the Briools by the scruff of their necks and their wet seats and plunked them down together on the coach box. Siem wriggled between them, pulled at the reins and clicked his tongue. But Vos, accustomed to a gentler hand, stayed there trembling, with bowed head and a pleading look in her bulging eyes. Kris craftily tried to take advantage of this delay by climbing down quietly from the box, but the beastly strong Geert Molenaar swung him up on the box again with one hand and gave the frightened Vos such a slap on her behind that the old beast shot forward whinnying. Then he roared with laughter as the Briools, not prepared for this jolt, tumbled down for the second time that day and landed with cries of anguish on the floor of the carriage beside the dead doctor. They were so terrified that they lay there motionless, hands over their eyes, mumbling prayers interspersed with curses. Old Vos finally galloped away after the slap on her behind, and Siem of Geert Molenaar, ordinarily not easily upset, tumbled from the box and fell head over heels in the ditch.

Man alive, what consternation on the island! Geert Molenaar followed the lurching carriage open-mouthed as it rattled on one wheel around a curve in the road, toward the village.

The roar of laughter hadn't died on his lips when he slowly realized that now three corpses might come riding into the village. But how to overtake the runaway horse? For the present he had enough trouble with his son, who kept sliding back into the muddy ditch. He reached out his hand to Siem and pulled him on dry land. "This is a strange case!" he muttered. "A darn peculiar thing, Siem!"

Siem didn't say a word. He rubbed the mud out of his nose and ears and with chattering teeth climbed onto the box of the milk gig. Then Geert couldn't think of anything to do but lead

THE CRAZY DOCTOR 11

Brown by the bridle to the gate where the road was wide enough to turn the gig around. At a stiff trot they went to the house, since Siem had to have dry clothes, and the three in the coach could no longer be saved.

The three in the coach lay fraternally next to each other, all three of them equally quiet. Old Vos ran on with flecks of foam on her mouth and bloodshot eyes. Unhesitatingly she took all the well-known curves with the speed of mortal fear in her stamping feet. It was only the heaviness of the three old men that kept the little coach from overturning. The doctor lay in complete tranquillity, squeezed in the center, looking up with wonder, as though he couldn't understand it. Next to him lay the Briool oldsters, hands pressed hard to their eyes, heads on the back bench and their legs dangling above the box. They would have screamed like stuck pigs, but the horror of lying beside a corpse paralyzed their throats. What a nightmare! Kris grew hot all over, and Teun felt the cold sweat running down his cheeks, but mistaking it for tears, he started moaning softly. That gave Kris the courage to break his silence, and cautiously at first, so as not to frighten the doctor, but then louder and louder, he called to Siem with his eyes shut. "Siem! Not so fast, boy! Siem! Hold on a bit, fellow! We're lying in the back, Siem! Pretty soon we'll be on top of the doctor!"

Teun groaned like an echo, "Siem! Siem!" It sounded for awhile like a double jeremiad. Then, astonished when no answer came, Kris cautiously opened one eye a crack, only to close it quickly again with a shriek. What he saw shocked him so terribly that he thought he was about to faint. The sparse trees flew past his tear-stained eyes, and there was no Siem on the box! Christ almighty, what misery! What a horribly cruel adventure to experience in your old age! Together on the bottom of a coach with the dead doctor between them, and nobody on the box to drive the crazy horse.

Trembling, Kris began to prepare himself for a blessed death. Did the numberless flasks of gin weigh on his guilty soul? Or the endless string of curse words? The good Lord would have to pity him greatly, otherwise he'd land in hell upside down! Oh God! Who could have expected it in the morning! They had started out so pleasantly together, contented with the whole world, and childishly happy with their crock of old gin. But in the fog they had met death, waiting for them with his horse. And now they were driving together with the grim Reaper out of time into eternity. How cruel life could be!

Teun, in blessed ignorance of the end close at hand, gradually grew astonished at the silence. "Kris!" he whispered, "Kris, are you still there?"

"Still!" sobbed Kris. "And you? . . . Siem is no longer with us!"

With a frightened cry Teun sat half-up, but a hollow in the road took care of him. He tumbled back to his horizontal position, and only the velvet pillow on the back seat closed out eternity to Teun Briool for a short while.

But Christ-in-the-Wilderness, what is he doing? How peculiar he is. Christ-in-the-Wilderness is busy behind his farm, hammering one nail after another into the broken-down pigsty. He needs no inch rule and no plumb. He repairs his pigsty as he repairs his whole farm: big nails, heavy beams, a support here and a prop there. Thus everything keeps hanging together solidly, and no storm will harm it.

So built his grandfather and his father. So too builds Christ-in-the-Wilderness, and Driek, his giant son, will not do it differently.

The shaggy farmer is busy behind his house and the blows of his hammer reverberate in the stillness, when with still a louder noise the carriage of the doctor comes careening along his courtyard, with four dangling legs on the box.

"Four legs," says Christ-in-the-Wilderness, as he scratches his beard. "A small heap of legs and nothing else! Something strange here!" And as soon as he has decided for himself, the silent giant goes into action. He tears open the stable door, where his most precious possession is busy inside eating hay. "Satan, boy," he says as he grabs his short tan whip, "get a move on here, there's something crazy going on!"

Not a word is wasted, for Satan knows his master. The black stallion runs snorting into the young day. And Christ jumps on Satan's gleaming back and presses his wooden shoes into the flanks of the fiery animal, who flies up the road at the crack of the whip as if the bearded devil himself were at his heels. The hirsute head of Christ-in-the-Wilderness lies grimly upon Satan's neck. His beard is tangled with the horse's jet-black mane, but head to head, their eyes looking straight ahead into the distance, they storm on to the village that lies so terribly close.

The legs on the box don't interest the giant; in some way bodies and arms must be attached to them. What occupies him fiercely is the exciting race, the runaway horse, and which one will win, his fiery Satan or the scrawny nag of the doctor. He curses inwardly, cracks his whip like a pistol and presses his wooden shoes more firmly into the flanks of Satan, but old Vos has sprouted wings and drags the carriage on one wheel around the curve of the road.

"If the carriage turns over, all those inside will roll out on the cobblestones," thinks the giant, "and what's inside goes to hell! Hurry, Satan, faster!"

Satan does more than run, and before they reach the village street they are neck and neck: Satan elated with the excitement of the deadly contest, and the frantic Vos flecked with quivering, steaming foam. With one glance Christ-in-the-Wilderness has taken in the abominably rollicking situation; three old fellows neatly stretched out next to each other, the middle one staring wide-eyed and the two on the sides with their eyes tightly shut. Christ-in-the-Wilderness isn't surprised; he takes things as they come and acts by intuition according to the demands of the moment. Three old fellows lying in the carriage; they'll tumble into eternity if Vos gets it into her crazy head to make a sideways jump and wreck the coach! Whatever the cost, he must get ahead of the maddened horse and stop it in its tracks.

But the road is too narrow; Satan cannot pass without being forced off the soft shoulder into the ditch. The farmer curses in his beard, and a hot fury mounts in his head because of the decrepit horse that won't move over for his Satan. "Sakkerdie!" cries Christ-in-the-Wilderness. "Sakkerdie!" And in his unreasoned fury he cracks the whip again. But this frightens Vos even more, and with her utmost strength she jumps sideways just as the whinnying Satan is about to pass triumphantly. The coach creaks in all its hinges with the unexpected turn, the legs on the box flail to the side as if they were trying to kick each other, and with a vigorous jump Satan just manages to keep himself on the edge of the road.

If Christ-in-the-Wilderness has ever been mad in his life it is now, with this humiliation! Satan, Satan would have to give in, on account of that miserable carcass that's running on its last legs. He, Christ-in-the-Wilderness, the roughest, toughest farmer on the island, must bow before a dumb animal. A roar like that of a tormented beast tears out of his beard. His spontaneous desire to save three old men has suddenly degenerated into an unreasonable passion for triumph. He kicks Satan in the flanks until the stallion leaps forward whinnying, and the impossible happens; the horses come alongside each other. The grassy side of the road crumbles under Satan's sharp hooves, but they catch up. Neck and neck run the crazy horses, and Christ-in-the-Wilderness, reckless with fury, raises the heavy lead end of his mighty whip, hits Vos on the nose and above the eyes, leans sideways to re-establish Satan's precarious balance, and grasping the broken reins, roars at Vos to stand still, God almighty, when he orders it! But the old mare reacts like one possessed; she'll step aside for neither farmer nor Satan. Biting at her attackers, she almost snaps off Christ's fingers, and runs into the village as the victor. Victor? Who? What? Christ-in-the-

Wilderness, bursting with humiliation as he sees the blood dripping from his fingers, grasps the whip at the wrong end and slams the heavy lead down on the mare's neck. Vos in turn bites Satan with her spittle-covered mouth; now they're running neck and neck again. Then Christ's scourge descends like a poker on Vos' head. Twice, thrice it thunders down on the weary body, and the old mare, at the end of her strength, runs on for a little way, until the grim Reaper grins. . . .

Then a great shout from a frightened and dismayed crowd went up in the quiet village. Dirk de Krotekoker saw the tilbury first, since he lived at the edge of the village. Dirk opened his mouth and closed it with a snap. Then he ran outside and followed the carriage in his socks. Trien van Zelm and the Houtermans and Trul, they had all seen it at the same time when the doctor's carriage with only a bundle of legs on the box came thundering through the village. They looked at the carriage and at Christ-in-the-Wilderness, who seemed as stark mad as old Vos; the mare was biting at him, and received in turn a booming blow on her open mouth. Then the villagers looked at one another, uttered a simultaneous roar, and began their pursuit. People came running from all directions with a great deal of racket and gathered before the doctor's house, where Vos, after a final blow from the furious giant, sank to her knees and lay in convulsions, with wide-open mouth and a steaming body. Blood ran dark red out of her trembling nostrils, and dabs of foam were smeared over the old carcass. "Well!" growled Christ-in-the-Wilderness. "That's that!" And he tied Satan to the knocker of the rectory next door.

A cry of horror went up from the crowd when they saw three dead bodies lying in the forward-tilting broken carriage. But two of them began to move, and that made the spectacle even more grisly. A few women ran away shrieking, but the snot-noses and street urchins, who always have to be out in front for everything, pushed themselves forward and shouted enthusiastically that it was the Briools actually peering over the edge of the carriage.

The Briool oldsters! They began to touch each other hesitatingly, and weren't convinced they still had mortal bodies until Simon Sas, the constable, plowed his way through the crowd and asked them harshly what it was all about. The crowd grew silent as the oldsters crawled awkwardly out of the coach and pointed with a clumsy gesture to the doctor, who stubbornly persisted in his silent sprawling pose.

"Dead," said Kris.

"Dead as a herring," said Teun, "and we're still alive; I'd've never believed it!"

Dead . . . The villagers doffed their hats, and a soft, subdued mumbling went through the rows of people, as if only now could they believe the doctor was really dead.

Dead . . . It's the most serious word that a simple person can utter. Even the snot-noses stopped grinning, and a few fellows, respectful and grave, began to send the bystanders away. The women dropped out, bubbling with curiosity but obedient by nature, calling their children to order with a furtive box on the ears or a ringing slap on the buttocks. The circle became smaller. The women remained a short distance away, talking in low voices, and farther off were the gawking school children. In the small circle around the carriage stood Christ-in-the-Wilderness, somberly licking his broken fist, and the Briool oldsters, whimpering from overwrought nerves. Christ-in-the-Wilderness unhitched the dying Vos. The good beast did not survive her master long.

The priest came and the men stepped aside and told what they knew, which wasn't much, because the Briools couldn't be calmed down and were trying to outdo each other sobbing. The tension and their frightful experience had been too much for the little old fellows, and they sat now shoulder to shoulder on the stoop of the doctor's house, trying to find relief in the tears that fell freely at last.

The priest bent over the doctor, gave him absolution, and closed the eyes that were staring ahead in surprise. Then the constable dug the house key out of the doctor's pocket and Christ-in-the-Wilderness carried the little old body inside. A mere nothing in his heavy fists, a bit of fuzz that God had blown from his hand to somewhere in eternity, to the silent island where all days are the same, where time seems to stand still and only death is reminiscent of the slow passage of the years.

The priest went inside with Simon Sas, the constable, who was the only representative of power and dignity there.

Truike Pothuis came hobbling and moaning along. How fat she was, that Truike! For over thirty years she had managed the doctor's household, and today as she was running an errand, the women met her on the street with the news about the doctor. . . . O God, O God! Truike wondered how she'd get in. But she got there and closed the door with a bang on the curiosity seekers.

Now only the dying horse was worth looking at, except the sobbing Briools, who offered quite a spectacle themselves. But later on the Briools went inside their own cabin when the dominie told them they'd catch cold in their wet pants on the freestone stoop.

The Briools continued to cry inside. They'd have to be done with their tears before they could give Simon Sas a report of their adventures, and not until evening did the tale go through the village of how the doctor had been found. The men laughed, in spite of all the misery of the Briools' death ride and the cold plunge of Siem Molenaar.

Quiet had gradually returned to the village. Vos was killed by the constable with a real pistol and was dragged off by Christ-in-the-Wilderness to the skinner. Christ-in-the-Wilderness, that hirsute barbarian, who knows how to earn money anywhere, but will never get rich. . . . In front of the doctor's blinds now hung snow-white bed sheets, and a strange doctor had come from across the Meuse, very near to Rotterdam, to verify his colleague's death. He needn't have made the long trip, because nobody doubted it. But Simon Sas, who with his long sword was in fact the representative of the Crown, had wanted it, and so it happened. He might just as well have fetched a doctor from Beyerland or Middelharnis; they were much closer. But Simon was a queer one. He always did things differently from ordinary human beings, and often he was right too.

So the doctor arrived from across the Meuse, and just when everybody thought he was going to stay, he left as surreptitiously as he had come. That was no way to behave, because Griet of Teunis Trul would be having a baby any day now, and one of the Houtermans was very sick indeed. There was a soul here and there to help into the beyond, and seven or eight were on the decline. In the village they know everything about everybody, and they all agreed there was a crying need for a new doctor.

A new doctor . . . Village life had gone on in its everyday way, year in, year out, for centuries. Over the island hung the stillness of the broad plain. Life moved along its monotonous path. A new doctor . . . The labor pains started for Griet of Teunis Trul as the old doctor was being buried, and Antje Houterman was surely dying. It was high time for a new doctor to arrive. There was uneasiness throughout the village and the polder. Something was missing. How would it go by and by, when Griet's hour was nigh?

But everything always straightens itself out here on the island. With Griet's hour came the new doctor, but what an extraordinary character! What a crazy doctor!

2

A pale, watery sun peered between two banks of gray clouds and winked at the polder. A monotonous green plain saw it, a dreary plain, intersected from meadow to meadow by straight furrows and coldly gleaming ditches, and by the narrow road that wound itself to the village, where the small clump of houses crowded anxiously around the little church with its steeple and cross pointing upward like the warning finger of an old man.

Beyond lies the big dike against the Dirty Hole where the green-brown water ripples along, moving outward to somewhere under the sky. Thus the little watery sun saw the polder, lonely and melancholy. A tree here, and off in the distance another tree. A farm scattered here and there too, like a forgotten toy. A depressing silence reigned over everything. One scarcely dared to whisper, for fear of being pointed at with the warning finger: "That one's raised a racket."

No, silence prevails in the polder, all around the village. In the village itself there is some noise of living human beings, but it's muffled and subdued.

Then suddenly came a noise as cacophonous as a crackling curse at a Sunday-morning church service. This is the way it was: Dirk de Krotekoker, that liar with his thousand afflictions, had gone into the polder with Tys de Toeter and Driek, son of Christ-in-the-Wilderness. They were off to work for Geert Molenaar. He was very busy, that proud farmer. He said he had enough work for half the village. But half the village didn't show up. Of course not, they all knew Geert Molenaar for an avaricious devil. Only a few farm hands would work there, fellows who had nothing to do—Dirk de Krotekoker, who seemed to raise his houseful of children on wind and water, and Tys de Toeter, who sold peat and brown coal during the winter. They earned hardly any money, and were happy when they could make a hard half-dollar at Geert Molenaar's. Driek of Christ-in-the-Wilderness was with them too, not because he didn't have enough work, for the pigsty still had to be finished and there was always something to repair on his little house, but Dirk and Tys had asked him to come along, simply because they felt safer. The rich farmers didn't dare scold and curse Driek of Christ-in-the-Wilderness as they did the other farm hands, for Driek was a hothead, over six feet tall and strong and tough like his father. The fellow had a couple of coal shovels for hands! He could crack down a grown man whenever he cared to.

As many tales were told about Driek of Christ-in-the-Wilderness as about his father. Everyone was scared of him, except the girls, who had discovered that Black Driek the giant became a bashful fellow when they ogled him. No, Black Driek couldn't faze the girls. Their giggles frightened him, and his big feet lost plenty of ground when the girls were around.

The three farm hands went through the polder, Dirk and Tys, the two measly little fellows with their worried little faces, and Black Driek looming above them. They talked about the cold and the high cost of living and all the things a farm hand talks about. Driek chewed his cud and every ten paces he spit out a neat brown circlet on the road. Tys was pulling at his pipe. He walked with hunched-up shoulders, his pipe pointing straight ahead. But Dirk de Krotekoker did nothing but walk and shiver and grouse. He wasn't allowed to smoke any more by orders of the dead doctor, and he was also forbidden to chew or drink. He really wasn't allowed to do anything, because he had two floating kidneys and a knot in his appendix, he said. There was probably something wrong with his stomach too, and he had a buzzing in his ears, and one eye looked in another direction. If one were to believe Dr. Walrave, there was nothing right with Dirk de Krotekoker.

But the little doctor, who'd been in good shape, was now as dead as a doornail, and Dirk was still walking pleasantly over God's good earth in spite of all his ailments. Yes, he did shiver a bit, and sometimes everything went black before his crossed eye, but it might very well be from cold or hunger. In any case, Dirk consoled himself with the thought that he was still walking and the doctor wasn't. So did Tys de Toeter, and Black Driek, who was stepping along like a dragoon. It really couldn't be called walking, the way that fellow moved. Tys and Dirk could hardly keep up with him.

"A bit slower would be all right too," grumbled Dirk. "We're not twenty years old any longer!"

Black Driek slowed up and pointed ahead of him. "A motor-cycle!" he marveled. "I'll bet my head that's a motorcycle!"

They stopped in deep respect for the approaching machine. As it came toward them from the distance, it quickly grew from a dot into a sputtering motorcycle that finally flew past with a deafening roar.

"Christ almighty!" panted Dirk. "What an instrument of death! They would . . ."

"He's turning around!" shouted Black Driek, who had whirled about when the noise stopped abruptly.

And the motorcycle really turned around at Melis Eilers' place

and headed toward them slowly, exploding crazily. The three re-
treated to safety at the edge of the road and didn't know which
to admire more, the exploding machine or the hairy ape astride
it. Because that's what he was, an ape. They didn't get a good
look at him until the motorcycle came to a standstill with a final
ear-splitting bang. A red machine, stinking of gas and oil.

The man set his short legs on the ground and held his back-
firing motorcycle in balance. He wore faded corduroy trousers,
Driek saw, and white scrubbed wooden shoes filled with straw,
as the farmers did. And still he wasn't a farmer. He was an ape
with a friendly face and hairy hands that rested on the wide
handle bar. Driek looked admiringly at them. He'd seen fists,
but these . . . Astonished, he looked at the grinning face and
then down at the hands again. How strong they must be! They
were three times too big for the little fellow, and the blue veins
were stretched across them like cables. But it wasn't that alone
which made the hands look so powerfully strong. It was the long
hairs that curled thickly over the shirt sleeve at the wrist, black
and shiny and continuing up to the fingers.

He was still smiling friendlily, sitting on the saddle of his motorbike. He pushed his glasses up on his forehead and looked at
the farm hands as though he were having the time of his life.
Short and broad-shouldered he was, in his blue blouse. Jiminy,
wasn't the fellow freezing in that outfit? He didn't even shiver,
marveled Tys de Toeter, who was hopping from one wooden
shoe to the other, in cringing admiration for the hairy man who
began to undo the top button of his blouse.

Now it was Driek of Christ-in-the-Wilderness who first broke
the silence. He laid a heavy hand on the square shoulder of the
man and bent toward him. "Listen, mister, are you crack-
brained, to go riding around on that thing in the dead of winter?"

That was Driek, you see, as unmannered as he was rough.
Afraid of the girls, but as rude to the fellows as only a son of
Christ-in-the-Wilderness dared to be. But the unexpected hap-

pened. The hairy ape didn't get mad. Oh no, he drew his ugly snoot into a broad grin and looked at the giant. Then he laughed, his mouth wide open, without uttering a sound. A noiseless laughter. No, he certainly wasn't a beauty, that crazy man with the whopping hands. The three were dumbfounded and stared at him nonplussed. Black Driek felt fury mounting to his head as he realized he'd been badly taken in. The man certainly came from the city, even though he wore a peasant's costume. He thought he was dealing with yokels and he was going to make fun of them! He'd find out differently. "Kid your granny," growled Black Driek, "but don't smirk at us, or I'll beat your teeth down your throat!"

The mouth closed, but the sparkling eyes continued to look laughingly at Black Driek. The stranger was going to say something.

"Quite nice, the way you react!" spoke the hairy man, and he did his best to hide his citified speech. "I stop to get acquainted with you, admire your magnificent body, and try to start chatting with you. But when I smile you threaten me with murder and mayhem! Aren't we misunderstanding each other, my friend?"

"I'm not your friend," snarled Black Driek, "and your chatter leaves me cold! I don't like freaks who snigger when you tell them something!"

"Well, at least that's plain language!" laughed the stranger. "I like your kind of fellow."

"But I don't like your kind at all!" countered Black Driek, still furious because he thought he'd been laughed at.

The man on the motorcycle now grinned somewhat more discreetly and buttoned his blouse again. "It is a little chilly," he conceded. "Next time I'll put on my coat, if you'd like that better."

The three looked at him suspiciously. For a moment they were lost for words. That fellow has his nerve! Moreover, he didn't even seem to be exaggerating; he wasn't shivering from the cold, but sat there as comfortably as if it were midsummer.

"What I don't get is, how can a man sit on such a deathly conveyance in the middle of winter with only a thin blouse on!" yapped Tys, trembling with the cold.

"Training, dear friend," grinned the stranger, "nothing but training! A human being can harden himself to anything, but I must honestly admit I don't feel so warm. So I'd better get on quickly, because I think they're waiting for me in the village. Oh yes, now we're back where we started; I didn't turn around for nothing. Can you people tell me where Trul lives? Teunis Trul."

"Are you *permetassie?*" asked Dirk de Krotekoker, unbelievingly.

"Perme—what?" laughed the man.

"He means are you a relative!" Black Driek explained in a not too friendly manner.

"I didn't get that far yet," smiled the fellow, "but I'm going to help increase his family. I've been called for his wife."

Driek of Christ-in-the-Wilderness sputtered forth a brand-new curse, and the baffled farm hands glared at one another. "You don't mean to tell me . . ." Driek hesitated, "that you . . ."

"But it's the truth," grinned the man. "I haven't introduced myself!" And he grasped Driek's hand so hard that his joints cracked. "Dr. de Geus is my name; I've come to take the place of my deceased colleague, Walrave, and the letter I got told me they were in a hurry."

The three farm hands were dumfounded. The comparison between the aristocratic little doctor and this hirsute barbarian was so appalling that they hadn't been able to find words by the time Dr. de Geus had turned his motorcycle around and with a grin was making his explosive way to the village. "It ain't true!" said Tys de Toeter after awhile. "How can *that* be a doctor!" Black Driek peered after the disappearing death-engine and rubbed his right hand painfully. "It's an ape!" he growled. "And strong as a bear! What a fellow!" Dirk de Krotekoker slowly shook his head and worried about his afflictions. "Poor Griet!"

he muttered. "And she has such a hard time getting them as it is! The poor soul will never survive this!"

But Griet survived very well indeed.

When Dr. de Geus came to the small, low house on the Natte Doezel, he didn't have to ask the way; a few women neighbors with wide, frightened eyes stood in front of the door, and the alley was alive with the raw, hoarse cries that came through the windows. "So, here's where Vrouw Krul lives," the doctor grinned most pleasantly. He had leaned his motorcycle against the wall and gently pushed the women aside to enter.

"Eheheh! What do you want?" snapped Mie of Kees Kuit, who placed herself solidly in front of the door, hands on her haunches, chin stuck out and her sharp eyes riveted on the stranger's face. "You surely haven't the nerve to come in here now?"

"Let me by," smiled the fellow undisturbed. "I must get to Vrouw Trul."

"To Griet? Now? . . . Well isn't that something! The poor creature is about to die!"

Dr. de Geus lost his patience and his grin. Resolutely he pushed the woman aside and lifted the latch. He closed the door softly, took off his wooden shoes in the hall and stepped into the stuffy room where the crying sounded even harsher than outside.

Two women sat in a half-darkened corner, shaking their heads sadly and telling each other how bad it was with Griet again, and how the last time it had been nip and tuck whether she'd pull through or not. "Just quiet down, neighbor! Just you quiet down! Everything'll be all right in the end, woman! When they're ready to come, they come, but it's a cross to bear just the same, I tell you."

And they pursued their conversation in whispers, staring and shaking their heads. Truike Pothuis was there too, her fat carcass preventing all access to the dark bedstead. When you've kept house for the doctor for thirty years you know everything, you're almost a doctor yourself, judged the women neighbors, so they had fetched Trui, now that the doctor was no longer there. But Truike was wobbling in front of the bedstead and shaking her big head; all she could do was to use soothing words, for she had never witnessed such a difficult confinement in all her long years of practice.

What a situation! And now there was no doctor and the midwife had gone this morning to Beyerland! Teunis Trul, the skinny little farm hand, stood sniveling before the bedstead, grasping Griet's clammy hand in his calloused fist. Shivering in his great confusion, he implored the good Lord to help, God damn it all, He had to help, because what could a farm hand do with a houseful of kids when Mother pulls out? The good Lord ought to take pity on him and not abandon him.

And the good Lord took pity. He sends His angels in the strangest forms. This time it was a hairy man who came sneaking in in his stocking feet and mercilessly, but with a broad grin, shoved the women out the door and sent Truike Pothuis to the kitchen to get hot water, lots of hot water, and a couple of clean towels if possible. Didn't they have any? It didn't matter. The stranger knew the poverty of the farm hands. Snip! snip! And his thick fingers opened up the instrument bag on the table and there were towels, shining-clean. Then he took out his disinfectants and washed his hands in the small kitchen as if his life depended on it. The room smelled of disinfectant and something else when he entered with his small bottles and shining instruments. He grinned at the trembling Teun, who stared incredulously at his hairy arms.

"And now you're going to help me, Father," murmured the strangely quiet voice, as if he were addressing a small, frightened child. "Do exactly as I tell you. And don't stand there sniveling, but act like a grown-up fellow!"

His fine voice buzzed through the small room where everything had suddenly quieted down, and the bewildered people began to accept with happy surprise the new turn of events. Even Griet, exhausted from pain and misery, felt the soothing influence of his personality. A hairy ape? Nonsense! An angel sent by God. The savior Teun had prayed for so roughly, but so fervently and desperately, went about things in the quiet room with a smile and the great love of an expert for his work. He didn't say much, the strange fellow, but he breathed such an air of well-being into the room that the small, frightened folk swelled with confidence and throbbed with happy expectation of the miracle that was about to happen. The mood now was joyous and emotional, because the good Lord had sent His angel.

His angel! Who said that? Who had come upon that crazy thought? When Truike Pothuis looked out of the corner of her eye at the shaggy man bending over the bed, standing in his socks and smiling like a lovelorn young lad, when she began to realize that she'd taken that comical figure for a doctor. . . . When Truike compared him to the fine aristocrat she had served for thirty years . . .

But the man didn't allow any time for comparison. He did his work carefully and quickly. He hummed at his hard job, and his humming hung in the room like organ music that calmed Griet and steadied Teunis Trul's hands and compelled Truike Pothuis to carry water and warm towels with humility and wobble silently back and forth in industrious obedience. The woman on the bed lay pale as a corpse, but her dark, feverish eyes looked up at the smiling face of the crazy doctor who, in the glow of the lamp that Teunis held up with a steady hand, exorcised death from a worn-out woman and ushered in life for a small, pink Trul who immediately demanded her right with a feeble little cry. Another small mouth for Teunis Trul to fill in the future, a new little Trul, the eighth . . .

And Griet of Teunis Trul, upon hearing the tiny cry, began to weep passionately with pure joy and relief. She didn't make a comedy of it, the thin, tired woman. She pressed no kiss on the hairy hands of the crazy doctor, and she didn't even thank him for saving her life or for the life he'd gained. No, she sobbed and laughed and closed her eyes for sleep. God! how tired and grateful she was! How glad she was, the frail Griet!

Truike Pothuis was busy binding her taut with pins, and she grumbled with pleasure that everything had gone so well and smoothly and that she had so capably managed her first confinement since the doctor's death That proud Trui! The semidoctor! She chatted with Griet and pressed and pinned her in and had a fine time. But Griet didn't hear anything. She slept, exhausted and contented, with a smile on her yellowish face.

And in the kitchen the doctor was washing his hands while Teunis Trul, blabbering with happiness, swung the pump handle.

"You're a crazy doctor," he mumbled modestly. "I've never seen such a crazy devil my whole life long!"

"I know it," grinned de Geus, "I know it, friend. A little more water, please."

"Now you mustn't think me rude," the happy farm hand excused himself. "I only mean what I mean, get me? I mean to say, dressed just like us! No doctor's suit at all, and wooden shoes too!"

"What does a doctor's suit look like?" de Geus wanted to know. Teunis Trul stopped pumping and his expression grew thoughtful.

"Well, how'll I say it, Doctor? Our old doc wore a fine black suit, and he was a real gentleman, see?"

The doctor did understand. He dried his hands on a large red handkerchief because there was no towel left.

"And he had a beard," Teunis Trul continued, filling his pipe.

"I have a beard too," de Geus grinned, and scratched his stubbly chin. "You see, friend, clothes don't make the man."

"That's just what I wanted to say," Teunis replied, laughing heartily, "and many thanks for your help!" And from pure joy, because life was so wonderful again, he slapped the doctor on the shoulder.

"Nothing to thank me for!" said the doctor, and skinny Teunis got such a slap on his shoulder that he shrank back with a shout of pain.

"Hush!" whispered the doctor. "Your wife's asleep!" Teunis Trul didn't even hear him. He was sitting on the chair rubbing his burning shoulder and looking with holy respect at the crazy doctor and the curtain of jet-black hairs on those white arms. God! What a guy he was! What an ape too! And suddenly Teunis Trul discovered that the doctor's skull was as bald as a billiard ball, so of course the hair had to be on the rest of his body instead. The two sat laughing heartily about it until Truike Pothuis came rushing furiously into the kitchen with the warning that they'd wake up Griet with their heathenish noise.

Then the doctor got up, wiped his glasses, pulled down the sleeves of his blouse and was ready to leave. He pulled a funny beret over his naked skull and shook hands with Teunis Trul. "Trul, good friend, take care of yourself!"

When Teunis pulled back his hand with astonishment there was a rix-dollar in it. With an odd feeling in his belly he stared up at de Geus. But that one had already gotten into his wooden shoes, and locked the door softly behind him to Mie of Kees Kuit, ugly old Mie, who was still waiting and shivering in the cold. He blew her a kiss and then pushed his heavy motorcycle around the corner of the Natte Doezel, where he started the infernal machine with a great racket. Griet van Trul had to sleep. She'd hear enough noise when her seven offspring came home again.

Griet of Teunis Trul slept. Teunis was blubbering a little in the kitchen, holding the shiny rix-dollar in his honest hands.

And the crazy doctor—he went sputtering into the polder as

twilight began to fall, where somewhere a great and somber house stood with closed blinds and many broken roof tiles. The notary used to live there, Notary Bibber, but he had hanged himself from the rafters. It must have been a gruesome sight for the people who found him. But it was even more frightening afterward, when the house remained empty and the dead notary went spooking every night in the garret! That was no matter for laughter! At night all sorts of nasty noises resound through the big old house, and the villagers who have to pass it shake from fright. Didn't Tys de Toeter see the notary himself floating over the roof on a stormy night?

And how about Dirk de Krotekoker? He was coming back from Middelharnis late one evening in his dogcart. Dirk had been drinking, but he wasn't so befuddled that he failed to see the hanged notary, with only a shirt on and a rope around his neck, hopping around the haunted house! In his terror Dirk almost beat his dogs to death, but the dumb animals couldn't move a leg; the ghost held them back with his hanging rope! Dirk fainted from fright and only awakened when the cart stopped with a jerk in front of his house. The faithful beasts had apparently succeeded in biting through the enchanted rope, and it was to this fact alone that Dirk de Krotekoker attributed his rescue.

So all kinds of tales are told about the ghost house. No one dared to buy it, nobody dared pass it at night. A mysterious blue light shines through the small heart-shaped apertures in the window blinds. Then the hanged notary is walking with a lamp through his room. . . . Woe to the poor farm hand who falls into his clutches! He is hanged!

But the crazy doctor—and you could expect as much from that one—was rumbling toward the haunted house; he was going to disturb the rest of his dead uncle. Uncle Bibber hadn't left him his ghost house for nothing! . . .

The motorcycle stopped with an explosion in front of the carriage drive. The gate creaked upleasantly on its rusty hinges as it opened stiffly. A long, quiet carriage drive in the stillness of the polder. Keys jingled—a door squeaked open slowly and closed with a dull thud. The dead notary now has company.

Dr. de Geus stands all by himself in the ghost house—and grins.

3

It must have given de Geus a funny feeling when he stood there all by himself in the dark hallway of the haunted house, knowing that only his dead uncle was keeping him company. The dead notary . . . Perhaps Dr. de Geus didn't even think of that. He stood still for a moment in the dark and smiled. He felt in his pockets for matches to find his way in the dark and light the gas. He couldn't find the matches quickly enough, so he felt his way. The walls felt damp to his touch and his wooden shoes sounded hollow on the marble tiles. Somewhere on the left of the hallway must be the door to the front room and, further on, the one to the kitchen. Funny, how long a hallway can be in the dark.

The doctor stopped for a minute when he felt the doorpost. Somewhere in the upper part of the house there'd been a noise. Not just a noise, but a big, raw sound as if somebody were shrieking. De Geus thought this strange, and, absolutely quiet,

he stood listening in the dark with a grin of astonished surprise.
He held his breath and waited motionlessly. Outside the wind
was raging. The wind . . . "It must have been the wind," the
doctor concluded. "It can blow through this house at random."
But just as he found the doorknob and was ready to enter the
room he heard the same cry, rising into a shriek and then slowly
dying out. At the same moment an icy draft like a chilly breath
passed along his face.

"Blessed Uncle Bibber!" he smiled happily, and took off his
wooden shoes in order to investigate the phenomenon. The villagers didn't seem to be so far off the track, after all, in their fear
of the haunted house. . . .

"Ad astra," grinned de Geus, and like a cat he slunk upstairs.
Had the dead notary heard anything? It was frightfully quiet
upstairs, and even the wind seemed to hold its breath for a
moment, dumb with admiration for the daring of this man.
Halfway up the stairs the doctor listened for awhile, not because
of the silence, but because he found it fun to hear his own
breathing and, when he held his breath, the beating of his own
heart. . . . Now the wind started to howl again, and it wasn't
fun any longer.

"Avanti!" said the doctor, and up he went, supple as a cat. He
could have been the spook himself, so stealthily did he climb the
stairs that never seemed to end. Then above the clamor of the
wind, the long drawn-out, shrieking cry sounded again, much
more loud and alarming now.

"Monsieur le notaire a grand peur!" the doctor asserted with
satisfaction as he bounded up the last steps, where another dark
hallway awaited him, and another flight of stairs. His eyes gradually grew accustomed to the dark. The moonlight dropped
through the stained-glass window of the staircase and fell ob-
liquely across his feet. No longer did he feel the chilly breath of
the dead notary on his face and neck. No, it seemed as if dear
Uncle was blowing all his might from the stairs to the attic. A
cold chill went through the doctor's limbs and he drew his

blouse closer about him, shuddering, tempted to go downstairs to make a fire and light, and have some warmth and comfort in the abandoned country house. But there was something fiercely occupying his mind, something he wanted to know, something he *had* to know. What in thunder was that horrible shrieking that he had heard coming from upstairs in the dark? And who'd had the courage to blow in his face so bitter coldly?

Resolutely he slunk up the next flight of stairs which creaked nastily under his stocking feet. He had barely stuck his head above the stairs and peered around from beneath his bushy eyebrows when once again came the raw, shrieking cry, immediately followed by a heavy blow. Instinctively de Geus shrank down from a sense of imminent danger. But he had to laugh broadly and noiselessly, because the yell didn't come from the dead notary, nor from one of his poor victims. The doctor had climbed to the turret that rose above a corner of the haunted house, and a shaky door, screeching on its rusty hinges, clapped back and forth with the play of the high wind. The door flew open and a broad streak of moonlight streamed silvery-blue across the attic. The door banged shut and everything was pitch dark again.

Still Dr. de Geus had seen somebody in the streak of moonlight that sent a strange shiver along his spine. Someone was standing at the farthest end of the attic! It was a large, dark figure that stared at him motionlessly and silently, and seemed to be waiting for the intruder to explain himself. Surely not the dead notary? But no, he walked about in his white shirt with the noose around his scrawny neck. No, it couldn't be the notary, the doctor judged. The devil! The door should blow open again and then he could make things out. But the door didn't shriek and it didn't creak and it didn't fly open, now that the new master of the house required it, and the wind held its breath to await coming events. The intruder did likewise. He stood as still as the black figure, waiting to see if his lordship would move closer. After awhile, when nothing had happened, de Geus started the conversation.

"With whom have I the honor?" asked the doctor. The dark one didn't breathe a word; he stayed there, black and motionless.

"You're not Uncle Bibber," said the doctor, "because he was small and skinny, from what I've heard, and he usually appears in undress."

The black one was silent. This began to bore de Geus. He took one of the many boxes that were scattered around the attic. He balanced the box on his hairy fists, aimed with half-closed eyes, and threw the projectile directly at the black one. It was certainly a master throw. Without a death cry, without a last sob, the silent black creature collapsed. Or perhaps his cry had been deadened by the thunderous clatter of the box on the attic floor, or by the shrieking of the shaky door that suddenly flew open again. The wind roared around the roof and the moonlight flowed in like milk.

"Not a bad shot, eh?" grinned de Geus; and then in an admonishing tone: "Yes sir, that's what happens when you don't obey the rules of courtesy!"

"Bang!" said the door. The moonlight disappeared outside, and once more the crazy doctor was alone in the dark. But he had seen enough to go back downstairs, grinning and reassured. Uncle Bibber of blessed memory had been a man of peculiar habits, he'd been told. One of them was the collecting of old trophies from the Middle Ages, lances, swords and an occasional suit of rusty armor. The black fellow upstairs had jingled too much as he fell to disturb de Geus. Living folk don't jingle when they collapse. The doctor knew that through his own experience.

"Tomorrow we'll have the tower door nailed shut, and we'll clean up the attic," he decided, as he went down the stairs humming. It was devilishly inconvenient that Uncle Bibber hadn't installed electric light in his fortress. Now his dear nephew had to grope his way downstairs, since an investigation of his pockets brought no results, and there he was without matches in a strange dark house. Downstairs he found his way to the kitchen, where a chilly, sickening smell met him. There was no use groping for matches any longer, he thought, cursing when he banged into some heavy furniture; the house had been uninhabited for too long to expect any comfort from it. Back in the hallway he opened several doors but thought it unwise to enter, since one of them must lead to the cellar, and if he broke his neck there was no doctor in the neighborhood to repair the damage. He returned down the hallway and opened the first door to the left; that would at any rate lead to the front room. He'd hold a council of war there.

The wind howled profusely around the lonely wanderer who roamed the haunted house in his damp stocking feet. The shutters rattled rebelliously as he landed in the front room and kicked the door shut behind him with a curse. Such a hateful reception was enough to rob even de Geus of his good humor. He was stubbing his toes on everything; still, he didn't want to go into the room in his wooden shoes, for at least the thick carpet felt warm to his wet socks. He'd take them off; they were soaked through from the chilly dampness of the marble hallway. He sat on something soft that might have been an easy chair, and pulled off his socks. With a wicked swing they flew across the room and landed somewhere at random, to be left to dry.

"Stupid of me to get here at night!" he grumbled. Why couldn't that skinny female have waited half a day longer for her Trulletje? Then his trunks would have arrived, and he could have hired a cleaning woman who'd light the fire and cook a meal and . . . Still, the thought of little Trul almost put him in a good mood again. Buried in the easy chair, his naked feet almost disappearing in the thick rug, he mused for a short while about his first delivery, and how happy the skinny woman had been and how uproariously relieved her man. But a moment later he longed for a cigarette, and grew furious again because of those hellish matches. Driven by his intense desire he searched all his pockets again, knowing it was useless. He found nothing. Uttering a word that made the shocked wind hold its breath, he grabbed a chair to knock to smithereens in his senseless fury. Then the bell rang, and de Geus was frightened out of his wits. A ringing doorbell shouldn't frighten anyone; it's just a commonplace household noise. But when the ring reverberates through the deathly quiet of a haunted house and brutally reechoes through the marble hallway, when a bell rings that probably hasn't rung for months, well, that's a different story. He put the chair he'd wanted to destroy on a table, for the time being.

The bell rang again, somewhat more discreetly than before, and this time the doctor wasn't frightened. "A human being!" he grinned.. "Perhaps a man, and they usually carry matches!" Humming, he stepped into the hallway, but the song died on his lips when his bare feet touched the cold tiles. Still, he had to keep going, since he couldn't find his socks and the man might get impatient and run away with the matches! He shouted anxiously that he was coming to the door. A soft growl came from outside. Finally the door swung open and a black figure stood in the moonlight, not like the black silent one upstairs, but smaller and somewhat bent.

"I don't give a damn who you are, but if you've got matches on you, come on in," the doctor welcomed him.

The black one seemed to have them; at least, he came in and stuck out a skinny old man's hand to de Geus. "Father Conings," he said. "Welcome to my parish."

It was silent in the hall, until the door was closed more noisily, perhaps, than de Geus had intended. "I'm freezing here," he excused himself. "Where are the matches?"

Two groping hands found each other in the dark, and between them rattled the precious little box that would bring light. How funny, just an innocent box of matches! Flip, flop, flip, flop, a pair of naked feet went along the dark hallway, followed by the small shuffling steps of the priest. Then the doctor said, *"Fiat lux!"* and the priest said "Amen." The doctor cursed because he burned his fingers before he found the lamp.

"A little more to the left," said the priest.

"Damn!" said the doctor. "The mantle's gone!" and sheepishly the two men looked up at the gaselier that had no mantle.

When the little flame had died, the priest started talking rapidly to keep the doctor from swearing anew. "I thought a few things would be missing," he said. "That's why I hurried over, my friend. It's cold and dark here, and I heard you arrived helterskelter."

"It's a well-shaped little Trul," said de Geus, happy again at the memory of the whimpering, rosy little doll. "About six and a half pounds, I guess. Sit down, if you can find a chair. Oh wait, here's one on the table."

"We shouldn't sit here," decided the priest. "It's so dark and cold, and I can hear your stomach rumbling. My parsonage is very comfortable, heat and light and food. Don't you want to come along?"

There was silence for a moment; the temptation was great for the harassed doctor. Then he spoke sarcastically to the priest. "Do you know I'm not a Catholic? That I don't want to have anything to do with your dear Lord?"

"Did I ask you about that?" the priest smiled, but the doctor couldn't see the lines of pain around his old mouth.

"I'm a confirmed God-denier," de Geus bluffed.

"The greater my pleasure to meet you," laughed the priest, "since I've never met one before."

"Besides, I've lost my socks," the doctor said, with less conviction. "I threw them somewhere in the room."

"Then we'll both look for them, my friend, because eternity is close at hand."

The two men crawled around in the dark looking for the wet socks. The priest struck his head against the table and said, "Ouch! Here, I found one!" The doctor struck a few matches and discovered the other one. Shivering, he pulled them on his cold feet.

"Just remember that I don't pray before my meal," he warned the other, "and that I use a string of curses a yard long!"

"Shall we go?" asked the priest, in a friendly voice. "Bertha is waiting supper for us."

They went outside into the moonlight and the strong wind. The doctor locked the door and grabbed his motorcycle by the handle bars. "Is that machine coming along?" the priest said, frightened.

"What did you expect?" the doctor laughed, as he put on his beret. "We can't walk, can we?"

"All my life I have walked," sighed the priest, "and it's only a short distance from here to the village." Then the two started arguing about it, and since the priest was in a good humor and the doctor was irritated with his wet feet, the motor was started and the priest climbed, trembling with fear, on the explosive machine. They made an agreement to go slowly; the priest had prepared himself all life long for a blessed death, but was not, at the moment, inclined to depart. The doctor feelingly agreed with him and they went slowly, according to their bargain, but the old man commended his soul to God as he sat there, convinced that he was risking his life and would have to pay for it.

But he didn't have to. Our good Lord took pity on the reckless priest, for, a few minutes later, the infernal boneshaker came to a stop in front of the parsonage and the priest climbed off with shaking knees. To the right and the left, curtains were pulled aside, and a strip of yellowish light fell into the dark evening. Here and there the villagers opened their doors to satisfy their curiosity about the strange noise in front of the rectory. Then they recognized the priest, mumbled a greeting and quickly drew back into their houses, ashamed of their nosiness. But once inside under the oil lamp and next to the glowing stove, they put their heads together and said that the world was certainly topsy-turvy, and what would the dean say when he heard that the priest had climbed onto that engine of death behind the crazy doctor?

The crazy doctor . . . Everyone knew by now about the advent of the crazy doctor. The news wasn't an hour old before it sped through the village like a running fire. The farm hands had come back from Geert Molenaar and talked about their meeting with the queer creature. And Teunis Trul had dashed out to spread his great happiness throughout the village, and told about the doctor and his superhuman strength and the great ease with which he'd helped the eighth Trul into the world. Truike Pothuis had added her two cents and Mie of Kees Kuit and Dirk de Krotekoker, that champion liar, all, all of them had carried the fame of Dr. de Geus abroad, until far out into the polder it was known that a new doctor had arrived. But upon the soul of Christ, what a doctor! A cross between an ape and a clown, but the case of Griet of Teunis Trul spoke well for itself, because they all knew what hard times she'd gone through in the past!

Unconscious of the wagging tongues, they went inside, the little priest and the uncouth de Geus.

Bertha, as curious as the rest of them, had been peering behind the screens, and she met them in the hallway with widened eyes. She meant to take the priest's coat and worn hat, but, flabbergasted, she grasped a void, her eyes riveted on the hairy face. That one was grinning at her amiably, and winked one eye beneath his bushy eyebrows. . . . "Bertha, my daughter," said the priest, "this is Dr. de Geus, who's now living in his uncle's house, Notary Bibber of blessed memory."

"May the Lord have his soul!" said Bertha, as was the custom, but she really didn't mean it; she was too busy taking in the doctor. Then she preceded them into the room hesitatingly, looking around a few times as if she couldn't believe her eyes.

It was a large, somber room with oak paneling and heavy beams on the ceiling. A gas lamp rustled, and the bright light spread over the glistening white table that shone with gleaming cutlery and crystal. The doctor smelled the aroma of fried bacon and his empty stomach growled. But he laughed broadly at Bertha when she pulled up a chair for him, and he told the priest he had a jewel of a female in his house. A jewel of a female, that's what he said. Bertha sniffed audibly as she shuffled out of the room, and the priest bowed his silvery head under the lamplight and stared smilingly at his white hands. They were lean and very small; three of them would have fitted easily into the doctor's bear-paw.

"She's a fine figure of a woman," the priest agreed, when he was sure Bertha wasn't listening behind the door, "and she can cook magnificently."

"Still, I wouldn't care for her," grinned the doctor. "I'd rather have something, something . . ."

But Bertha's arrival with a pan of steaming soup cut off any further explanation. "Bertha, my daughter," said the doctor, who already felt quite at home near the roaring stove, "your soup smells murderous!"

"I'm not your daughter!" snapped Bertha, "and my soup smells like bouillon, with your kind permission." There was a silence. The priest sighed, the doctor scratched his bald pate, and Bertha, who didn't want to be his daughter, nevertheless served his soup.

"Thanks so much, puss!" said the doctor. Bertha stared at him with eyes of steel and tightened lips. Then, in a hot temper, she served the priest and shuffled out to the kitchen.

"Boom!" said the door.

"*Benedicamus Domino*," said the priest.

"Damn!" said the doctor as he burned his tongue. "This soup is hot as hell!"

"With all our united efforts we cannot extinguish hell," smiled the priest, "but this is easier." And when they had eaten their soup he poured red wine into the glasses. The wine sparkled under the lamplight.

"To your daughter!" said the crazy doctor, as he lifted his glass.

"To my new friend!" spoke the priest, as he looked reflectively at the red goblet that trembled for a moment in his hands. Then the doctor drank with his eyes closed and a sigh of contentment. The priest looked at him over his glass.

"A strange person," he mused, and his clear eyes shone with mirth, "a strange person, this new doctor. May God bless him!" They drank the wine like connoisseurs and enjoyed it in silence. Somewhere a clock ticked. The wind howled outside.

Then Bertha came again to spoil the mood, with rattling plates and a look of steel. She shattered the spell of contentment and peace, there under the lamplight. For a moment it was like a cold breath of wind in the room, as she busied herself with resentful hands and sullen face. But Bertha left, and peace returned with the floury potatoes and golden-yellow bacon.

"Still, she's a jewel of a female," sighed the priest, as if his friend had maintained the contrary. The doctor laughed without further comment. They ate and listened to the wind and the roaring stove and the quiet ticking of the clock's pendulum. Then the priest poured the sparkling wine again and the two men began to talk. First about the new little Trul; she had to be christened early in the morning.

"It's a great pity!" sighed de Geus. Not that the lamb had to be christened; after all, that was Teunis Trul's business. But that every year there was a new small Trul! When you couldn't take care of seven children already, how would you be able to feed ten or twelve later on?

The priest glared at him with his startlingly clear eyes. "I don't know that any of them has ever died of starvation!" he said.

"As if that were the only thing to be concerned about!" growled the doctor. "Kids need more than good food; they need a warm bed and blankets and clothes. They mustn't pine away or get sick! They must . . ."

"Did you see Teunis Trul's seven children?" interrupted the priest, his eyes shining. "There aren't any healthier or rosier-cheeked youngsters in the whole village!"

"Then they don't look like their father!" said the doctor, trying to make his point.

"And not like their mother either," the priest agreed. "Where
they get their rosy cheeks from, God only knows! No, my friend,
I never worry about the blessing of children; there are worse
things."

The silence weighed between them. They ended their meal,
and the priest bowed his old head over his white hands, and
prayed. The doctor looked at his sparse silvery hair and bony
hands and worn-out cassock. They would have to get used to
each other. Their opinions were so far apart. "There are worse
things," the priest had said, and the doctor felt what he was al-
luding to. He thought of the time when he himself folded his
hands in prayer before every meal. That was long ago, but it
couldn't be forgotten, nor talked away with a glass of wine and
a good cigar.

"There are worse things." And he thought of the woman who
lived somewhere in Holland in a large cold house, where hatred
had grown between two young people because no happy child's
laughter resounded in those stately rooms. . . .

Bertha came to clear the table, and the rough de Geus was no
longer amused with her sullen face. He sat opposite the priest in
an easy chair by the stove, silently smoking his cigar. The blue
smoke ringlets rose to the ceiling.

The priest began to speak. His voice rang warm and profound
through the room, and the doctor listened contentedly. The
priest talked about the villagers; about the farm hands and their
bitter poverty and the wealthy farmers of the polder. And about
Dirk de Krotekoker, that big liar, and the little Briools. He
talked about Christ-in-the-Wilderness and the Houtermans and
Giel de Tuut. They all had their turn, his good parishioners. He
talked about all of them, the little priest, and said something
good or funny about each one.

They laughed a lot that night. The priest laughed so loudly
that the room was filled with sound, and Bertha in the kitchen

was angry at the merriment she couldn't understand. The doctor laughed soundlessly but with no less enthusiasm; his stomach shook violently and his whole ugly face was a mask of joy. Afterward, they drank coffee and filled their pipes. And the little priest kept talking until the doctor was familiar with all the needs and problems of the village. Then they went outside into the strong wind for a breath of air. Bertha peered out from behind the screens in her nightgown and pointed at her forehead. "Stark crazy!" Then she fell back in anger on the bed, and the bed creaked in protest.

4

It wasn't right the way this new doctor behaved, all the villagers agreed on that. Oh, he was a bit queer, but that didn't matter; who wasn't? There are many strange people walking around on God's good earth, and the village knew at least six or seven of them who had a screw loose somewhere. But they were the ordinary funny people, like Christ-in-the-Wilderness and Dirk de Krotekoker and Keetje Houterman and Giel de Tuut, and a few more of the customary odd ones who are familiar sights in every village. They could afford the luxury of doing crazy things because they were just common folk. But a doctor is someone who's looked up to by our people, a learned man, one who's absorbed a lot of knowledge and can instill confidence, like the priest and the dominie and the dean.

The last doctor had been a gentleman from head to toe; he wore a top hat and a silver beard, and he drove in a carriage and talked like a gentleman from the city. Was it any wonder that the whole village shook its head in dismay when the new doctor put in his appearance? And the priest, what did he see in such a half-baked fellow? The villagers couldn't make head nor tail of it, but the next Sunday, when nine o'clock mass was over, the priest again stepped out into the polder to the haunted house. The doctor had sputtered past on his machine with his blue blouse flapping in the wind. Loudly he greeted the villagers, who timidly acknowledged his salutation and stared after him in dismay. Then a little later the priest came by. He hadn't dared to risk himself more than once on the boneshaker. The village would have been really shocked—in full daylight. As if they didn't know already that he'd ridden on it the other night! The news had made the rounds some time ago, and they were still gossiping about it.

All right then, but another morning the doctor was in his haunted house and along came the priest and a little later a large truck from somewhere beyond Rotterdam. Four hefty fellows jumped down and began hauling things off the truck. They hollered and cursed, but under the doctor's instructions everything was quickly carted into the house, and the priest stood there looking on and laughing and not saying a word about the swearing. Then they went inside, the doctor and the priest and the moving men, and everyone had a drink to celebrate the moving, and still another because it was so devilishly cold, and finally one more for the new little Trul, because the doctor still found it a curious case, that first case of his.

The villagers were looking on and enjoying the excitement, commenting to each other about this crazy moving. Not one decent piece of furniture had been carried inside, no cabinets and no easy chairs, not even a bed. But suddenly Dirk de Krotekoker realized that the haunted house must be full of the dead notary's furniture, and the doctor didn't have to buy any. All the white, shiny things those fellows had carried in and those big trunks and boxes, they must be the doctor's instruments and books and all the other stuff that a learned man requires.

"Learned man!" Tony van de Brant spat contemptuously on the grass. "First I'll have to see if he *is* a learned man," he growled. "Learned men wear top hats and they walk sedately and dress up! This funny bird wears corduroy pants and a blouse just like you and me! Where's he hiding his learning, then?"

Well, shrill Tony didn't reason very clearly, but it was pretty effective anyway, for the villagers didn't appreciate being delivered into the hands of a doctor without a top hat, a doctor wearing wooden shoes and corduroy pants and a blouse. How could you say "Yes, Doctor, sir" or "No, Doctor, sir" to a laborer in wooden shoes?

"I'll be damned if I will!" said Giel de Tuut, "I won't say 'Doctor, sir' to him. He doesn't look the part to me!"

"You don't have to," said Kobus the sexton, coming up to them. "The priest calls him 'that ape'."

They laughed surreptitiously about that, amazed that he made the remark so openly. A few looked slyly at the haunted house, wondering if the priest had heard it.

But the sexton stuck to his guns and said he'd heard it himself. "The priest came over here right after mass," he smirked, "and when I asked him if he didn't want a bite to eat before he left, he says, no, Kobus, says he, I must go and call on our new Escul-ape! Well, and then he went into the polder!"

"Ho, our new Escul-ape!" the men snickered. Escul-ape. He was certainly a strange beast; that wasn't such a bad discovery of the priest's. Or had the lazy sexton invented it, perhaps? . . . They looked at him suspiciously, but the moving men had climbed into their truck, and the driver sounded his horn so sharply that they all started. They gave the truck a wide berth, and the chugging monster disappeared into the polder. Now there wasn't much doing in front of the haunted house, and the little fellows returned to the village, arguing busily. At least it was a diversion for poor peasants who had no work during the bitter winter. They were the poorest of the poor, who had plenty of time to watch the moving and chatter excitedly about that phenomenon by the name of Dr. de Geus, who might as well be an Escul-ape or a crazy clown or an impostor.

"Just imagine if he really wasn't a doctor at all!" said Dirk de Krotekoker, and he thought fearfully of those thousand aches and ailments that could be fouled up by an incompetent who messed with their insides.

But the others laughed at him openly.

"Of course he's a doctor!" Jochem Sloor said decidedly. "Only he's a crazy doctor, and I for one know he's not going to mess with my body! If I get sick I'd rather crawl on my knees to Mid-delharnis than let that fellow in my house!"

They agreed with him warmly. Yes, that was their solution and, satisfied with the decision, they trudged into the village, shivering with the cold and firm in their agreement to boycott the doctor.

But Dirk de Krotekoker was the first to get sick, that very afternoon! Writhing with the pain in his guts, he was lying in bed when Driek of Christ-in-the-Wilderness came to fetch him for a job on the farm. Dirk's wife met him at the door with a worried face. Black Driek knew there was truoble.

"It's the old trouble again," said the wife disconsolately. "Dirk is ailing." Black Driek knew the symptoms; the whole village knew that Dirk de Krotekoker was held together by complaints, that several times a year he was about to die, and only got better when everyone had said the prayers for the dead at his bedside.

"Don't be silly," Black Driek comforted her as he walked beside her into the house. "Weeds don't die; Dirk wants to be waited on, and that's why he's the priest's most difficult customer."

But when Black Driek stood by Dirk's bedstead and saw the small fellow writhing and grimacing, his crossed eyes sunk in his yellow face, he hardly recognized his old friend. He scratched his head and muttered a curse. A few pale children sat in a frightened group, quieter than they'd probably been for months. They stared at each other silently with white faces. It's bad with Father again, they thought, and maybe this time he'll really die. It was a terrible thought, because they all loved Dirk, who was a splendid father. The mother started to cry in her apron and the children sniffled in response. This time it would really happen, and they were very frightened. The two smallest urchins didn't understand it at all, but they cried a bit because the older ones did. The little fellows listened in intense anxiety to the moaning from the bedstead, and they sobbed again and piously folded their soiled little fists as their mother had told them to do. And before the bedstead stood Driek of Christ-in-the-Wilderness, the large man that all schoolboys feared, but these youngsters weren't a bit afraid of him because he came so often to their father.

Driek stood in front of the bed with his hands in his pockets and stared dumbly at the little heap of misery that was called Dirk de Krotekoker.

"It won't be long now," moaned Dirk between two twinges of pain. "I'm done for, Driek! I'm pegging off for sure!"

"You've said that lots of times," mumbled Driek. "Weeds don't die, Dirk; don't worry, boy, they'll fix you up yet!"

"No, this time it's the end," the little fellow gasped. "They're floating again!" and he sank back on his blue bolster with a groan.

"Float . . . ? Who's floating?" Driek growled. But he didn't wait for Dirk's answer. The whole village knew that Dirk de Krotekoker had two floating kidneys which had brought him to the edge of the grave many times, but which always floated back into place again when the priest brought him the Holy Oil.

"You know what I'm going to do?" the black one promised generously. "I'll get the priest and it'll be over in no time."

Dirk mumbled something incoherently. His eyes sank back in his head and sweat appeared on his brow.

"Do you really think you should?' his wife asked timidly. "I don't have anything ready, and it'll have to run its course. This is only the beginning; it'll surely be a few weeks before he needs the priest."

Black Driek looked at her. Then his eyes wandered to the little man in the bedstead who lay there so miserably and didn't seem to be breathing.

"Well, we'll turn things around and start at the end," he growled. "Dirk won't be satisfied until the priest comes. I'll get the family together to say prayers, and he'll be walking on the street tomorrow, just you see!"

The plan only mildly interested Vrouw Krotekoker. Calling the family together for a fellow who'd been lazying on the road that very morning, and who perhaps would be drinking his pint again tomorrow . . . No, she thought, that was going a bit too far.

"Let's try the new doctor first," she said hesitatingly; "after all, Griet Trul pulled through just fine."

"Yes," reflected Black Driek, "that's all well and good, but Griet was having a baby and Dirk isn't, as far as I know."

The tortured Dirk wanted to put in a word then, but a new attack clamped his mouth shut. Instead he turned his crossed eyes and stretched out his hand in a gesture of refusal.

"You can drop dead," he groaned when he had regained his breath. "I don't want a crazy doctor to touch my body! I'd rather suffer than let that fellow mess around in my stomach! I'd rather . . ."

But no one ever learned what the small scared Dirk would rather do, because his chatter suddenly changed into a raucous cry. The children stiffened with fear and then burst out collectively into fresh wails. The mother slapped their ears nervously and then said with a strange tenderness that they ought to pray a bit, because this time it was very bad with the floating kidneys of Father Krotekoker. Dirk didn't make another sound, and Driek slunk quietly out the door.

"He's in bad shape again," he said to de Geus when that one

opened the door himself. The new doctor looked at him a moment and started to grin.

"What the hell are you laughing at?" Driek said angrily. "This time he'll go for sure, if you don't get there fast!"

De Geus didn't need any further explanation. He understood things quickly, and the priest had told him a great deal, especially about the taciturn Christ-in-the-Wilderness and his giant son.

"Then we better get going," he decided. "Where did it happen?"

A surprised look appeared on Black Driek's face.

"In bed, of course! Where do you think? It's Dirk de Krotekoker again."

That was enough for de Geus. He went inside humming and came back with his instrument bag. "Here, light one up," he smiled, and offered Black Driek a cigarette.

"Thanksmerci," said Driek, searching for matches, but suddenly the doctor pointed a shiny revolver at his head and fired, before the frightened Driek was able to jump aside. A small flame came from the revolver and they lit their cigarettes from it. Driek trembled a bit, and when he noticed this he grew furious. Did the fellow think he could make a fool of him? He'd have to get up earlier if he thought so. "You're a crazy crackpot!" Driek growled as he inhaled deeply.

"I've heard that often," smiled de Geus. "Are you coming along?"

"On that machine?" Driek snarled. "Not on my life!"

The doctor stared at him in surprise. "You're not afraid, are you?"

It was the wrong thing for the small man to say to the giant son of Christ-in-the-Wilderness. No one had dared say that to Black Driek without being punished for it, because it was his great pride that he'd never been known to be afraid. He threw the cigarette furiously on the grass and stalked arrogantly toward de Geus, who was starting his motorbike. He laughed at the angry face of the village giant, and yelled above the roar of the machine to jump on behind and show him the way. But what did Black Driek do? Purple with anger, he grabbed the death-wheel by its saddle and slung it with a jerk of his trembling fists into the road bank.

It was very quiet on the polder. The doctor bent down to pick up his machine and turned the throttle. The machine was silent. Then the short man advanced very slowly on Black Driek. They stood chest to chest. The small doctor scarcely came up to Driek's folded arms, but his usually friendly face was scowling.

"What do you mean by that bad boy's trick?" he snapped.

Black Driek didn't move. Looking below his crossed arms, he stared contemptuously at the doctor's beret. "Who do you think you are," he snarled, "to say that I'm afraid? Not a single fellow in the village would dare say it! Get along, or I'll crack you down."

Dr. de Geus had plenty of reason to be offended, but there was a sick person waiting for him who mightn't hold out much longer, according to the latest report. So he controlled his itching fists and suppressed his desire to knock the peasant yokel from the road. A patient like Dirk de Krotekoker was no small matter, and you couldn't let him croak just to satisfy your hurt pride.

"Serious patients come first," sighed de Geus, and pulled his motorbike away from the bank. He climbed on the saddle and started the motor. Driek of Christ-in-the-Wilderness watched all this with a grin of satisfaction.

"Who's afraid now," he snorted, "you or me? Take care, little fellow, that you don't abuse Driek Bladder again, or there'll have to be a new doctor, and this time a real one!"

De Geus looked up angrily. Then he pulled out his watch.

"I'll be back in fifteen minutes," he said in a friendly voice. "Wait for me here, will you?"

"Wait? What for?" growled the giant.

"To give you a hell of a beating, something your old man

should've done long ago!" smiled the little doctor. Black Driek uttered a curse and his fists swung through the air, but the motorbike belched gas and smoke from its exhaust and disappeared sputtering into the polder. Black Driek, the bruiser, the mighty colossus, watched the machine out of sight, trembling with rage. With a groan he tore the gate of the carriage drive from its hinges and threw it across the road. Then abruptly a great calmness came over him.

"In fifteen minutes!" he mumbled. "Good! In fifteen minutes! Then we'll have some fun!"

He picked up the cigarette he'd thrown on the grass in his anger. With folded arms he leaned against the pillar in front of the driveway and thoughtfully smoked the doctor's cigarette. He stood there, still as a frozen guard, in front of the haunted house, but an ominous glow shone in his eyes. . . .

A girl came walking along the road. She came from far away, out of the polder. Click-clack went her wooden shoes over the hard frozen dike, and from far off their noise could be heard in the still air. Her name was Mieke Dulk and she was about seventeen. She was a nice Mieke with dimples in her cheeks as well as on her white throat. The boys from the polder called her beautiful Mieke, and they were right, the enamored fools. Mieke had flirted with them all, because she was a passionate little thing for her age. But the girls had no hold on bashful Driek of Christ-in-the-Wilderness. They laughed at the way he blushed when they leered at him. They laughed at his big boy's bluff that he didn't care for girls, and they thought that he just couldn't find the words to say clever things.

But the beautiful Mieke now came walking out of the polder, and in the gray wintry day she was as fresh as a breeze in May. Of course she saw Black Driek standing there, though the big boob tried to hide himself behind the pillar of the driveway. Her dark eyes glinted mockingly when she saw him there, pretending indifference but reddening down to his neck as he chewed his cigarette butt. She came straight at him and her voice was like a song in the stillness.

"Boo! What's this? Not Black Driek himself for sure?"

"The same!" growled Driek, as he spat his butt into the bank of the road. He looked at the pretty girl before him. He saw the dimples on her white throat and the mocking lights in her eyes. He liked looking at her, and at the same time he hoped ardently that she'd walk on to the village. But Mieke did nothing of the sort. She looked at the iron gate that lay across the road, and then at Black Driek in astonishment.

"Did you manage that?"

He nodded curtly.

"Then you must be beastly strong!"

"That I am!" His chest expanded.

"Why?"

What kind of question was that for a girl to ask!

"Because it's me!" growled Driek.

Her burst of laughter resounded in the silence. "That's not what I mean, braggart! Why did you do it?"

Black Driek looked at her moist red lips from which her breath steamed, and at the wealth of her gold-blonde hair. She showed her sharp white little teeth as she laughed. That disturbed him even more.

He nodded toward the doctor's house. "That's why," he muttered, "and in a little while I'll beat the hell out of him, the skunk!"

Mieke's laugh died on her lips and a thoughtful line appeared above her nose. Her dark eyes shone with a malicious fire. "Just remember that I'll need him first!" she snapped. "Don't you touch him before I've seen him! Do you think I walked over the polder for nothing?"

Black Driek looked at her nonplussed. Here was a new complication to think about. This fresh and lively girl, this lovely creature came walking out of the polder because she wanted to see the crazy doctor. It was very strange. Pretty Mieke was a sweet thing, though evil tongues called her man-crazy, and now she had to talk to the doctor, and he had to give him a beating! In just a quarter of an hour, he'd told him, they'd fight, the two ruffians. What was more important, pretty Mieke or de Geus' insult? Driek had to make a difficult decision. "Why do you need the crazy doctor?" he asked roughly.

Mieke's eyes shone with malice again. "Oh, you'd like to know, eh? Well, it's none of your business! Are you a doctor?"

Driek was stuck with that one.

"He'll be here in fifteen minutes," he began hesitatingly, searching for words, "but first we're going to fight: I don't think there'll be much left of him for you, because I'll knock him to pieces, you see."

"You'll do what!" sneered Mieke. "As long as I'm here you won't touch the doctor!" She planted herself in front of him and lifted her angry little face. She almost had to stand on tiptoe to be able to look him furiously in the eye. She knew that Black Driek couldn't bear it when she looked straight at him; she knew the big yokel was just a bashful child up against a smart girl. But what did Black Driek do? He looked at the pretty thing in confusion and grew aware of the great silence around them and of her wet mouth so near his face. He saw her rosy cheeks and the yellow flame of her hair around her face. He saw so much loveliness there in the broad stillness of the lonely polder that in a sudden passion he drew the girl to him, almost crushing her in his strong arms, and kissed her wildly on her red lips, in the hollow of her throat and then again on the small mouth that started to shout furiously. Mieke resisted him with an angry strength and sudden fright. She kicked his shins and yelled. But his greedy mouth was on hers and his strong arms were around her, so she let things happen, still looking at him with surprise and thinking it funny that Black Driek should behave like this. Actually she wasn't too annoyed that the strongest man of the village was kissing her and that she drove him wild until she fled breathlessly from his arms. She sprang away from him giggling behind the heavy pillar of the driveway, waiting for him to pursue her. Then she'd slap his face or scratch his greedy lips until they bled. . . .

But Black Driek, did that big lummox enjoy it? When she stuck her head out beyond the pillar and looked for him with sparkling eyes, there he was, standing grumpily on the same spot and staring at her with a troubled angry glance as if she were the one who'd insulted him. She shivered a bit and involuntarily her eyes wandered over the road where the dusk of an early winter evening was falling. All the fun was gone for pretty Mieke, who knew she was alone with the ruffian. Her small mouth was set and she shuddered.

"Why do you stand there—like that?" she giggled rather lamely. "Don't look at me in that funny way!"

For a moment there was a shrill undertone of fear in her voice. She had lost her bravado.

Black Driek looked down and clenched his fists in his pockets. He stood there motionless, but in his head there was great confusion. "You ain't going to that fellow," he growled. "You've got no business there!"

"And why not?" Mieke wanted to know. "Is it any of your affair?" She came up to him calmly, now that she felt the danger was past, now that the big oaf stood there again like an awkward schoolboy, now that she knew he was helpless against her derisive laughter. "I'd like to know what you got to do with it. If I have to go to the doctor then I have to, ain't that so?"

Driek looked into her mocking eyes and he was lost. "I—I don't want you to," he muttered stubbornly, "because you shouldn't. . . . That fellow's not to be trusted, and I'll bust him in the nose!"

Her laughter danced like a glass marble through the silence, and Driek blushed down to his neck. He drew his head into his shoulders and walked back and forth, ashamed of the sorry figure he cut. He was miserable and furious at the same time. "I'll knock him to a pulp!" he said. "I'll . . ."

"You'll do nothing!" snapped Mieke, having gotten the upper hand again. "You'll wait decently until he's finished with me!"

"But then we'll fight it out!" Driek grumbled to save face. "When he's through with you he'll have had his last patient!"

Mieke nodded her head a bit. She'd let the boaster have his say. She felt chilly in the first evening freshness and hopped back and forth on her feet to keep warm.

"If he stays away much longer I'll have to go home in the dark," she sighed. "It's good the doctor lives here, otherwise I wouldn't dare go by the haunted house in the dark."

"Haunted house!" said Black Driek contemptuously, "the notary's dead and there's no such thing as ghosts!"

They were silent for a long while and they both stared at the old house, its gray shape looming against the dusk. From somewhere in the distance came the cry of a late bird; then there was silence—and the cold!

Dr. de Geus came roaring along in his customary noisy fashion. From a long way off they could hear his motor and see the pale light shining in front of his handle bars. He sat in his saddle, grinning as always and calm, as if there weren't a single cloud on his horizon. He halted his explosive machine in front of the barred gate that lay straight across the road. Then he swore a mighty oath, and Driek a mightier one as the hot anger rose in him again. The doctor looked at the giant and the giant at him, as if they wanted to tear each other apart, but the girl was there, the blonde girl with her flame-red sweater. She was cold and there was something she had to talk to the doctor about, the crazy doctor. . . . It mellowed him when he saw her standing there like that, tender and delicate in the light of his motorcycle. The beret slid from his bald pate and he greeted her politely. Out of the corner of his eye he saw Black Driek glaring at him, but not saying anything because of the girl.

"I'm Mieke," she said, "Mieke Dulk, and I want to talk to you. That's why I came way across the polder. We've got to talk before you start fighting; that hulky guy is strong as a bear, and if you're going to box it'll be all over and I'll have to go home."

The doctor looked at the girl and laughed. Then he glanced at Black Driek and saw the dark anger in his eyes.

"It's too bad," he said. "A serious patient comes first, you know."

Driek mumbled something.

"Well, serious, serious," giggled Mieke, "it ain't that bad; it's only, er . . ."

"Light a cigarette in the meantime," said de Geus, and he offered Black Driek his case. "You'll have to have a moment's patience, my friend."

Then the "friend" did something foolish and stupid. He knocked the cigarette case out of the doctor's hand. And the doctor did something violent, something unbelievably smart.

He stood up in his saddle and let him have it, so quickly and furiously that his hairy fist hit the chin of Black Driek with a dull report before anyone knew it was coming. Mieke let out a shriek, and Driek a muffled sigh. Then he lay full length across the road with closed eyes. It was a terrible sight in the dusk of evening. Mieke stared at him with wide eyes, and they were very beautiful then.

"There are limits," de Geus said amiably, "there are limits, my friend, and you transcended them."

The friend didn't say a word. He was knocked out. The doctor stepped over his motorbike and stood it against the bank of the road.

"A moment, miss," he said sweetly. "We'll go inside in a moment."

Mieke nodded silently. She stared with growing admiration at the strong doctor, who fastened the gate on its frozen hinges and slung the silent Driek over his shoulder like a bag of flour.

"May I go first?" smiled the grisly barbarian. He went first and Mieke followed him. . . . She followed the two strongest fellows she had ever known, but one was as limp as a dishrag and the other was actually whistling as he opened the door of the open house and invited her in with a grin. Pretty Mieke hesitated with one foot on the doorstep. She shivered and looked into the dark hallway. Then she looked at the grinning doctor and then at Black Driek, who hung across his shoulder as pale as a dead man. All this, combined with the darkness that was descending upon the haunted house, was too much for the frightened and excited Mieke. She suddenly forgot what she'd come for, and uttered a fierce cry that rang across the frozen polder. Then she shot out of her wooden shoes and ran as if the bearded devil himself were at her heels. The flame of her hair above the red sweater was the last the surprised doctor saw of her as she disappeared into the dusk. Bending down, he picked up the small wooden shoes and put them neatly together in front of the threshold. Then he slapped limp Driek familiarly on his buttocks and went inside with his sweet burden. Bang! said the door, and Uncle Bibber of blessed memory had company again. . . .

5

So life continues its slow process, its daily routine. Even the crazy doctor with all his funny tricks cannot change that. Hours and days and weeks follow one another with regularity. After the night comes morning, and upon the morning, day. Nothing exceptional happens. The farmer takes care of his animals and he does his chores in the barn, now that it's so bitter cold outside.

But after the day comes evening, bringing even in its obscurity some light to the life of the villagers. Then there is talk and gossip beneath the yellow lamplight and around the roaring stove. They fill their pipes and their tired, lazy voices fill the low-ceilinged room until they stretch out yawning and go to sleep. There is talk about the cattle and the cold and the poverty in the village. About the cattle. Of course, what else would a substantial farmer talk about? About the new doctor. In the small houses of the farm hands and day laborers they chatter about him. The important farmer has no time for that. He takes care of his cattle and worries about the frost that eats so deeply into the soil, and his money that must always be better invested. Those are the problems of the big farmer.

But the field workers and the day laborers, the common starvelings of the polder, they dispose of their time talking among themselves so they won't feel the hunger gnawing at their innards, and also because at the moment they're amused by the crazy antics of that doctor, the Escul-ape.

The young men, the lanky boys, they act differently. They go out of an evening and gather beneath the linden tree behind the church, even during this bitter cold. They have no worries because the girls come too, giggling, their eyes sparkling. There in the dark under the mighty tree the youths gather to make love, to laugh and joke in the night. But there aren't so many of them, for it's only a measly little village and the small ones must stay home at night, lying abed while the adolescents are beginning to live. They all like it under the old linden tree; in wintertime it's hard to find the lonely road to the polder in the dark, and they are shielded from the wind because the little church stands in the way with its flying buttresses and deep niches.

But this night they aren't courting or kidding. No, there are problems to be solved and plans to be laid that make the girls giggle nervously and the boys glow with pride in their daring. Driek of Christ-in-the-Wilderness is among them. He has a dirty plaster on his chin, but he doesn't want to tell how he got it. It would be very difficult for him to admit that de Geus, the new doctor, floored the village giant with one blow, and that later on he found himself on the threshold of the haunted house with a pair of small wooden shoes in his lap. He had certainly been too dizzy then to challenge de Geus anew, otherwise he wouldn't have shuffled so calmly into the polder, carrying in each pants pocket a small white wooden shoe. . . .

But now it was evening again and his dizziness had disappeared and the brute strength had returned to his muscular fists. Now there was fury about the dreadful humiliation; floored, right under the eyes of the liveliest girl from the polder! . . . Pretty Mieke was there too, and worked on Driek like a red rag on a bull, because she was giggling secretly at everything he said, and she didn't breathe a word about what had happened the previous night. She'd told none of the boys how dishonorably Black Driek had been knocked out. She was very grateful to him for bringing back her wooden shoes, or perhaps she remembered a little nostalgically how passionately he had grabbed her and kissed her on the lonely road. . . . Who knew what was going on in that fickle little head? You could never tell about such a strange pretty thing, certainly not when your name is Black Driek, and you're glad you can't be seen blushing in the dark. But Mieke stood there with a bunch of her girl friends and turned on the boys with great daring. "You haven't got the nerve!" teased Mieke. "None of you would dare to go into the polder and to the haunted house at night! When the clock strikes twelve you'll all have fled, 'cause you can't face the dead notary and the doctor!"

"Sure we can," boasted Gerrit Grauw. "There's nothing to it. We're not afraid of the spook, and I can floor the little doctor myself with my pinkie, what do you say, Driek?"

Driek spat contemptuously on the ground but wisely kept silent, because you could never tell about pretty Mieke.

"There's no daring to it," Siem of Geert Molenaar agreed with his friend. "We wouldn't beat it for twenty spooks; but they come so late, y'see, that's the trouble! At six in the morning it's already another day for me, and that's why I can't wait till midnight for a ghost that mightn't show up anyhow. As for de Geus, I'll take him on just as well in the middle of the day without waiting half the night in the cold for him. Let him call us yokels once more and I'll knock him to smithereens!"

"He certainly didn't do that!" said Sientje Kranebil timidly. "Not the doctor; he's much too nice to everybody for that."

"He did for sure!" cried Mieke to the contrary. "He said all the farmers in the village were yokels! Driek, didn't he say that?"

Black Driek growled his assent. He knew that Mieke lied till she was blue in the face, but did he dare say so to this excited bunch? He was much too happy that she hadn't told about his humiliation, and so he backed her up loyally. "That's exactly what he said," growled Black Driek. "He said that man for man we're yokels, and when I wanted to slap him down he'd already jumped on his motorbike and beaten it."

"That's just the way it was!" agreed Mieke, and she giggled so mysteriously as she said it that the black one felt himself blushing to the roots of his hair. It was a good thing it was so dark, otherwise he would have betrayed himself. That pretty Mieke with her crazy stories! Why was she trying to rouse and excite the boys? Did it please her to turn everyone against the doctor? First she came walking into the polder from half an hour's distance to see him, and now suddenly she was his bitterest enemy. What a fickle creature she was. You could never tell about her. The boys couldn't either. One evening she'd be courting one, and the next another, and when a boy would get the taste for it she'd let him stand there like a boob and then giggle and go away. Such a sweet Mieke. That fluttery little thing. But just the same the boys fell for it every time, because she was so pretty and such a desirable girl to flirt with for at least one evening. So all of them had been through it, some even two or three times, since free boys were a scarcity these days, and Mieke had to start anew every time she'd made the rounds. With the exception of Driek of Christ-in-the-Wilderness who'd never gone out with her of an evening, and it bothered her that he was too bashful to pay court to a girl and that yesterday in front of the haunted house he'd let her go after a flare of recklessness. That vexed her! "You can't get Driek of Christ-in-the-Wilderness!" teased her jealous girl friends. "He's not aware of any girl."

"Can't get! Can't get?" boasted Mieke. "I don't want him,

he's too uncouth for me; but if I wanted to, he'd crawl for me, even to—to the haunted house!" she said recklessly.

And that was how the whole miserable thing began. Geertje of Giel Pik, that skinny, yellowish girl, had gotten the idea.

"Want to bet," she said, "that you can't get Black Driek to the haunted house at night? All of 'em are too afraid to go!" And now the whole bunch stood under the linden tree, and it had become a question of prestige for pretty Mieke to prove that Driek would crawl, even to the haunted house at midnight, and for Black Driek to show that he wasn't afraid of the devil or his old mother either. Now they stood in the dark behind the little church and the words grew ever more violent in the wintry evening.

"Yokels, he calls you!" bawled Mieke. "Peasant yokels, that's what he said! You can ask Black Driek!"

"Well then, I'm surprised Driek Bladder let it go at that," Melissie Poker said quietly. "I wasn't there, so I needn't be so concerned, but if he'd said it to me . . ."

"I *won't* let it go at that!" barked Driek, high and mighty because of the girls' admiring glances, and seething again at the memory of his shame. "Do you think I'd let myself be insulted by that ape? If I meet him tomorrow he'll be a dead Escul-ape!"

"If you're a man you'll go right away!" challenged Mieke, enjoying herself thoroughly. "But you ought to take a few fellows along; you know how beastly strong the little doctor is!"

Eh, she'd almost made a slip of the tongue that time. Driek blushed and began talking loudly and excitedly lest the boys go into it further.

"All right, I'll go to the haunted house. Who wants to come along? You don't have to," he added hopefully. "I can handle it by myself! I'll go there and rattle his blinds, and when he comes out I'll say to him, you ape of a doctor, tell me now who's a yokel, you or me! And if he says you, I'll blow him out of this world!"

"And if he says me?" grinned Melissie Poker. General laughter under the linden tree.

"Then I'll let him live a while longer," smirked Driek. Thus it was decided. De Geus would have to watch his words! "Me" or "you" had now become the question of life or death for the Escul-ape. Melissie Poker and Bram de Bolk withdrew, not caring to give up their night's rest for the crazy doctor even if he *was* written off as dead. They went home and promised to be there for the funeral. Tys of Giel de Tuut and Gert of Kees Kuit felt the same way, and the girls thought it was too late to go into the polder so they left, giggling nervously. Only pretty Mieke— and it was to be expected of such a little witch—was all aflutter with impatience and was coming along to witness the slaughter, if one of the boys would bring her home when it was all over, since she lived at quite a distance into the polder and didn't dare walk alone past the haunted house at night. Driek generously took this task upon himself; after the account was settled he'd sweep up the remains of the doctor, clean his hands after accomplishing a dirty job, and deliver Mieke safely home. The big fellow decided it that way, and that was the way it would be.

The four of them headed for the polder. Only the most powerful of the village remained: Black Driek, Gerrit Grauw and Siem of Geert Molenaar, three fellows as big as trees. And between them walked pretty Mieke, slender and delicate, but proud in her knowledge that she was the instigator of the crazy scheme, that these big fellows ate out of her hand, so to speak, and did exactly what she wanted them to do. She was going to show Geertje of Giel Pik and all the girls of the village just whom the boys would go down on their hands and knees for! She'd show them that Mieke Dulk could do as she pleased with boys, even with Driek of Christ-in-the-Wilderness. For it had never really occurred to Mieke to slay the doctor like a pig. She only wanted to show them that, just for her sake, the big fellows would go to the haunted house late at night and would go home again like good boys when she ordered them to do so. Thus Mieke had figured it would happen. But the way through the polder is long and lonely. Could she help it that Siem and Gerrit, the excited pair she was bravely walking between, took turns kissing her? The two boys actually seemed drunk with joy and behaved as if they were going to a wedding instead of a funeral. They kissed her resoundingly and said foolish things and kissed her again and again. A mood of expectant glory stirred in their overheated heads and their fists started to itch. These fellows were so bold that pretty Mieke asked herself with a heavy heart how she could send them home like good boys. If only something didn't go wrong, there at the haunted house.

And it did go wrong, of course! Black Driek; was it jealousy of his bold friends or grim fury at his recent defeat that made him walk along by himself in that dark mood? Ignoring the gay suitors, he walked ahead of them, a little bent and grumbling to himself. His chunky figure was silhouetted against the road that was now feebly lighted by the moon. The powerful Driek walked alone in a rage and grew even more excited than the two boys who laughingly kissed the girl beneath the moon. He clenched his sinewy fists in his broad trousers pockets and glared straight ahead as if he were impatient to reach the haunted house.

The moon was mirrored in the frozen ditches all around and shimmered from the glazed tiles of the blessed notary's roof. A milky light hung over the turret and sparkled from the gilded weather vane. The four of them looked at it, at the roof drenched in moonlight and the somber building beneath it. The blinds of all the windows were closed but through the small heart-shaped apertures dripped a bit of yellow light. They knew that behind those blinds was Dr. de Geus in his solitude and courage, the hirsute, virile fellow who dared to live all alone in the dead notary's house, who went to bed there at night. . . .

Mieke shivered at the thought and started to giggle nervously. The boys looked at her in astonishment, startled from their own thoughts; they all felt real admiration for the doctor, who had the courage to do what they didn't dare to.

"Why do you stand there sniggering?" growled Black Driek.

Mieke laughed even more. Her laughter danced brightly in the clear frosty night, perhaps even reaching the driveway to the doctor's house; possibly that gay, light sound had penetrated the closed blinds.

"I'm laughing because of you," she chortled, " 'cause I got you into this! For me you walked into the polder and came to the haunted house, and Sientje Kranebil and Geertje of Giel Pik said you wouldn't do it for me!"

"We didn't do it for you," growled Driek. "We came on account of him there, and now he'll get the axe!" And grinding his teeth he started up the driveway.

"But it really ain't true at all!" shouted Mieke, scared and trembling at the thought of her rashness.

"It's true, all right," growled Driek over his shoulder, "and now he's going to get it! Come on, boys!"

The boys came, following their brave leader, heads sunk in their shoulders, fists clenched and their eyes directed fiercely at the haunted house. Mieke paled. Dear Lord! They'd believed her, the yokels! They'd swallowed her stuff like sweet cake and their courting had made them hot-headed and now they were going to murder the doctor! "It ain't true!" yelled Mieke anew, and breathing hard she followed the boys. "It ain't true, all that I said! It was just a joke and you mustn't do anything to him!"

"Shut up!" Driek hissed at her, for they were near the house now and carefully slunk closer to it.

Mieke's heart pulsed in her throat. "Dear Lord," she sighed, "dear Lord, how will it all end?" With heavily beating heart she stood halfway up the driveway, hoping ardently it was just a joke to the boys too, hoping they were teasing her and would turn around when they reached the house.

But the three didn't turn back. Noiselessly they slunk over the lawn and stopped on the doorstep in front of the heavy door. Black Driek was their leader; so he'd always been, thus he must remain. With a quick gesture of his hand he motioned to his two friends to stay where they were. Then he shot out of his wooden shoes and climbed soundlessly along the blind until he stood in the window frame and peered through one of the little lighted hearts. He didn't stand there for long. The next moment he was on the ground again and back with his comrades.

"We're too late," he grumbled disgruntedly. "We'll have to come back another time; the blackguard's standing there in his underwear." He didn't want to admit he'd been frightened by the black tufts of hair curling around the doctor's shirt and the naked strength of those athletic arms.

As though backing him up, the little hearts in the window-blinds grew dark. Why hell yes, de Geus must've gone to bed! There they stood, the three strong youths, staring in disenchantment at the haunted house wherein that crazy lonely doctor was surely climbing the stairs, humming as was his wont and unaware of any danger.

"There he goes!" whispered Gerrit Grauw, a trifle frightened. "If I didn't know better I'd say . . ."

"That it's the dead notary!" completed Siem of Geert Molenaar. All three of them looked up at the little stained-glass window of the staircase, along which a small dancing light moved, now and then disappearing behind a wall, flickering again at the next small window a bit higher up. Ever higher the light slid along the windows of the turret until it suddenly went out, and the haunted house lay darkened and lonely in the wide polder.

Silence reigned all around. From somewhere came the bark of a farm dog, and behind them the gravel crunched in the driveway. It was Mieke approaching hesitatingly, quivering with curiosity as to why the boys had abandoned their dark project. But they misinterpreted her arrival. They thought Mieke would laugh at them for losing their nerve. And they all started outdoing each other in boasting, for a dear, lively girl like Mieke works on your heart with her mocking glance.

"I don't give a damn if he wants to go to bed!" said Siem of Geert Molenaar sturdily. "If he called us yokels, then he'll have to bleed for it, even if he's in his underpants!"

"Righto!" grumbled Gerrit Grauw, because pretty Mieke was glaring at him. "That's it, Siem, he'll bleed, even in his undershirt!"

But Black Driek, the tyrant, had peered through the little heart of the window blind and seen the doctor standing in his shirt in all his naked strength. Rough Driek had been a bit frightened, and now he rubbed his chin thoughtfully where the dirty plaster was stuck. Whether from kindheartedness or something else, at any rate, the big fellow now suddenly opined that it really wasn't right, three strong men against one little doctor. They ought to go home and fight it out another day. Mieke was warmly of the same opinion and thought she had won her plea and that now she could send the boys home sweetly and would be taken home herself by the black one through the wide, still polder. But she hadn't counted on the fighting spirit of Siem and Gerrit. Now they were aroused and didn't want to go to bed before they avenged the insult.

"Three against one?" growled Siem of Geert Molenaar. "Who says three should fight against one? We'll ram in his door like we said, and when he comes downstairs he can decide which one he'll fight, because we're all three just as eager for it!"

It couldn't be avoided, and no matter if Mieke got excited and threatened and begged, or Driek tried to instill milder feelings against the poor little doctor, it was all to no avail. The emotions were aroused, the fists itched, there had to be a violent fight.

So there was a fight.

Siem of Geert Molenaar was the one who tied the bell on the cat. Suddenly he stepped over the crunching gravel with a great deal of noise, and pulled at the bell. Loudly it reverberated along the hollow marble hallway, and it sounded as if all the ghosts had broken loose at the same time. Mieke shivered with fright at what was about to happen and withdrew anxiously to the darkness of the driveway. There she waited with pounding heart for the course of events. The three youths loomed large in the moonlight. Everything was quiet. . . . Now it was Gerrit Grauw's turn to tear the bell from its chain, and again the haunted house reverberated with fierce-sounding noises. The sound hadn't died away when somewhere in the turret above a window was opened and the moon was mirrored on the bald pate of Dr. de Geus, who was peering down, garbed in his white shirt. "Who's there?"

"We are!"

"Who's we and what do you want, friend?"

"We ain't your friends! We're the yokels and we're here to fight!"

"A moment then, yokels, and I'll be downstairs!"

"Bang!" went the window, and the yokels looked at each other in some confusion. They hadn't expected such a quick answer. And how friendly the doctor had sounded from his turret! "A moment then, yokels, and I'll be downstairs!" Just as if they'd come calling on account of a very sick patient. Well, that moment would take some time, because before the doctor had dressed himself . . .

"We must be careful!" warned Driek. "Maybe he'll come with a pistol! He's got one!"

He didn't come with a pistol and the moment didn't last long; it didn't last at all, and before the black one had had his say, they heard the door chain rattle and de Geus stood on the threshold in his full glory, broadly grinning and almost naked. He was really a formidable sight in his light apparel that exposed a lot of black hair and made one suspect there was even more.

"Well, here I am," he grinned jovially. "So it's not friends this time?"

There was a moment of silence. They couldn't digest this so quickly. Then Siem Molenaar took a step forward.

"You called us yokels, eh?"

He stood large and threatening before the small man. The little doctor didn't blink.

"At first I called you my friends; that's my custom, so long as I'm in a good mood, but later on you seemed to insist on being called yokels, then I used the word, sure."

"It's fine talk," grumbled the furious Siem, "but we won't be pacified by that, understand? We came here to fight!"

"I'll be glad to oblige you!" smiled the little man. "Come inside, friends, it's rather chilly here in the doorway!"

"There are three of us, you understand!"

"My house is big enough!"

They entered, all three of them, and Dr. de Geus closed the door behind him humming, carefully fastened the chain and looked at the sturdy fellows who stood somewhat abashed in the vestibule, surprised at so much bravado. "Where'll it be?" sang the little man. "Here in the vestibule? Or no, let's go in the hall where there's more room and I can light the gas."

Plunketyplunk! went his bare feet ahead of them.

"Does one of you gentlemen have matches?" They had, and the four of them stood under the hissing light of the gas lamp.

"We're three against one," Gerrit Grauw hesitated, "that won't do; tell us who you want to fight!" Immediately he regretted his gracious gesture when he saw under the gaslight how the doctor's muscles bulged between the tufts of hair. For the love of Christ, if only that ape-man didn't pick him! But it wasn't that bad; the doctor was a devilishly sporting fellow.

"I think it's fun to take you three yokels on at the same time," he smiled. "The three of you! On guard!"

The next moment, the groaning Driek was grabbing at his stomach and the hallway trembled with a terrible racket. Dull, thumping blows were exchanged with lightning-like speed, and the four pent-up fellows, grunting and breathing hard, fought below the turret steps. Black Driek regained his composure with a furious yell and threw his full length upon the rough doctor, who had just parried a blow from Siem Molenaar and had put Gerrit Grauw out of battle with an uppercut. "That's number one!" growled the little man, who didn't have a friendly look any more, and then Driek hung on top of his shoulders bellowing like one possessed, but without much effect, as with a quick dive and a left hook the doctor regained the upper hand and flung the village giant against Siem Molennar, who was just fighting in. Now the doctor fought with his back against the wall. His chin creaked under the heavy blow that Black Driek threw, but he planted a naked foot in Driek's stomach, steadied himself against the wall, and attacked violently and deftly. The hallway resounded with a raw yell. Now only Siem Molenaar was left, but he produced the white flag and asked if he might withdraw undamaged because tomorrow was an early day and a girl was waiting outside for him who didn't dare go home alone such a long way through the polder.

The doctor was nursing his chin and looked with great satisfaction at the two prone figures on the floor. "*Vade in pace!*" he said to the trembling Siem. "Go in peace, you protector of virgins. Wait, I'll let the gentleman out!" And courteously he plunkplunked to the door which he held wide open for Siem Molenaar. With a sigh of relief the boy stepped outside, but just as he was passing the Escul-ape, the ruffian twisted his nose a bit as a teaser, so that the blood spouted from it.

"Greetings to the virgin!" grinned the crazy doctor. "And hold your handkerchief before your nose!"

The disconcerted Siem said something phenomenal, but he had the courage not to renew the battle. "Go to hell!" he said to Mieke, who asked him sympathetically how everything had gone. "There's two corpses lying there," he said, "but the doctor isn't one of them!" Then he took the trembling Mieke home, but all the long way through the polder he couldn't kiss her on account of his bloody nose.

And de Geus put a plaster here and a bandage there, speaking friendly words to the two dizzy fellows who looked at him out of drowsy eyes. Later he let them out.

"Come back tomorrow with six of you," he suggested. "That'll be nice. And thank you for a pleasant evening!"

So courteous was that crazy doctor . . .

6

But anyone who thinks that Dr. de Geus came to the village in the polder just to fight, doesn't hit the nail on the head at all. He only did some fighting from time to time, almost for pleasure, or because the yokels had challenged him, or perhaps to get rid of his surplus vitality. You can figure it out for yourself; a strong, gay fellow like that is really a rarity.

In the beginning the villagers thought it strange that no woman was around the haunted house. But still, they could understand it well enough; when even a brave man didn't dare go past the house at night, how could a woman stand to live there? After all, a haunted house was a haunted house.

But when the haunted house had been occupied for a few months, and the doctor still hadn't hanged himself and hadn't been murdered, the somber place gradually lost its sensational appeal. Then the villagers dared to go into the polder at night, and the haunted house became known as the home of the crazy doctor. The crazy doctor; the name stuck, in spite of the praise the poor peasants bestowed on him, in spite of the fact that the little giant proved to be a serious human being where his job was concerned. Hadn't he given every poor farm hand a fever thermometer and explained to them how to use it? The priest had recommended it and the dominie too, and both had said that such a thing could help in promoting good health.

If there's no fever you're not sick.

It was some time before they learned how or wanted to use such an odd thing, but the women got the drift of it first and saw its miraculous quality, registering all by itself to tell you whether you were very sick, or just a little, or not at all.

And here and there the doctor had distributed pocket lights to put over the dark bedsteads. Then there was more light in the beds during a confinement or a serious illness. He'd said even more, Dr. de Geus had. He said the field workers should wash themselves and teach their young 'uns to swim. Strange, that the priest agreed with him in all these things. You wouldn't expect it from such an old and little priest.

But Driek of Christ-in-the-Wilderness had smashed the thermometer and had stuck the pocket light in his pocket, and every time he passed the haunted house at night and knew that Dr. de Geus was at home, he let the beam shine on it.

Look, see how he lives in his peasant clothes all alone there in the big house, and yet he must be a very learned man; this is what the villagers couldn't understand. There was renewed talk every evening under the lamp and behind the stove. They mumbled about it and guessed there must be a big secret behind it all, behind that man and his strange behavior. Why didn't he wear decent clothes befitting a doctor? Because he couldn't afford it? Nonsense! A poor man doesn't distribute shiny guilders to needy wretches when he's called in for a difficult job. And a doctor who sends stiff bills to the miserly rich farmers so that they fall back scared and furious, a doctor like that isn't poor. For that's what de Geus had achieved, to the great joy of the poor farm hands and to the fury of the tight gentlemen farmers. Teunis Trul and Daantje de Bietser and Dirk de Krotekoker and quite a number of small folk with cabins full of kids and hunger in their eyes, he'd helped them all, with their growing broods or with guts tied in knots or with floating kidneys, for nothing. And along with that he gave them money surreptitiously, and as a result some of the starvelings tried to get a little bit sick when they were broke.

There was talk about how good the new doctor was, in spite of all his eccentricities, and how cheaply he exercised his practice. These things came to the ears of Sebus Lens. Sebus Lens was an old, ailing little fellow of about eighty. He was considered one of the richest farmers of the polder. But he was a nasty old Sebus; he was dying gradually but he wouldn't die because he was too miserly to give up his last free breath.

Sebus Lens, the old penny-pincher, listened with shining eyes to the stories about the new doctor and how cheaply he helped Dirk de Krotekoker to cure his floating kidneys. Sebus' bony claws curled greedily when he heard that Dirk had been given some money on top of that.

"It's the gospel truth, Sir!" boasted Dirk, who had come to Sebus to do a job. "It really happened. In the afternoon I was ready to give up the ghost, and toward evening that crazy doctor came with his miracle pills and I had to take one every hour. That night I was a little better, and in the morning I swallowed a dozen slices of bread, no joking, twelve breadpills! And guess what I had to pay? Nothing, not a red cent! Not that I had any, of course, but the best part of it was, he gave me a rix-dollar in the bargain! That's for the kids, says he, to get over their fright."

Well, Sebus Lens, the old miser, thought the world of Dirk de Krotekoker's story. He thought it was damn fine, and so tempting that he became ill that same evening and started to moan and groan.

"Now the old miser's going to croak at last," said the nephews and nieces hopefully. "Now we'll have our inheritance!"

And with that happy prospect they brushed their woolen clothes and the nieces polished their golden headpieces, because this time Uncle Sebus was really going to die. . . . But the old rascal didn't die, because he was counting on de Geus. Uncle Sebus crawled into bed in his woolen undies as if he were in great pain. But there was nothing the matter with the old joker as he peered through his eyebrows at the nephews and nieces who came running there hopefully in their Easter getups.

"Children, I'm almost done for," groaned Sebus. "I'm going to cross over to the other side!"

"That's very sad," cried the chorus of nephews and nieces, "and we'll pray for you and miss you when you're delivered from your pain!"

But the nephews meant it just as little as the nieces who were already leering around at the cabinet and all of Uncle Sebus' lovely things. The old fox took it all in, the croaking penny-pincher, and thought to himself, "Just wait, you scum, I'm going to fool you; I'll live another twenty years or more!"

So there was the whole hypocritical family gathering when the doctor entered with his bag of secret stuff.

"Dr. de Geus," he said, "pleased to meet you."

As if they didn't know. Sure, everybody in the village knew the crazy doctor! There was plenty of gossip about the eccentric fellow and the nephews and nieces had heard it too. But they also knew—and this disturbed them not a little—that in spite of his funny antics he was still a damn clever doctor. They weren't at all pleased about it. Just imagine, if he fixed up Uncle Sebus for another year or so, all their plans would be spoiled!

Dr. de Geus looked with a friendly grin at the collected relatives, looked at the moaning little fellow in the bedstead, and hummed as he took his instruments out of the bag. The sad relatives watched curiously as he produced a stethoscope, a set of lancets and other puzzling instruments, and laid everything out neatly on a white towel.

"It looks pretty bad, doesn't it?" one of the nephews asked, his voice trembling with apprehension that the doctor would say no.

"It looks very bad," said the doctor gaily. "He'll probably die." The faces of those present cleared up, and Sebus in his bed really began to perspire. His eyes bulging with fright, he stared at the clown, who was actually pulling a pair of rubber gloves over his huge fingers. What would happen to him now? Was he going to be skinned alive? Was the fellow ready to operate, while he was simulating his illness? . . . "And now all of you get out of the room," said the doctor with his friendliest smile. "I'll have to operate and none of you has the qualifications to assist me."

The three nieces uttered three shrieks and lifted their ample bodies to the room above. The four nephews followed in their stiff shirts, but the oldest couldn't bear to leave Uncle Sebus in the hands of that uncouth barbarian without first wishing him strength and a speedy recovery.

The old fellow mumbled something indistinguishable, but he thought to himself, "You're just like the others! You're all hoping I'll peg off, but I don't want to!" But whether he wanted to or not, the strange doctor continued calmly with his preparations for the slaughter, and Sebus Lens had worry aplenty. "It ain't that bad!" he said, trembling. "It's just a bad cold! I feel better already!"

Dr. de Geus grinned as he stood before the bedstead.

"I'll decide how bad it is, farmer! I'd keep quiet if I were you, because any excitement may hasten the end. Take off your shirt!"

"But, but I—I . . ." spluttered Sebus with mounting fear.

"Are you the doctor or am I?" Now it sounded much less pleasant. "I certainly ought to know what ails you! You're very sick, man! You have *morbus simulitis*, and you can die from that in a few hours if you don't do exactly what I tell you!"

Sebus' eyes bulged out of their sockets and in no time at all he had taken off his shirt, exposing his old man's body and waiting in fear for the things to come.

"It's awfully bad, my friend," muttered de Geus as he approached the bedstead and started feeling around Sebus Lens' flabby skin. "Secondary simulitis! It looks very bad for you!"

Cold sweat broke out on old Sebus.

"Is—is it that bad?" he shivered. "Will I—will I die from it?"

"We'll have to wait," said the doctor encouragingly. "I won't know until rigor mortis has set in. In other words, when you've crossed over to the other side," he added with a smile.

"But I don't want to cross over to the other side!" whimpered Sebus, who suddenly found life mighty attractive. "I still want to live another twenty years, do you understand? Twenty years and not a day less!"

Dr. de Geus looked reflectively into the distance and then started to clean Sebus' stomach with a wad of cotton and something wet that smelled of the hospital.

"Twenty years is a long time," mumbled the doctor, scratching his stubbly beard. "Oh well, let's wait and see if you pull through this operation. Then we'll know more about it."

He took a shiny lancet and pricked its point carefully in Sebus' belly-button.

"But I don't want to be operated on!" groaned the old miser. "I don't want to!"

"All right!" came the harsh answer. "Then we'll meet again somewhere in the beyond! Put your shirt back on!" And Dr. de Geus emphatically pulled off his rubber gloves and prepared to put his instruments away. It was so quiet behind him for a few seconds that it seemed as if Sebus had already departed for the beyond. Then there was a sniffling sound and the croaking of an old man's voice. "Doctor . . ."

De Geus turned around. "Are you still lying there naked? I thought you didn't want an operation!"

The bedstead creaked and Sebus sat up like a naked Buddha. "Do you know for sure that I, er—have simbelitus?"

The doctor closed his instrument bag and nodded seriously. "I'm never wrong in my diagnosis."

"And uh—that in a few hours—to the other side . . ."

"Oh, it won't be so bad," the doctor encouraged him warmly. "You lived like a true Christian, didn't you? Shall I fetch the dominie? Perhaps I can still . . ."

Emotion—or was it something else?—prevented the sensitive doctor from saying more, and with bowed head he walked to the door.

"But I don't want to die!" sniffled the little man in the bedstead. "Listen, Doctor! Listen just a minute!"

Dr. de Geus came back, sat down with a deep sigh next to the bed and waited.

"Can I only be cured through an operation, Doctor? Does it have to be?"

"Well, have to be, have to be . . . In our country, yes. Here we can only cure simulitis by a major operation, but I've heard about a learned colleague in Boston who cures the illness with powders."

"Get me those powders!" begged Sebus.

The doctor looked at him in surprise. "Do you know where Boston is?"

"I don't care, just get me those powders!" The frightened little farmer clung desperately to the small bit of life that was left him. "I've got to have them!" He breathed hard. "Even if they cost a guilder! Or even ten!"

Dr. de Geus grinned from ear to ear and slapped his thigh from pure joy.

"Even if they cost ten!" he moaned. "Fellow, what do you think my American colleagues are? Philanthropists? Do you realize those powders will have to be flown over if I still want to save your life, and that'll cost at least five hundred guilders?"

The old miser blanched. "Five—hundred." He stared at de

Geus with horror. "Five—hundred . . ." he whispered to himself, and tears appeared in his mean little eyes. For a few seconds he hesitated between the five hundred guilders and the beyond. But maybe he hadn't lived like a true Christian, because the beyond didn't appeal to him much, and suddenly he thought of his bulging safe and that it was better to live with five hundred guilders less than to depart for the beyond in possession of it. Still he wanted to bargain. With his sly eyes half-closed he whispered hoarsely, "Couldn't you make it a few ten spots less, doctor? After all, I'm only a poor farmer, and five hundred guilders is a heap of money."

"Of course, my friend," said Dr. de Geus, "I can cure you for half the money, even for less than half; after all, an operation isn't that expensive, only . . ."

"But I don't want to be cut open!" the little farmer broke in. "I want those powders and nothing else!"

He now felt the pain eating viciously into his body, and it certainly wasn't his imagination! The simbelitus was acting up terribly, and in his unholy fright Sebus Lens begged for the powders that would keep him for awhile from the beyond.

The doctor stood up with a satisfied grin. "So I'll order the powders from Boston."

"P-please!" hiccupped Sebus. "And tell them to hurry, or I'll peg off!" Perspiring with fright and imagined pain, he lay in the corner of his bedstead. He didn't even have enough courage any more to bargain for ten guilders less, so fearful was the miserly old farmer of his approaching demise.

De Geus tried to cheer him up with a few encouraging words, and promised he would hurry the order. He'd probably have the precious powders by the next evening. The Americans were damned quick when it concerned very sick patients. Sebus Lens should really keep up his spirit, for maybe he'd still be a bit alive when the powders arrived. Perhaps it wasn't very nice of the crazy doctor to tell all these stories, because now the skinny little farmer shrank with fear and waited in dread for the death he had seduced with his mockery. Ah, Lordy, Lordy! Life seemed so beautiful this morning when he'd listened eagerly to Dirk de Krotekoker who'd earned a rix-dollar, a hard silver rix-dollar by being sick, and now, now Sebus Lens, the most miserly farmer of the polder, lay there almost passing out and thankful that for five hundred guilders he could save his perishable body. Now he had a heavy attack of simbelitus, and could only hope that the expensive powders would arrive in time! That's the way old Nick punishes the scoffers who try to take him in; that's how death, tempted by a miserly farmer grasping for an easy rix-dollar, avenges itself.

The nephews and nieces came in good spirits to the sick room when they saw de Geus crossing the yard. They went down the stairs on tiptoe from the room above, because if their sugar uncle had been operated on he needed rest, perhaps even eternal rest. . . .

But they were bitterly disappointed, for the patient was peering with his mean little eyes, and saw their faces glowing with happy expectation. He took it upon himself to start the conversation, to the great shock of his loving relatives.

"Don't count on inheriting anything from me soon!" snarled the deathly ill Sebus. "Just hang up your best clothes for awhile, because you won't be able to celebrate yet; I'm not dead by a long shot!"

"So I see," said the leader of the relatives with not a little bitterness. "You look as if you had eternal life!"

"I only have a little simbelitus," said Sebus, trying to be grandiose, "and it'll pass with common powders."

"With powders?"

"Yes, with powders from Bois," sneered the old man, "and they cost five hundred guilders."

General consternation.

"And he calls them common powders!" shrieked niece Guurtje with alarm. "Uncle Sebus, you're not a complete fool, are you?"

"That's what you'd love, eh?" roared the simbelitus sufferer.

"No, Uncle Sebus ain't completely a fool, and that's why he'd rather buy the powders for five hundred guilders than have you grab for the cabinet! And now I need rest!"

He got his rest. Silently, but with embittered faces and deep disappointment in their greedy hearts, the family went homeward, the three nieces in their shiny gold and blood corals, the four nephews in their Sunday caps. They trudged in their white wooden shoes through the polder toward their huge farms. They didn't curse and they didn't use foul language, they were too pious for that, but nobody would dare to assert that they favored the new doctor. . . .

Moreover, de Geus had no need of their favor. He didn't count on the good hearts of the rich farmers, for he knew that with all their riches they were poor as lice because they had no love in their hearts. He simply speculated with their safes, making them a bit lighter for the benefit of the poor field workers.

And it came to pass that three months later, four powerfully wealthy farmers and twice as many fat farmers' wives began to suffer from all kinds of secret illnesses. It usually started with harmless symptoms, a bellyache from a too-greasy bone, or a hangover from too much to drink. Innocent things, one would venture. But look out! A mishap seems to hide in a small corner, but de Geus profited from it. And he made a goodly sum of money.

He made so much money that one day his motorbike no longer seemed good enough for him. Then he left for the city with his infernal machine and drove up to Rotterdam on a fine summer morning. The sun was working wonders with its light in the ditches on both sides of the polder road, and behind the dike the Dirty Hole lay stinking in the heat. The cattle stood lazily at the edge of the water and stared dumbly at the gay fellow who was singing to his heart's content as he came rumbling over the dike. The crazy doctor sang of summer sunlight and love, and his voice resounded over the flat polder, where everything now was gray-green or flowering. The horses in the meadow threw up their hindquarters and broke into a gay run, joyful in the warm summer sun but fearful of the explosive machine. But de Geus raced ever farther away until he disappeared singing behind the horizon at the end of the polder and seemed to ride beyond the world, so long did his trip last. Then he came to Rotterdam, where the people took him for a farmer although he had a small snake on his handle bars, the symbol of a physician.

He didn't stay in Rotterdam very long, because Teun Briool, the younger of the twins, as you know, was very ill and needed his care. That evening Dr. de Geus was already back in the village, but if Truike Pothuis hadn't providentially hung out over the lower part of her door and looked at the teeming village street, nobody would have known, since faithful Winnetou, that remarkable explosive machine, no longer announced the approach of the doctor with a fearful racket.

No, he was riding in a car! In a super-de luxe body with shining accessories, noiselessly suspended above the cobblestones. An auto the likes of which Truike Pothuis hadn't seen all her lifelong days, fiery red and sparkling with newness and nickel finishing. Inside was gray velvet or something of the kind, and there sat, no, floated, Dr. de Geus with his shirt open at his chest and a smile of blessed happiness on his face. He flung a jovial greeting at Truike Pothuis and asked her what she thought of it —his car, he meant. But all Truike could say was "Beh! Beh! Lordy, Lordy!" . . . And by the time she was over her first surprise the doctor had already given it the gas with his wooden shoe and the beautiful car went swinging along. "Lordy! Lordy! Save my soul!" sighed Truike Pothuis. "What a car! Ain't it a beauty, though! That crazy doctor must make an unholy amount of money, otherwise I don't know how he manages it!"

Well, the stone-rich farmers knew all about it, the skinflints who'd been mercilessly soaked, in a manner of speaking, so they could be delivered from all kinds of secret ailments. At any rate, as long as you could lengthen your life, a few hundred less in your bulging safe was preferable to an early death from a Latin ailment. They couldn't make him out, the rich farmers, those miserly penny-pinchers; still, they couldn't blame him for anything, because in the end it was they themselves who, moaning with fright or suffering from an imaginary ill, asked for the foreign pills and powders and ointments. De Geus never suggested they should take these expensive medicaments; the Dutch ones were good enough. But what can you do when you feel the throttling claw of death around your throat or somewhere in your belly? If the Dutch cure might take months, or even threatens to come too late? Life is beautiful, though a farmer has reasons for complaint, and even when your cupboard is filled with clinking coins, you're quite willing to part with some of them to get your health back in a few days' time.

That's how the rich farmers felt when they were in the doldrums and their relatives were already counting on their inheritance. But the farmers, at least those from the polder, were ingrates, because even though they begged for miracle drugs in their agony, they were scarcely in good health again before they scolded the doctor when they met him and growled as they realized that he'd bought that shiny car with their precious money. Who can tell what the truth was? There was so much gossip about the crazy doctor. But the small farm hands and the poor of the village loved and respected him. They said they'd never been so well taken care of, and they knew who to go to when they were at the end of their rope.

Didn't Griet of Teunis Trul drive her youngest about in a real perambulator, while she'd trudged all seven little Truls on her skinny arms through the village?

And Tys de Toeter? All his life he had walked around with a kind of gramophone shell that he would hold to his ear to hear with, and you had to holler into the tooter if you wanted to tell him anything. But now the little old fellow walked proudly around with a small silver knob in his pulled-down ear, and from that a black thread ran to his blouse in which he kept a small brown box, a secret machine, that must have been invented by one of the doctor's American colleagues. The marvelous little box hadn't cost Tys de Toeter a cent, and now people could talk to him the same as to everyone else. What a curious thing! Out of gratitude Tys gave the doctor his tooter, and de Geus used it as a funnel for his gasoline. So Tys didn't need to feel he'd gotten the marvelous ear-bell for nothing, because every time he met the doctor somewhere, Tys asked, "And Doctor, how's the tooter?"

And de Geus said, "Fine, my friend, it helps me a great deal; I'm really glad we made the exchange!"

But Tys, the old rascal, what did he do? He made a pitiful face and complained, "Yes, Doctor, I was really attached to that beautiful tooter. . . . Yes, when two people swap off, one is always the loser!" Then old Tys would blow his nose in a large red speckled handkerchief. And de Geus, who had probably paid a hundred guilders for Tys' ear-bell, reached in his back pocket and grinned, "There, you old thief! This is to compensate for the loss of your tooter." So crazy was our doctor that he gave even more money away, and so ungrateful was Tys de Toeter that he couldn't withstand the temptation to renew the game every time. . . .

Until one morning he was found stiff and dead in his bed. The doctor must surely have seen it coming, because he was always so kind to Tys and so tolerant of him, but the news hit the villagers like an unexpected thunderbolt. On the wings of the women's wagging tongues the grisly story flew through the village.

"Have you heard the news? Old Tys is dead!"

"Say, neighbor, did you know yet? Tys de Toeter had a stroke; he's all stiff and the little machine is still in his ear!"

"Neighbor, they say that Tys de Toeter has pulled out! The woman Mutje found him when she came to clean his house. He was all purple and the county constable is holding an inquest!"

So the lonely death of Tys de Toeter became known to the village; so the rumor went through the polder, where nothing ever happened and where each bit of news was eagerly grabbed to bring life to the drab surroundings, even if it was only the news of a dead person. . . .

A little later the crazy doctor went to old Tys' cabin. And still later the dominie arrived. The two of them met at the corpse of the little old fellow with his one small and one very large ear. They looked at one another, those two, and gauged each other's thoughts. Neither wanted to bow before the other, because they couldn't stand each other. One was a dominie and very religious, and the other a doctor and a mighty bad man who cursed terribly and was never seen in any kind of church. Which one of them would buckle under and politely say good morning? Neither of them. Each did his own work, the dominie for Tys' soul and the doctor for Tys' skinny body, for which little could be done.

"Lay 'im out, he's off to Nick," the doctor said after awhile to Truike Pothuis, who was busily fussing around. He was purposely rough because the dominie was watching him. But the dominie said disapprovingly, "Fie, man! He has passed on to a better life. The Lord has taken him unto Himself and he has gone into eternal blessedness."

"Indeed?" sneered the doctor. "How do you make that out?" The dominie directed his eyes skyward and kept his silence. He was a good man. The crazy doctor gathered his instruments together and went out. Then he uttered a very bad oath, because he was so wicked, but in the presence of death he always knew how to behave, out of respect for something that he couldn't fathom for all his knowledge.

Later on they were all present at Tys' funeral. The sun shone mercilessly on the black clothes, and the bonnets of the farmers' wives. That's a funny thing about our village; a living farm hand doesn't count, but once he's dead the whole polder population gathers there in their best togs and the women with their gold and blood corals. It's a feeling of unity they have that makes them help one another to the other side.

Standing next to the coffin was almost unbearable in the heat, but the dominie spoke eloquently for at least a quarter of an hour. Moreover, he had a fine voice. When the grave had been filled, the crazy doctor came carrying Tys' tooter. He pushed its narrow end into the fresh soil and in the wide opening he stuck a beautiful geranium. With that Tys de Toeter was completely out of this world, and all the villagers went home satisfied. It had been wonderful. . . .

7

He is a many-sided person, Dr. de Geus. He can do many things and he excels in almost everything. He is a devil of a fellow in curing the sick, cursing, making friends and enemies, fighting and singing, helping souls into this world, and repairing car tires. All this he accomplishes by himself, as though it were the only way to do it.

Because of his great loneliness the villagers thought that maybe he couldn't make love, didn't know how to impress a woman. But look out! Just let Dr. de Geus shift for himself; he knows his stuff and he lives his life as he pleases. Of course, all that is no excuse, for in all his kindness to the poor he's still a very bad man, a godless dog, and as we express it here, a cursing beast. Yet he never neglects to warn his great friend the priest when one of the few Roman villagers begins to act strangely, or his bitter enemy the dominie when somebody shows an inclination to leave for the beyond. No, they can say what they

want, those talkative, sensation-loving villagers, he never neglects his duty. In the middle of the night he's always ready for
his patients and the small souls he helps into the world with a
curse for his effort. He also grimly assists them out. He doesn't
believe in God at all, and as for the dominie, who's such a fine
human being, he could tear him apart, the villagers maintain.
But when he comes to Teun Briool at midnight and sees that
neither miracle potions nor Latin powders can help any
longer, he jumps into his luxurious car and drives to the dominie. He rings the good man out of his bed, and when the
dominie's wife sticks her head in curlers out of the window, he
says in a friendly voice, "Call your master, it's a far-gone case
again!" A moment later the dominie steps out into the night,
shivering with his coat collar turned up. Then the doctor politely holds his car door open and the dominie steps into the
back. They don't say a word to each other, the two learned
men. The dominie doesn't even ask where they're going. Usually he knows anyway, for he too knows the village through and
through and is acquainted with his flock everywhere in the polder.

Silently they drive through the night. The dominie sits in
back and is already saying a small prayer for Teun Briool, who
has started on his last trip. And in front de Geus holds the
steering wheel. He's growling to himself because old Teun
thought life was so jolly, and now he has to leave it. That's how
the two men are, the good dominie and the bad doctor, both
on their way to help that emaciated little Briool in his great
need.

And later on, when they've found out that he's a tough little
Briool who can fight off death for days, they step silently into
the car again, hostile but correct. Then the doctor delivers the
dominie to his wife and leaves without saying good-bye. How
did this hostility between the dominie and the doctor begin?
Oh, nobody knows the cause of it; perhaps the learned gentlemen don't know themselves. The doctor is so intuitive that

from the start he makes a man his bosom friend or his bitterest enemy. To do this he needs neither congeniality of spirit nor any visible reason. He has enemies before he knows or wants them. The same way with his friends. Now look at the priest. That holy, pious man, who has never allowed a bad word to cross his lips, sits night after night in de Geus' haunted house, or the doctor sits with him in his old parsonage. It's a funny thing, the way those two dissimilar people are attached to each other. Our little priest is a saint and the doctor is a bad 'un and a cursing beast. Is there any rhyme or reason to that?

Is the priest trying to convert the ruffian? Do they speak at night about the church, and God's holy articles? Twaddle! If the priest ever started on that, the friendship would soon be over; the doctor maintains rigidly he's a hardened atheist and doesn't want to hear anything about the church. Yes, it's all right so far as that little broken-down building is concerned, where the priest says mass every morning, the little building that's almost falling apart because all the rich farmers are Protestant and the poor farm hands can't keep it up. The doctor doesn't resent the small building; he's already given quite a bit of money to have it repaired, because the priest is his friend. But the Church with a large C, God's Church, that's the one he doesn't want to hear about, and it saddens the priest.

And still the two of them sit together nightly and laugh and talk and argue very seriously about learned things that the villagers wouldn't understand. Bertha, the priest's sour housekeeper, wouldn't either, though she does her utmost to spy on the man. They talk a lot in the language that the priest says mass in and which the doctor uses to make out his prescriptions and describe the American ailments. They also speak Dutch, for it would never do to tell a booming joke in Latin.

The priest should have known better than to get mixed up with a ruffian like Dr. de Geus. Convert? Ha! They drink beer from large mugs, holding them up against the lamplight and saying all kinds of crazy things. "*Ad fundum!*" says the crazy doctor, and he empties the whole pint in one swallow into his thirsty throat and wipes the foam from his stubbly beard with the back of his big hand. The priest sits there smiling a bit and drinks his beer in thoughtful small draughts. Then they fill their pipes and sit listening for quite awhile to the monotonous ticking of the clock. Until the doctor growls, because he has started to reflect, and this he doesn't want to do. He doesn't want to think. He only wants to be gay and have fun, for life is so short anyway, and when you're dead it'll be all over and you can only regret that you haven't enjoyed life more, haven't made the most of it.

The priest just sits there and lets him say those foolish things. Perhaps the priest is neglecting his duties terribly when he doesn't hush up that wicked man and doesn't interrupt to tell him how it is after death and that you have to be good to be happy in the hereafter.

No, the priest lets the doctor talk and talk and talk. Until the doctor suddenly pounds the table with fury: "Damn it all! You just let me talk all by myself tonight and you say nothing and simply sit there and nod yes and amen without knowing what I'm talking about!"

"Do you know yourself, friend?" asks the priest, and his small, clear eyes are fixed on the hot face of the doctor.

"Perhaps not," the other growls. "Maybe I'm just talking to convince myself."

You see, that's how honest Dr. de Geus is, notwithstanding all his badness. And a moment later he speaks again, more quietly now and with a bitter undertone in his voice.

"There was a time when I believed in God's goodness and His love for mankind. My old man used to laugh sardonically when we were on our little knees before a chair at night saying our evening prayers, and Mother would tell us all kinds of beautiful things. Mother was a brave soul, and if there were a merciful God He wouldn't have allowed the poor creature to be treated so badly; He wouldn't have let her be pestered into the grave at such an early age. Now you tell me!"

But the priest said nothing, he knew the doctor wouldn't be through with his story for quite awhile yet, and that tonight he needed to spit out all his gall at our dear Lord. And so they were silent for a time until the doctor started to talk anew.

"When I was small I didn't understand why Father always sneered and nagged Mother that way. I didn't know then that Father had learned to hate the church and the devout as only an embittered person can hate. But later on I grew to understand many things, when I myself had had the bitter experience of a loveless marriage and a God Who pays no attention to all your pleas.—Are you still listening, or are you thinking to yourself that I'm crazy anyway?"

"I'm listening, friend," said the priest in a strangely warm voice. "I'm listening carefully, and I know you're not crazy— and you must have suffered much in your loneliness. . . ."

"But damn it all, I'm not lonely! At least not the way one imagines a lonely person to be! I've always had a bunch of friends around me, and lady friends as well!"

"And still you were lonely, my friend!"

"Well, as far as that's concerned you may be right. . . . I was lonely in the midst of all that noisy to-do, and during some of the wildest parties I'd sometimes beat everything to pieces and kick all the scatterbrains out of my room, because all their crazy racket and their drunken behavior suddenly appeared insane to me and a sharp travesty of all that was good and noble in man. I was still so naïve then that I thought I was better than they were and was facing life honestly. Later on I understood that none of us is honest, that the whole world is a bunch of damned hypocrites! You aren't honest either; you sit there with a face that seems to be agreeing with me, and in your heart you're praying that sweet Jesus will convert me! That I'll fall on my knees and say, beat me, kick me, as You did then!"

A deep silence hung over them as de Geus stopped talking and stared bitterly at the floor. The priest didn't defend himself or say that God was good nevertheless. He knew it would fall on deaf ears that night. The doctor had much more need for his own loud, excited speech than for the priest's words that he couldn't believe anyway. The priest sat deep in his easy chair with bowed head and crying heart. The light of the lamp cast a yellow glow over his old head and slight figure. Perhaps his slender white hands trembled a little, but that didn't mean anything. Opposite him sat the embittered doctor, the man who was so gay during the day and had an encouraging word and a silver guilder for every poor wretch, but who now felt the sorrow stick in his throat, and couldn't be quiet till he'd first aired all his rancor.

The silence lasted for minutes. Then, almost whispering, the doctor began to talk again.

"There was one I never kicked out of my room, who stayed when the others had left scornfully. She stayed with me when I felt melancholy and disillusioned, and she bore my rudeness like a common slut. I know, I treated her badly, maybe because I loved her so much. . . ."

The doctor looked pensively ahead of him and his gaze grew milder as he thought of something that was clean and good to remember.

"She wasn't beautiful, Janette, but she reminded me of my mother, of her patience and quiet affection. Maybe that's what I hated most about her, that she never lost her temper, never flung insults in my face or drew my attention to my terrible behavior. I hated her servile nature, and still I liked her. . . . Our greatest stupidity was to marry, later on, even though we knew we didn't belong together, that our marriage would land on the rocks. . . ."

Short, scornful laughter sounded through the room. Or was it an outcry from a violent pain? The priest looked up frightened, but the doctor didn't notice it. He sat with his head in his big hands and continued hoarsely with his confession, the sad story of his miserable marriage. How he'd been hypocritically married in the church to keep up appearances, so that his wife, who'd been raised a Catholic, would be happy at least this one day.

"And she was happy," he said cynically. "God almighty, how happy the child was with me! Out of pure happiness she wanted to have a baby that first year. That was all right with me, but He prevented it!"

"He? . . ." The priest looked up with surprise.

"Now don't act as if you didn't understand me," sneered de Geus. "In those days I still believed in a good God, when the spirit moved me. I attacked Him with the mud of my arrogance, but when I needed Him I was cowardly enough to kneel in the dust and ask Him to bless my work. Ha! Blessing! I got just what I deserved, one blow after another! A wife who soon faded and grew sad in her loneliness. A practice where I helped kick one child after another into the world, and like a damned soul I began to think of birth as something denied to me! All the others propagated like rabbits, but our marriage stayed childless! I yearned for a child as much as my wife did, but year after year she got older and sadder and I grew more embittered. Then one day I said innocently that we were both damned, that our marriage was becoming a hell, as a punishment for my turning away from God. You see, I still believed that He could break or make a human being! So I became very devout in my own way. I went to church, I threw my money to the hungry huts, and I put the choice up to God: to show us His power, or otherwise to resign Himself to the idea that I thought Him dead and powerless."

"You challenged God!" said the priest, and for the first time his voice sounded more reproachful than sad.

"Yes, I challenged Him," de Geus answered hotly, "and if He had the power you people so willingly endow Him with, it would have been a small effort on His part to give us the child that would save our marriage and bring me crying back to Him!" And shrilly he added, "But He didn't do it, because He couldn't! He had no power over nature! Here He had a splendid opportunity to show His worth! He's nothing! One of your fictions to keep imbeciles well-behaved and to give significance and content to your life! God? Bah! I spit on that fairy tale."

He words sounded fierce in the stillness of the room, and an angry and indignant man was staring at the priest, who had gotten up slowly and leaned on the table. "Friend!" spoke the old man. "Friend . . ."

But it sounded like a sob, and the words didn't want to come. They couldn't shape and arrange themselves into the warm, eloquent argument the priest should be giving now. Everything was so confusing, and his old head felt dizzy with all the thoughts that assailed him and tumbled and overtook one another in his shocked mind. So he was silent after the rebellious outburst of the other man. Only sadness hung be-between them now, and the despair of the powerless priest. . . .

"Friend—" the old man stammered—"you can't—say that. . . ." And painfully he added, "You hurt me with, with those words—you must . . ." But a desperate gesture emphasized the priest's impotence. He had never been an orator, but he implored God with all his soul to give him the gift of eloquence. . . .

"Then show me where I'm wrong," cried the doctor, "or else go to hell; you shouldn't have anything to do with my kind of animal! When I first met you I told you that I wanted nothing to do with sweet Jesus, that I'm an atheist! You didn't believe me! Now you'll have to believe me!"

The priest took a step forward with difficulty and laid the trembling hands on the doctor's shoulders. De Geus glanced up at him. He looked rebelliously into the faithful eyes that shone moistly in the light of the lamp.

"It's all right, friend, I'll believe you," whispered the priest.

"I'll honestly believe you're an atheist—as soon as you believe it yourself!"

For a long while they looked deep into each other's eyes. Then the little priest gave a tired smile, and the doctor bowed his head. In spite of all his rebelliousness he didn't have the courage to look into the serious eyes and say again that he really was an atheist. No, the doctor rested his head in his hands and sat very quietly. And the priest went back again to his chair, sad but not defeated. Everything would turn out all right with that unhappy man. God's hand had lain heavily upon him, but still hadn't crushed him. The strong, furious de Geus needed greater blows before he'd bow humbly before a God Whose existence he could not obliterate with all his learning.

"Why did He kick us that way, then, if He exists and means so well with human beings?" growled the doctor without looking up. "Why did He plague us and help our marriage go to hell when we might have been so happy?"

His voice was soft now, almost a muffled sob in the stillness of the room. Gone was the bold arrogance he had shown when he hurled his insults at the heavens. The doctor was tired. But he didn't want to give up the fight, and still resisted, like a sniveling child who wants to be in the right. The priest watched him sitting there, bowed and disconsolate because of his ardent longing that had not been realized. "A child is the most beautiful gift God can give to human beings," mumbled the priest, looking shyly at his friend and anxiously groping for words that wouldn't upset the doctor and make him spit fire again. But the doctor didn't move. He sat there in his dull defeat, letting the words flow over him without wanting to understand their meaning.

"The child is not created by the will of two people alone. . . . God must give His blessing to it. And birth is always such a miracle," stammered the priest, and he closed his eyes spasmodically in a desperate search for, O God, please, the right words! Now please, just this once, the gift of eloquence!

The priest clenched his hands and grew pale. His old voice sank to a feeble whisper. "The—the child that . . . O God!"

Surprised, the doctor looked up from his reflections at the old man, who . . . "What?" said de Geus. "Are you crying?"

The clock ticked hatefully loud. The gas lamp hissed. Two men sat together in silence. Then one of them could no longer bear the ticking of the clock and the hissing of the lamp and the enervating silence. He got up slowly and stepped heavily into the chilly hallway. Now the other one had a chance to regain his composure, and surreptitiously he rubbed his eyes with the sleeve of his cassock. What a miserable sight, to see a man cry in his impotence. An old man who begs so desperately for the blessing of eloquence and then finds that God does not give in to his pleas. Such were the doctor's thoughts as he walked softly along the hallway, and in his stocking feet went down the cellar stairs with a heavy heart. A flickering match lit up the cellar, and another, and a third burnt the doctor's fingers so badly that he uttered a strong expression and then regained his composure. He couldn't stay depressed for very long. Damn it all, he wasn't a small boy who cries because he can't grasp the moon! So the crazy doctor groped around for the dusty bottle, and a moment later, almost gay again, he returned to the room where our priest was waiting with a delighted expression on his face.

"I found it!" cried the priest, and his voice trembled with joy.

"Me too!" laughed the doctor. He put the wine bottle on the table with a bang and licked his burned thumb.

"I found myself again and the bottle too, though it almost cost me a finger. Come, old mate, don't let's argue any more. I behaved like a spoiled girl and I don't want to think about it any more. *Carpe diem!*"

De Geus laughed broadly and cleaned the bottle and let the

light of the lamp sparkle in the tinkling crystal. Then he poured the amber wine into the glasses, a satisfaction to the eye as well as the tongue. But the priest had a hard time hiding his disappointment about the fine words he'd finally found and couldn't use because the doctor wanted to enjoy himself and drink away his melancholy mood with the old bottle.

The priest nipped at his delicate chalice and slowly shook his gray head. His eyes wore an expression of weariness and sadness.

"I've always been too slow," he sighed. "The most beautiful thoughts occur to me when nobody asks for them any more."

"Keep them for another time!" laughed de Geus. "Or write them down and arrange them alphabetically so you can find them when you need them again!"

The priest smiled sadly and the doctor offered him a cigar. He became as noisy and gay as usual, and the priest knew he was too late, that the hour of grace had passed and the chance for a serious conversation was gone. The doctor had pulled through one of his rare moods of depression. Now he would be contented again for months and live like the happy barbarian he was, a jolly heathen, who found life much too happy and short to brood over it.

"We must be patient," reflected the priest, and he took a sip of the cool wine. "Too bad I was so slow and found that beautiful thought about God's mercy and the child too late. . . . But God's mill grinds slowly. God will eventually get de Geus. It'll take some time. . . . Perhaps if I could have told him that God offers His mercy to those who ask for it humbly, that He sometimes lets a human being wait in order to test him. . . . After all, de Geus hadn't undergone the test; he got rebellious when he didn't get his wish soon enough, and then wanted to force God. The good Lord doesn't let Himself be forced by His insignificant creatures. We must kneel in the dust before Him. But what does de Geus do? He kneels in the dust for a moment, and then he jumps up and says, 'And now, God, now I must have your mercy, immediately, or I don't want it any longer! Give me the child I've begged you for; give it to me right away, or we're friends no more!' . . . Yes, yes," thought the priest further, "that's the way it happened. My friend is too proud, and if only I dared tell him so now, that he must bow his tough head, and that he—that he—for a child . . ."

The little priest's face cleared. He sat up straight in his chair, because now he would tell his friend all the things he had thought over quietly; that he would have to start anew—that he should direct his life toward God again, and together with his wife, the wife God had given him . . .

"Listen, my friend," implored the priest, "listen to what I'm going to tell you!"

But de Geus laughed out loud and emptied his glass.

"Bottoms up, friend," he laughed, "and I'll pour you another. Let's drink to life, that really is so wonderful!"

And they drank. They clinked glasses and looked at one another from behind the yellow chalices. They talked about Teun Briool, who was such an old tough, and about many other things a priest and a doctor of a small village can talk about. Afterward the doctor brought his friend home in his car, and said to Bertha, who opened the door with a surly face, "Hello, sweetheart."

Bertha said "plouf!" It was the strongest curse that had ever passed her maidenly lips.

But the priest stood in the stillness of his room and thought of the many things he wanted to tell his friend. He listened with bowed head to the starting of the motor and heard de Geus drive away into the night. From far away he could still hear the sound of the horn, but to the priest it sounded like the cry of a soul to God. . . .

The doctor drove alone in the night. A lonely human, he grinned, but not from pleasure. Silence and loneliness were beside him on the seat. And the longing slumbered in the back.

"A woman," said the crazy doctor to himself. And with that thought he finally plunged into his bed. A woman . . .

8

And the woman came. . . .

But it wasn't the woman that Dr. de Geus meant, not at all!

At that time the waiting room of the crazy doctor was always crowded with patients. His reputation had grown, and from the far end of the polder the people came with their common ailments, with their gut-aches and festering fingers, with rheumatism, hemorrhoids and all the ills a peasant can suffer from. They came from near and far to the wonder doctor who had an ointment or pill for every ill. Sometimes he cured them just with his hearty laughter or his rough banter, and the others' troubles he pinched out of their bodies until they lay there shrieking with pain. But the pain only lasted a moment and they went home cured.

The ones he could help no more were the old wrecks who stayed at home in their bedsteads and were later buried by the poor with a bunch of dandelions on their graves. Those were the hopeless cases that irritated de Geus, because he couldn't keep the flicker of life going. But he wasn't blamed for such cases. The man who has lived his time must make room for someone else. Thus it had always been; thus it would remain in the polder.

But the doctor's waiting room was filled to overflowing every day, and there was nobody to open the door for the patients. The wide front door remained invitingly open from seven in the morning till after ten. Inside the doctor in his white apron was busy with his shiny instruments. He'd say to a farm hand who entered his office, "Come on in with your festering thumb, I'll cut it off!" But his whole grinning countenance promised just the opposite. And to Kobus Kriel, who was finished, he said, "Get out of here! Get dressed in the hallway; there's no time for it here!" And Kobus Kriel trudged into the hallway in his underwear and dressed himself, which took quite a long time. The silently waiting throng heard Gerrit Grauw holler behind the closed doors. He had a festering thumb, everybody knew that, and now he was being terribly mistreated by the doctor. A little later Gerrit Grauw came out sweating and pale and the barbarian roared again, "Next!" And a new victim went into the office with a sick feeling in his stomach, but full of confidence in the ruffian who had a remedy for ailments and hadn't yet needed to send any patient to his colleagues in the city.

So the patients lined up and filled the waiting room, where it smelled of pigs' manure, heavy tobacco and wet clothes, and where you could cut the blue smoke with a knife. The men smoked and kept a pent-up silence. The women looked around and were quiet from fright. But the young girls snickered among themselves, because funny stories were making the rounds about the crazy doctor who lived all by himself and still had such fiery eyes and a smiling mouth and a pair of shovel-like fists that were like velvet when it was necessary. There was a lot of gossip about him, especially among the young people. But who could tell how much of it was pretty Mieke's doing? Pretty Mieke, who had presented herself to the young doctor at the very beginning, and who no longer dared come to his house after he had chased her roughly out of his office and bellowed after her that nothing was wrong with her? . . . That she'd better hurry and marry a hefty peasant, one who'd break her of her strange ways, and if she ever dared show up again he'd send her into the street just as the good Lord had created her! That was what the furious doctor had hollered after pretty Mieke. And he added she ought to be glad he gave her the time to get dressed again! Since that day strange stories had made the rounds among the young folk, and pretty Mieke, who suddenly didn't have a thing wrong with her at all at all, blackened the doctor's name whenever she got the chance. Such a funny Mieke! Such a pretty and passionate body! . . . But now in the waiting room sat the menfolk in their wooden shoes, and their pipes smelled worse than the manure on their clothes. The women were darning socks while they waited or knitting sweaters of gray wool, and as their fingers moved they whispered among themselves. And the young girls sat with red faces and shining eyes, giggling, because where there's smoke there must be fire, and was it altogether a lie what pretty Mieke said about the weird doctor? . . .

Geerte of Gilles Bieteblauw sat there too. Geerte was tall and skinny, a neat, hard-bitten wife. She noticed that a cobweb hung from the ceiling and the picture frames were thick with dust and one could hardly see through the window glass because it was so filthy. But in the office where she let her scrutinizing eye wander, everything shone with cleanliness, and hard as she tried, she couldn't find the tiniest speck on the instruments. "Who keeps your things clean?" she asked.

The doctor looked at her and laughed abundantly. "Are you coming for your troubles, or for mine?" he wanted to know.

"I ain't sick," admitted Geerte. "I just wanted to . . ."

"Next patient," roared the doctor, and he gallantly held the door open for her.

And Geerte found herself standing in the hallway. Abashed, she realized she had spoken a bit too promptly. Is this what she'd waited for an hour in the waiting room? Hadn't she chased that lummox of a man of hers into the polder to look for a job while she went to find a house to work in? Spitefully Geerte looked around her in the half-lighted hallway. The front door was wide open, and beyond it the rain hung like a trembling curtain. It sizzled and splashed on the thick clay and in the bubbling ditches. Like a cover, like a heavy screen the rain domed the earth and the endless polder. Geerte didn't venture into it. She hadn't counted on so much splashing wetness, and retired shivering to the hollow-sounding hallway, where the stillness was accentuated by the monotonous ticking of the big clock's pendulum and the steady whizzing of the rain. She looked at the many mud traces on the marble tiles and felt like crying. A grubby mess of muddy tracks led from the front door to the waiting room, and in front of the next door stood eight pairs of dirty wooden shoes in a neat row.

" 'Tis an ungodly shame," sighed Geerte, who kept her own childless cabin spick and span, "an ungodly shame, the way this beautiful hallway looks. That fellow neglects it something awful!"

She listened to the dull hum in the waiting room and to the sharp cries in the office beyond and to the melancholy rain. Then she got tired of it. She hesitated as she pushed the slightly ajar door open. "Jiminee!" shouted Geerte, and clasped her hands together. "Damn! How can a learned man live in this!" And resolutely she stepped into the room where the remnants of a hasty breakfast stood on the table, where corduroy trousers lay in brotherly embrace with a repaired auto tire on an easy chair, and an overfilled ash tray together with a sticky gin glass were sad memories of a lonely evening—of a lonesome man. Geerte closed the door behind her and clapped her hands again in astonishment. But this wasn't helping at all, so she started to boil big kettles of water. She rolled up her sleeves. Grumbling and fussing, she began to scrub and polish as if somebody were forcing her to do it, as if she didn't feel the greatest joy about a kitchen that gradually became shiny and clean, about a room where a normal person could feel at home again. Piles of plates and cups she washed, dishes covered with weeks-old remnants of food. God! to think that a fellow all by himself could have dirtied so many dishes, always using new ones instead of washing the dirty ones first, like a decent Christian person. "The man is daffy!" fussed Geerte, as she scrubbed the pots and pans. "A complete fool!" And she crawled on her knees through the room and wiped and rubbed until she was hot and flushed and could mirror herself in the parquet floor.

Then the front door slammed and she saw de Geus drive his car from the garage. On a wet day like this, he followed his last victim out of the office in his blouse with a fresh cigarette sticking out of his stubbly beard. But he smiled at little Dorus Wys and asked him if he wanted a lift to the village, because it was raining buckets and little Dorus looked like a drowned cat. Noiselessly the shiny car drove over the driveway, and suddenly Geerte felt insecure, now that there was no longer any sound in the somber house of Notary Bibber of blessed memory. For a moment she had a fleeting thought of spooks and ghosts, but she dismissed it in her irritation about the dirty hallway, where muddy wooden shoes had left their tracks. She fetched buckets of water and slaved and polished and rubbed until the hallway shone with cleanliness, and when she looked down at the tiles she could almost tell the time by the large clock with the long pendulum. But in the stillness of the haunted house the clock suddenly started to stroke. Twelve hoarse broken sounds echoed through the sepulchral hallway, and frightened Geerte so badly that with a cry of anguish she disappeared into the living room. How this stillness could work on a person's nerves! The clock had certainly struck at least four times this morning, but then Geerte had been so busy in the kitchen and the rooms and too much in a hurry to pay attention to the striking clock.

Twelve o'clock; the doctor should be back from his sick calls before long, and then he'd need a bite to eat. So Geerte peeled the potatoes and rinsed the vegetables and cooked the bacon and stood there in the newly shining kitchen, cooking as if she were in her own home. She covered the table with a dazzlingly clean bed sheet—she couldn't find anything better—and in the center between the shiny eating utensils she set a bunch of dandelions pearly with raindrops. The flowers struck a festive note in the doctor's somber abode, and Geerte only regretted she couldn't fling the windows wide open to let in pools of sunlight as well as the terse notes of a blackbird. No, the rain fell monotonously from a gray sky, and no blackbird sang from the pear tree and no sun smiled over the polder. It was really a shame; it would have heightened Geerte's pleasure in the things she had done for Dr. de Geus. If only that man would come now, because the bacon was sizzling in the skillet and was getting all crisp and yellow, and the good aroma of the midday meal filled the clean house. The potatoes would soon be done, and she almost had to pour the water from them. If only the doctor would come now! . . .

But it was getting toward one o'clock and the doctor did not appear. Geerte was getting nervous. The potatoes were steaming dry and the bacon was sputtering over a low flame. Darn it all, what a pity that the man was staying away so long. In her disappointment, her hands were awkward as she worked; she was afraid the precious food would burn. All the pleasure was gone for her, now that de Geus didn't come in time to enjoy her cooking.

When the clock struck two, Geerte was crying a bit next to the vase of dandelions, and at half-past two she said crossly to herself, "He can burst in now, for all I care!"

She extinguished the flame under the browned bacon. She dumped the cold potatoes into the slop bucket. She threw the vegetables in the refuse bin and loudly blew her nose. Then she stood in the hallway fumbling at the front door that refused to open at first.

Later on she trudged into the polder with a disconsolate heart. A tear ran over her leathery cheek. Or was it only rain? It came straight down from the sky, like a window shade. The rain sang its monotonous dirge over the flat polder and drenched her to the bare skin. It didn't matter to her. She paid no attention to it, nor to the puddles that splashed dirty brown water over her wooden shoes. She felt a deep and dark hurt about the doctor who ignored her good care and failed to clap his hands in pleased surprise for the work she'd accomplished on the sly. Thus she approached the village that seemed moribund under the continuous rain. She passed the church and the rectory, where she saw the doctor's car gleaming in the rain. Geerte stared at the car with a miserably sick feeling in her stomach. Then she went on like a cat soaked by the rain.

"I should've known," she blubbered, "I should've known a bachelor like him would eat at the rectory when all his pots and pans are dirty. . . ."

In her own clean cabin Gillis was snoring with his stocking feet on the rod of the furnace. She let him sleep and stole upstairs for dry clothes. Later on she came and sat next to him in the cane rocking chair, shivering from cold and misery. Gillis continued to snore, and Geerte had no words in her sadness. She too put her feet on the copper rod of the furnace in which some peat was still smoldering. Then it was really quiet in the childless cabin of Gillis and Geerte. Her eyelids grew heavy. The rain beat monotonously against the window. Her head nodded forward upon her flat chest. They slept in their chairs, those lonely, quickly aging people. The furnace became colder but they didn't notice it. An almost imperceptible smile played around Geerte's dry lips, and Gillis snored open-mouthed with a deep and peaceful noise.

The doctor nearly fell backward with surprise when he came home and saw the brightly laid table and the clean house. He looked around the room dumfounded. He didn't believe in ghosts and even less in brownies. So he started looking all through the house as though someone were hiding there, but the house was as empty as always. It was really a riddle. And the riddle became even greater when, coming down-stairs again, he discovered the cold potatoes in the slop bucket and the burnt bacon stuck fast in a pool of hardened grease. "My good lady friend waited for me with the noonday meal," concluded the doctor with a grin. "That's damn interesting!"

But he didn't bother his head about it any more; there were pills to be made, potions to be prepared and powders to be weighed. Woman or young girl, pretty maiden or old farm hand's wife, whoever did the job for him would probably come tomorrow to collect her wages, he decided, for like every other place, things weren't done for nothing in the polder.

A moment later he had forgotten the whole incident; the drugs required his attention. There was a lot of work here for a country doctor who was swamped with patients and who had to attend to things all by himself. He stirred with the mortar, he weighed the milligrams attentively, he mixed the powders and prepared ointments of all colors and odors. He hummed as he handled the retorts and cast a sideward glance at the receptacle that started to bubble. He made a face at a small bottle containing a dirty yellow liquid, and at another small bottle he growled satisfaction. He busied himself like this for several hours in his quiet pharmacy. He was still working when dusk descended on the polder. Across the fields rang the plaintive lowing of a cow being driven to its enclosure. The rain that had flooded the late-summer day began to fall heavily again. It wouldn't end today; it was an orgy of water. The coldly shimmering puddles mirrored the dark sky where a blackbird flew with a shriek that resounded over the desolate polder.

Fourteen small boxes were neatly arrayed, from the smallest to the biggest, with nervous scrawls written on them. Beside them lay the little boxes filled with powders and carefully counted pills. And small bottles everywhere; bottles with eyedrops, with ear-drops and with boric acid, with nice and evil-tasting prescriptions, bottles with instructions for dosage, such as "one drop three times a day" or "one tablespoon every hour." All had passed through his hands, through his hairy fists that now trembled a little with weariness. Dr. de Geus rubbed his eyes and stood for a moment with his bald head pressed against the cold window that was clouded by the dusk and the splashing rain. Then he sighed deeply and turned away shivering. The work was done for the day. At most, he might be called to a late patient. That would provide some distraction, for he felt miserably lonely and a deep melancholic mood had come over him while he had worked. It had crept into the room with the chill and the monotonous dirge of the rain, and had stood beside him as he'd carefully weighed his powders and thought about his patients in the polder. Now it weighed on his tired shoulders, now it pressed upon his beating head and tired eyes. It was the silence, the despair of desolation. "Don't think! Don't think!" he told himself grimly. "If you think you'll start drinking again, and when you drink you go to hell! Don't think!"

But he did think. He stood in the darkened room and his hands held the receptacle that still felt warm. He was scarcely aware of standing there and looking through the window into the dark evening. He didn't realize that it was raining buckets and the chill was all around him. He stood there in his white apron with the receptacle in his hand. For how long? A quarter of an hour? . . . An hour? . . . The night was black on the window and there wasn't a single star blinking in the whole firmament. Nothing but silence and rain. And the loneliness of a man all by himself.

If the receptacle hadn't dropped out of his hand into splinters he might have stood in the dark for hours. Now he came back to reality with a startled movement. Slowly he went into the living room, still in his white arpon, an odor of Peru balsam on his clothes. He came to the living room where the dandelions stood on the bed sheet with the shiny eating utensils around them. He didn't see them. Darkness can be a blessing. Sometimes it's warmer than light. The clock ticked lazily in the stillness. There was no fire in the hearth, but it was good to be in the dark and to sit down in a deep easy chair.

Thoughts came again to this lonely man. He no longer pushed them back. He suffered them. Thoughts of a woman going about her tasks in the quiet house, a ranging creature who would bring color and light and warmth into his lonely life. She would be beautiful and noble in stature. He saw her moving proudly through the room and coming to him and bending over him with a smile so tender and a mouth so red and seductive. He tasted the fragrance of her hair, silky soft. Her eyes were deep as the sea as they gazed into his, and she pulled his head toward her bosom. And he would tell her how lonely he had been in the dark chilly house, and how good it was to be together now, very close together and one in thought and desire. He stretched out his arms yearningly. But she wasn't there. He sat alone in the dark. And outside the rain taunted him with its tedious rustling over the flooded land. She was not there. All by himself, the lonely fool, who had come here to bury himself amidst the peasants and farm hands of the polder, who had allowed himself to be forgotten because he wanted to flee from God, God Who had pursued him in the city and would find him here as well.

Nervously he jumped up. He must chase these thoughts away. The light hurt his eyes when he lit it, but as he grew accustomed to the brightness he stared about him in surprise at the clean table and the shiny silverware and the dandelions. He saw how neat the room looked, and noticed at the same time that he still wore his apron. The thoughts came again. Oh yes. A woman had done it. . . . A woman. What woman? It didn't interest him because it couldn't be the woman of his dark thoughts. It might have been a peasant woman, or a fresh peasant girl with the fragrance of the country about her; she failed to beguile him, for she belonged to the polder that he hated throughout all those lonely evenings. He paced about the room, trying to tear himself away from the unsettling thoughts. He lit a cigarette and smoked greedily. He mustn't think! He mustn't think! If you think you go to hell. Why didn't the priest come now to talk and laugh with him? Or why didn't they call him to the bedside of a dying patient, or, as happened recently, a sick cow? Wait, he might go and have a look at Teun Briool. The old cobbler didn't want to die. He'd been lying there moribund for weeks. He'd drive over to see him.

He started to take off his white apron and stroked his beard thoughtfully. He might take a shave; that would be a distraction. He might get a fresh bottle and drink himself into a stupor so he could fall into bed like a block and forget everything. But then he remembered how Jane Stolk's time was almost there, and they might call him tonight for the delivery. Then he'd have to be sober. There were dozens of things he could do, but he did nothing, he was tired. . . . A little later he sat in his easy chair again with his head in his hands. He held his eyes tightly closed and tried desperately to think of nothing, to sit there numbly and gradually sink away into forgetfulness.

The clock struck half-past ten and the wet cold stole from the chilly hallway into the room and lay at his feet. He shivered but didn't move. He looked up and stared into the yellow light until it began to hurt his eyes, and once again his

thoughts enmeshed him in a seductive intoxication. A woman
. . . For a moment he had an image of Janette as she had
looked in their childless home, a pale and forbidding face,
graying hair and agitated white hands. But he pushed the
thought away. That wasn't the woman he wished for. She
would be young and beautiful, with a well-developed form
and a fresh, rosy face with full red lips, a mouth always ready
to laugh, and smiling eyes and . . .

It was a pity, the way that lonely doctor yearned for a sweet,
sweet creature to bring sun and joy into his solitary life. Perhaps it was a bit ridiculous at forty years of age to long for a
pretty girl to fill the silence of his evenings and the emptiness of his sleepless nights. But God had made a weird person
out of him. Or did he have a weird impression of God? . . .
God, Whom he saw as a kind of tyrant Who took pleasure in
the sorrow and impotence of His creatures. Always he saw God
Who crossed his path and blocked off his way to happiness
and peace. It was always God Who snarled at him: "Not
you! For you I have nothing good in store. Others may
achieve happiness, but not you; I've got it in for you!" Sometimes God would meet him tauntingly with beckoning
hands and an all-promising smile on His shrewd countenance.
But just as the doctor was about to grasp the proffered hand
and shout from pure joy because he, too, would be given happiness, then God withdrew His hand and laughed: "Ha! Not
you! First get down on your knees and bite into the dust and
humiliate yourself before My image and then . . . I'll still not
make you happy!" That's the way the doctor looked at God.
And he had gotten down on his knees and humbled himself
and begged for just that wee bit of happiness, just that one
thing. . . . Was it then so difficult for God to grant him
that? Couldn't God do everything? Why not, then? . . . The
doctor heaved a deep sigh. "You've spoiled everything yourself with God by your dissolute life!" But the next moment
doubt assailed him again. He hadn't led a worse life than

many others who had happiness and a sweet wife as well as children, had he? "Not by a damned sight!" growled the crazy doctor within himself. "Others tell the church to go to hell and commit adultery and everything goes right with them. . . . And when I was still running to church and lived honestly with my wife and did more good than I could be responsible for, still there was no child that we both longed for so much, and Janette grew sour before her time and there I was, with all my knowledge and good will, and all of it useless!" It was a vicious circle. Always God stood in his way and demanded that he humiliate himself. And it was God again Who laughed at him after his humiliation and pious moods and shouted to him that he'd have no happiness, in spite of everything. He implored God. God remained deaf. He grew rebellious and declared God impotent. God punished him by withholding the love he begged for so ardently. So it always came around to the starting point: God didn't want to see him happy; God hated him. . . . Why? . . . Where had it all started? . . .

The tired doctor passed his broad hand along his forehead. He couldn't find a way out of it. It was as though he were staring himself blind at a blank wall. There were bitter lines around his mouth, the mouth that in the daytime could laugh about every poor farm hand who was happier than he was. But now it was night, and the silence and the loneliness of the night tortured him. He got up. He was boiling because of his impotence. He wanted to cry out in despair, or smash everything around him! But neither one nor the other could change his destiny. He would be lonely as long as it pleased God—forever! A scornful laugh curled his lips as he stood beneath the lamplight and listened to the stillness around him. A mighty force rose in him, a sinister resistance against God Who wanted to tyrannize him, Who was deaf to his pleas and had burdened him with the damnation of loneliness. Resistance rose mightily in him and burst forth from his mouth with a raucous cry: "Never! You'll never defeat me, God, never! I want to live, do you understand? I want to live deeply and violently and be happy like the others. I'll steal happiness if I don't get it, and I'll make my own way as I choose! God! God! . . ." Thus the foolish doctor shouted as he ran amuck in the big silent house. His fists were clenched and the veins were swelling on his angry brow. He smashed a chair to smithereens on the table, as if to seal forcefully his alliance with his pride.

Then a great calm came over him. The storm which culminated in his rebellious shouting seemed to have abated. For awhile he stood looking at the pieces on the table and the dandelions miserably floating in their pool.

He smiled bitterly and didn't even question the possibility that he might be going mad in this heavy silence, or wonder whether it was right to shout in this way against God. No, he smiled scornfully and repeated his decision in a whisper to go his own way from now on and not allow God to bully him any more. He would shape his own life, and his happiness too, and the small fear of God that had always smoldered within him he would throttle as he went along. Why not take what was not given him? Didn't the world lie open before him? Were there not many who had wanted to share life with him? Was there no woman for him who wanted to relieve his loneliness and wash it away with the golden radiance of her being? He thought of one who had unconsciously given body to his lonely reflection, who wanted to make his dreams a reality, if he only took the trouble to grasp what God had denied him. . . . What, God? Wasn't he through with Him? He would make his own way now. He would get her, pull her into his pirate's world.

"Tomorrow!" the rebellious doctor promised himself. "Tomorrow I'll start my life anew!" And he left the room where the silence stared after him with a shudder. Boldly whistling, he climbed the stairs. He would shape his destiny! Tomorrow it would happen! He looked in the mirror at his laughing face, but it seemed to him old and neglected. He looked at his blue blouse that hung open at his chest, and rubbed his stubbly beard. He shaved himself, humming, and made faces at himself in the mirror as he rubbed in the milky foaming soap. "Tomorrow," he promised himself, and the shining knife scraped the stubbles from his chin. Tomorrow . . . He finished his shave. His skin was taut and smooth. He laughed. Then he took off the colored blouse and corduroy pants that he'd worn to be a peasant among peasants. He could be an urban gentleman as well, why not? He'd always been a dual personality within himself. He'd feared God as a small boy fears the bogeyman, but dared as well to hate and despise Him in grown-up fashion. Now he would make his own way, and outside appearance was important. He dressed himself in a handsome gentleman's costume that had humg in the closet for a long time now as a memento of the city gentleman he had once been. Ties that Janette had tied for him, and the dress shirts her white hands had smoothed out before she put them in a pile in the linen closet where she stood with a harsh pale face.

Janette . . . No, he pushed the thought away. She appeared unreal to him, now that he was dolling himself up in the middle of the night for another, a younger and gay creature who still hadn't given up laughter. He examined himself in the mirror again and saw that everything looked all right. There he stood, smooth-shaven now and dressed as a gentleman in his fashionable suit. He smiled at his image in the mirror and cursed out loud, with embittered boldness and mischievous pleasure. The stiff collar choked him and beneath it the tie and the gold stickpin gleamed noticeably. "A masquerading monkey!" he grinned with spiteful pleasure. "A vain fool!" Then he started to undress, humming. Everything disappeared in the closet again between other city clothes, neatly folded and arranged. Now he was in his underwear. He blew out the light and dove between the damp sheets. It helped him to lie there quietly and look into the darkness and think of her who would be an illumination.

"Tomorrow, old fool!" he said scornfully. "Tomorrow I'll start anew. God or no God, I'll go it alone."

And then God sent him to sleep and shook His wise head slowly. But the crazy doctor didn't know; he slept with his smooth face on the white pillow and dreamt that he possessed the power to regulate his life. The rain splashed outside on the flooded polder over which God stretched His almighty hands. . . .

9

The morning came peeping through the gray clouds in diffused sunlight and fanned out in rosy hues. The broad polder was gleaming in its abundance of wetness: coldly shining puddles and damp brown soil next to patches of brilliant green where the cows ambled lazily, their steaming breath standing out before them. Between the green, brown and black of the rich clay the rough dike wound its snakelike way, and over it hobbled the peasant carts with dazzling milk containers that reflected the wet sun. Behind the dike lay the Dirty Hole with its lapping water, and beyond it all the rest of the world. About that the villagers were in complete ignorance. They had grown up in the polder and it was all they knew. The polder was so infinitely big; you could walk through it for hours, perhaps for days, before you reached the end. Who could tell? And it was completely surrounded by dikes and beyond them the water that shut them off from the world.

Oh yes, there was something else. There was a small, warped little fellow who lived at the foot of the dike, next to the Dirty Hole. His name was Tony the Ferry, because his ferryboat was the connecting link between the polder and the world. His house was a miserable little broken-down cabin, its roof barely sticking out above the lumbering dike, and there lived Tony the Ferry with his skinny wife and his two louts of boys. What did they do there in that small, dirty cabin beside the Dirty Hole? Eat, sleep and eat again, and wait for the clock to strike, for every time the dilapidated clock on the mantel struck the hour, little, irate Tony would jump up and shout, "Hey! Boys! we're off!" And off they went. Tony with his nervous, bandy legs leading the way, climbing the high dike, and behind him, in their lazy gait, the boys. When Tony, breathing hard, had crawled to the top of the dike he looked down venomously and shouted at his loutish sons, "Git a move on! Pretty soon they'll be waiting again!" And spry as a young fellow he slid down the other side of the dike to the Dirty Hole where the ferry lay. Then he stood peering, shading his short-sighted eyes with his hand, and scolded the louts who kept people waiting, because every hour on the hour Tony's duty was to sail his ferryboat to the other side of the Dirty Hole if there were farmers wanting to cross over from the polder to the outside world, or vice versa. That's how Tony and his louts made a living; they were the connection from here to the other side, once every hour, fourteen times a day, neither more nor less. But from the top of the dike the louts had already noticed there was nobody to be seen on the other side of the water, so they slowly followed the coal-dust path leading down from the dike.

"There ain't nobody," Aai shouted to his excited elder. "We can stay here now."

"Don't contradict me," little Tony barked. "When it's time to sail, we sail. By the time we get across, somebody might be waiting there!"

"There's nobody never!" growled Jochum. But, duty bound, they stepped onto the flat ferry, because it was their destiny that from eight in the morning until nine in the evening they had to cross the Dirty Hole every hour. The louts were willing to give a hand only when the weather was very bad and they discovered nobody on the other side. But venomous little Tony was a man with a sense of duty who crossed every hour on the hour, weather or no weather, though there were days when nobody availed himself of his services. Neither Tony nor his boys ate any the less for it, because the state, which has to be represented somewhere above the Meuse, paid them for it. So they were, so to speak, government employees, though it was no skin off their rears, but you have to rely on government employees, or at least that's the way Tony the Ferry looked at it.

So they crossed over in their flatboat which could hold a horse and wagon, some bicycles and at least ten people. But as far as Tony could remember the boat had never been filled up, and he'd been at it for forty years. Oh yes, once! Ten years ago they had to cross over twice, because the car of a potato farmer had arrived at the same time as the gig of Geert Molenaar. Then they had made two crossings within an hour; a day never to be forgotten!

"There ain't nothin' again," growled Jochum, as he hid a large wad of tobacco behind his molars. "We might as well stay on this side and only cross when we see somebody over there!"

Tony paid no attention to his grumbling; he was accustomed to it for years from his boys; they just couldn't see that a government functionary had to stick to his duty and never lie down on the job. Groaning with effort, he hung onto the wet steel cable that bobbed into sight out of the Dirty Hole in front of the ferry and disappeared in the water again a little distance behind. With slow, shaky steps he would walk to the end of the ferry and just as he was about to step into the water he'd hold back, to start again from the beginning. Then Jochum would take over and after him Aai. And the three of them would take their spell of walking over the ferry, from stem to stern and stern to stem, until the lumbersome mammoth would bounce against the other shore, where they had to wait five minutes for eventual passengers. With his steel watch in his hand and his near-sighted eyes directed to the shore, Tony would count the minutes, for he was a government man and the soul of punctuality. The louts would jump off on the other side and sit on the little landing stage that slanted down to the shore. On that landing stage stood a signboard: "Crossings every hour on the hour; carriages ten cents; bicycles three cents; passengers one cent; children under fourteen free." So the state had put up this signboard and Tony fulfilled the order, faithfully assisted by the louts.

"Nobody in sight? Then back!" barked Tony, when the five minutes were over, and back they went. Five minutes going, a five-minute wait, five minutes to sail back. Working a quarter of an hour every hour and three-quarters of an hour rest. That was the order of the day for Tony the Ferry, day in, day out, year after year.

But now there was something that would disturb their routine and upset them violently. Lazy Jochum was the first to see it. He said with alarm, "Damn!" and quit pulling, so that Tony, bent low and crookedly walking along the line, collided with him and broke his short earthen pipe. Tony uttered an even much worse curse and was about to scold Jochum malevolently when he saw the reason for all the cursing. The three of them looked at the polder and let the line sink in the water in their astonishment. The unwieldy ferry floated to a standstill in the middle of the Dirty Hole and they peered to the other side as if they were seeing ghosts. Actually, there was nothing to be seen but the car of Dr. de Geus that was waiting on the landing stage to be ferried across. The doctor sat behind the wheel and impatiently tooted his horn. Everything was otherwise serenely still except for the lapping of the dark water around the ferry.

"But we won't do it!" Aai growled rebelliously. "He's too damned late."

"Yes, he's too late," Jochum echoed, "he'll have to wait for the next crossing."

Tony the Ferry scratched his small head. Now this was really a peculiar case. A crossing once every hour, that was his duty and he wouldn't deviate from it, but twice in fifteen minutes; the state had given no instructions for such a thing, to his knowledge. Again the horn sounded over the water, and the crazy doctor jumped out of his car and began to swing his arms excitedly. The fellows couldn't make out what he was saying because the Dirty Hole was very wide here, and the wind direction was toward the polder.

"Let 'im get the pest," snapped Tony, who didn't want to be made a fool of as a government employee. "Let's sail; next crossing is at eleven o'clock!"

"Does he know about it?" growled Jochum, and the three of them grasped the cable again and started their walk from the front to the back and the back to the front. The unwieldy boat crawled slowly through the water and the stem of Tony's pipe stuck out venomously from his face into the daylight.

"He can get the pest for all I care," he repeated a few more times. Then he pushed the ferry against the shore, and there they saw new cause for surprise, because it wasn't the crazy doctor who stood laughing beside his car. But it must be he; they recognized him on account of his grin and his bright eyes. Everything else about him seemed strange; a fashionable outfit like the urban gentleman wore who came to visit the island once a year. A suit with knifelike creases in the trousers! And shiny shoes and a hat, and a tie around his neck and a fashionable gentleman's topcoat! Their eyes bulged with surprise! Was that Dr. de Geus? Bald pate and hairy arms, all had suddenly disappeared beneath city togs. They shrugged their shoulders in disdain. Was that their doctor? He looked like a dressed-up monkey! Now you could see the world stood on its head! At first they'd been surprised that the new doctor didn't wear a silk hat and a high stiff collar as well as a Prince Albert, all befitting a doctor, and now when they were just getting used to his peasant clothes and his crazy habits, now that he had become one of them, here he was, looking like the others, dressed like a city slicker. Tony found no words for it, and glared at the doctor while the louts beat it, disappearing behind the dike.

"It's curious!" said Tony finally. "It's damned curious!" And shaking his head, he prepared to follow his sons. This was a mistake. The doctor allowed everybody his idiosyncrasies, but now he felt he'd been sufficiently gaped at, so he stepped into his car.

"Will you take me across?" It sounded friendly, but Tony produced his big watch and solemnly shook his head. "The next crossing is in about forty minutes," mumbled Tony and off he went, climbing the dike.

"What the hell!" Now Dr. de Geus suddenly got mad. "What do you mean, lazy pig? Take me across, I say! What's that boat good for otherwise?"

It was suddenly a mighty lively Tony who climbed the dike with nervous steps and slid down the other side. There the louts caught up with him and the three of them went snorting to the shack where Mietemoei had coffee brewing. With one jump Dr. de Geus stood beside his car, but then his good humor got the upper hand over his fury, and he looked laughingly after the crabby little fellow who was in such a hurry to get inside.

"I'll get you, Charon!" grinned de Geus. Smelling adventure, he hummed as he got into his car again and drove slowly down the landing stage and onto the slightly sinking ferry. He undid the strap they had fastened with a loose knot. Then he took off his neat overcoat and the new suit and laid them in the car. He put the newfangled hat on top of them like a funeral wreath on an honorable corpse, and now his bald pate was very naked in the stiff wind. He undressed even more; rolled up the sleeves of his dress shirt so that the wind played with the black hair on his arms. He rubbed his hands and drew the steel cable out of the water to ferry across to the other side. Then he thought it over. It would be much nicer if he left the ferry on the other side for his own convenience; tonight he'd be coming back from the outside world to the island, and he wouldn't give Tony the Ferry the pleasure of a victory. So he climbed up the landing stage and came to where the steel cable was attached to the shore. But what the devil! It wasn't so easy! At the foot of the rotting little jetty, almost half a fathom beneath the murky water, the cable was wound around a pole, green with slippery weeds, that protruded above the water. On his belly, the big rascal hung groaning over the jetty and jerked at the steel cable, but in vain; even the crazy doctor's strength was limited.

"Now we'll see what happens!" he raged within himself, and breathing hard he jumped from the landing stage onto the ferry. In the back of the car he had an auto jack, a small, handy thing that could lift tons. A moment later he was flat on his stomach again, wriggling until he had pushed the auto jack between the pole and the cable knot. And now he had to turn. Slowly the knot got tighter—and tighter. Then something creaked; something snapped. Another turn and the steel thread broke in two alongside the jetty with a short, dry crack. The auto jack disappeared at once into the depths of the Dirty Hole, but the crazy doctor didn't care. He was happy that his efforts were rewarded; now the ferry could only be pulled in one direction.

The ferry! . . . What the hell! The lumbersome mammoth, freed from its shackles, began at once to swing and sway, and was already two meters away from the shore. With a shock the doctor realized the joke was on him. He leapt with flying speed, his toes barely landing on the edge of the ferry, and he had to claw at the stern to keep from plunging into the Dirty Hole. But he'd made it, and he realized with malicious pleasure that the ferry was drifting rapidly with the current away from the shore. He was just about to take it easy and enjoy his triumph when he discovered to his renewed shock that he wasn't victor yet by a long shot. There was a heavy current in the Dirty Hole and the boat drifted to the west. In this way he'd never reach the jetty on the other side, but would run aground somewhere beneath Goeree. He managed to catch the end of the line that was about to go overboard in small jerks. He grabbed the steel cable in his strong fists and began to pull with all his might. Now the ferry lay still, the line was taut, and slowly the cumbersome thing started crawling toward the other side. Dr. de Geus threw the wet line across his shoulder, and his shiny white dress shirt got black with the wet and the muck. Like an experienced ferryman, he walked back and forth across the ferry with small measured steps, bending over the line. Once when he came to the end he nearly forgot, and almost fell overboard, but he regained his balance and walked out front again to start anew. The boat, freed from the shackles that had tied her to one shore, thought about living a carefree life and bobbed gaily on the current, always trying to float away to the beckoning sea. But the crazy doctor wasn't going to be caught off guard; he pulled with all his might on the steel cable. He pulled so strongly and so devotedly, that only when it was too late he noticed a small black tug approaching him at a distance of six hundred feet. Its whistle gave forth an anguished shriek with white steam pouring out of its funnel. The deckhand stood on the prow pale with fury, and the captain bellowed was the ferryman gone stark crazy to dare cross over right before his barge line and did he think the Dirty Hole was made just for him and did he have a brain left in his bean and . . .

But then, seeing that a collision was unavoidable, he fumed his order for "full speed astern," so that the wake was churning and foaming behind his string of barges.

The doctor, though surprised, was hardly aware of acute danger, stopped pulling for a moment, spread out his arms like a traffic policeman and signaled to the tugboat captain that he'd have to sail behind him. When they had passed each other at a hair's-breadth distance and the ferry bobbed violently in the wake of the tug, captain and deckhand both hung over the railing and called the insane fool every name in the book. But the Dirty Hole has only a narrow channel, and for the time being they needed all their skill and energy to keep the ship on its course and free from the grounds. When they had succeeded in this, the crazy ferryman waved at them from afar and bellowed loudly, wishing them a safe voyage and a safe trip home, and was everything all right on board? Such a crazy doctor! Such a bold rascal! Spring couldn't have gone to his head; it was a raw fall day and the clouds hung gray and threatening over the world. But Dr. de Geus had his fun. He moored his ship to the jetty with a final pull and began to disembark in his car. He now sang loudly about "Dear skipper, sail over me." The song flew in fragments over the dark water where it was pulled apart by the wind in tumbling sounds. Then, sitting on his haunches on the shore, the doctor washed his hands that were dirty from the cable and dried them on his shiny white handkerchief. He put on his gentleman's coat over his wet shoulders, planted the newfangled hat way back on his naked skull and, masquerading as a gentleman, he started his car whistling and drove straight ahead into the world to meet great adventure. . . .

"Now we're off!" said Tony the Ferry, when the clock on the small cupboard had struck eleven. He stood up on his short legs and reached for his cap.

"You're lazy good-for-nothings!" mumbled Mietemoei. "To let the doctor wait that long. After all he is a learned man, and who knows why he's going to town! Maybe for a sick patient in the polder, or who-knows-why!" Jochum stretched beneath the low ceiling and yawned. "Learned or not," he growled, "when it's time to sail we sail, but twice in succession —nobody can order us to do that. The crazy doctor knows very well we cross on the hour and he's got to be on time. What do you say, Aai?"

Aai didn't say a word; he was trudging in his wooden shoes behind Tony, a bit scared, for he was convinced the doctor would be raving mad and he'd heard plenty about the phenomenal strength of the little fellow.

They went outside. They climbed the dike and then all three looked at each other dumfounded. Tony rubbed his eyes but didn't dare say a thing, fearing that his short-sightedness might be playing tricks on him. But when he saw that the boys stared down in astonishment, he realized it was a bitterly serious matter, that his ferry had been stolen. Stolen, Holy Saints!

They slid down the dike behind one another and stood for awhile cursing and scolding and looking toward the other side where the louts saw the boat moored to the jetty like a cruel mockery. Tony didn't see it; there was a gray haze before his old eyes. He was trembling and swallowing nervously as if a great disaster had struck him.

"And the cable's gone too!" shouted Aai, lying down on his stomach on the jetty and feeling nervously in the water. "He took our cable and everything, damn it all, the wretch!"

Tony shook his head, completely dazed. "A bewitched fellow," he stammered. "A bewitched fellow! How is it God-possible for a man to cross the Dirty Hole all by himself, and without a cable at that! It's the devil's work, boys, sure as I stand here!"

"Hah!" growled Aai. "That fellow's as strong as an ox; no telling what all he can't do!"

"Coming back!" jubilated Jochum, who'd been thinking deeply. "We'll learn him, the dirty wise-acre, if he thinks he can trifle with us by fastening our ferry on the other side! When the gentleman comes back from the city he'll want to cross to the polder again with his car, but he'll be sorely disappointed, that scum! Come on, Aai, we'll get Noltie Damhuus' boat!"

Aai's face brightened. He had understood his clever brother. "You just go home, old man!" he cried to Tony. "We'll get even with that city slicker!" And he joined his brother, spitefully pleased about the trick they were going to play on the doctor. He'd stay on the other side all night, and as far as they were concerned the following days too. In vain he'd stand on the jetty shouting and raving; they'd fetch back the ferry and remain deaf to his cries.

"We'll learn him!" he laughed with his brother as they ran together to Noltie Damhuus, an eel fisherman who owned a tarred flat-bottomed boat. "We'll let him stand there all night long in his shirt, and tomorrow we won't ferry him across, and not the day after and not ever! Let him stay in the city with his tricks." That's what the louts decided and that's the way it would happen.

They borrowed the heavily tarred boat from Noltie Damhuus and rowed to the jetty to get the old man. Because Tony, of course, hadn't gone to Mietemoei. He was pacing the dike impatiently and cursing Dr. de Geus, who always had a trick or so up his sleeve, and rarely anything good. But now they'd learn him! Now they'd make him pay for his tricks!

The three of them rowed to the other side, and venomous old Tony was quite himself again when he stood safely on his ferryboat that he'd sailed as lord and master all these forty years. They tied the broken cable to Noltie Damhuus' flat-bottomed boat, and the two louts rowed back to the island to fasten the cable again with a couple of big knots to the protruding pole of the sheeting pile.

Mietemoei came to peer over the dike with her tawny face. "Where's that bunch keeping themselves?" she cried; the food had been cold for a long while, and the fellows could have been drowned three times over.

"We're coming!" jubilated Aai, crazy with recklessness. "We're almost finished! That half-crazy doctor stole the ferry, but we'll make him pay for it!"

Mietemoei came trudging down the dike. She didn't understand a word of what the boys were talking about, but she was very worried. "Let the doctor pay for it," she'd heard, and she knew it meant disaster and mischief. There'd been so much talk in the polder about strong fellows: of fellows strong as trees who wanted to measure their strength with the doctor, but one by one they had come home the worse for it.

"You're crazy in the head," she worried. "You mustn't get in that man's way; he'll break every bone in your bodies!"

"He got in our way," grinned Jochum, "and he won't dare do it a second time!"

Then they pushed off. They sailed to the other side where Tony was waiting impatiently on his ferry. "It's been almost two hours!" moaned Tony. "During that time we should've been three times across."

"We ain't crossing no more at all," grinned Aai. "There ain't no people anyway and that doctor can get the pest for all I care; we won't cross no more today!"

But Tony wouldn't hear of it.

"We won't take the doctor along," he agreed, "never no more, but we've got to sail; we owe it to the state."

The boys grinned. They had never seen the state. It was an empty name to them and didn't concern them a bit. But they had their revenge and it was palpable. They stepped onto the ferry and tied Noltie Damhuus' flat-bottomed boat behind it. Then the three of them pulled the ferry to the other side where Mietemoei waited for them shaking her head. "What's going to happen?" complained the little woman. "What are you going to do to the doctor? I see murder and mayhem coming, I'm telling you, and the potatoes are cold." Tony didn't say a word. The fear of de Geus had got hold of him too, and a little worried, he trudged inside behind Mietemoei. But the boys in their recklessness moored the ferry to the jetty and went to return Noltie Damhuus' flat-bottomed boat.

"For the time being we'll have to do without a doctor," they boasted to Noltie. "The skunk stole our ferry and now we don't want him on the island no more."

Noltie spat out his chewing tobacco and disdainfully shrugged his shoulders. "Oh, you don't, eh?" he jeered. "Well, if the doctor wants to come back, he will!"

"But never in his life on our ferry!" boasted Jochum.

"We'll see," said Noltie, and with that the affair was settled for Noltie Damhuus. His faith in Dr. de Geus remained unshaken. Those louts of Tony the Ferry didn't amount to beans.

Inside Mietemoei's cabin they were now enjoying the prospect of the defeat of the crazy doctor. They'd let him stand all night long in the cold, and perhaps tomorrow too and the day after. But the clock struck three and Tony got up.

"We're goin'," said Tony.

"And I'll be damned if I will," said Aai.

"And me neither!" growled Jochum.

Mietemoei started to blubber and Tony barked furiously. It was no use; the louts remained quietly seated and smoked their pipes. Then Tony trudged out the door all by himself, silent and a bit more bent than usual. They saw him crawl up the dike like a poor dog, and three times he slid back in the slippery grass because rain had begun to fall from a leaden gray sky. At last he stood on top of the dike and they saw the wild wind catch hold of his blouse and almost push the little fellow against the whole world. Then he suddenly disappeared, sliding down the dike toward the ferry. The boys watched and didn't say a word. And Mietemoei saw, with a lump in her throat, how her Tony was now all alone beneath the gray sky in the blowing wind. Suddenly she stood up furiously and her coal black eyes sparkled in her lined face.

"So you ain't going?" she snapped at the boys. "You let your old father shift for himself?"

"We ain't goin'!" growled the louts.

"Then I'll go!" hissed Mietemoei, and venomously she clattered out the door. The boys were too abashed to answer. With open mouths they stared after Mietemoei as she crawled up the dike in her flapping skirts and disappeared under the sky to the other side.

"I'll be damned," snarled Aai. "They'll come back; they can't do it without our help." But the two oldsters didn't come back. Mietemoei met Tony at the ferry, where with heavily hunched shoulders he was loosening a strap, a sad expression on his face.

"What are you doing here?" he snapped, thinking that she too wanted to keep him from doing his duty. "Go on back; I'll sail anyhow! I've been doing it for forty years and I won't quit now."

"You can't do it all by yourself!" blubbered Mietemoei against the increasing wind. "It'll break you!"

"Everything can be done that must be done," barked Tony. "Go back and tell those good-for-nothings they're deserters the state can't depend on." But Mietemoei didn't go back. She watched her old fellow hanging onto the steel cable and unable to pull the lumbersome boat away from the shore against the storm. It was a pitiful sight, the stooped little fellow exhausting himself for the sake of a useless trip. Mietemoei resolutely shouldered the cable behind Tony. "If the boys won't do it, the old'ns will show them what they're worth," she panted. Tony didn't answer. He had a lump in his throat; his emotion was so strong he couldn't even utter a "damn it," but he rejoiced in his heart for his brave wife and because now the state was being served just the same. The thought almost gave him the strength of a young man, and together the two oldsters, bending and moaning, pulled the cable as the ferry slowly crawled to the other side. When they got across, another disappointment awaited them; there was nobody to avail themselves of their services, and nobody could profit from their inhumanly hard job.

Mietemoei, exhausted, sat on the jetty trying to catch her breath. The wind played with her sparse hair that hung along her bony face in strings, and the rain splashed down mercilessly. And Tony stood on the ferry with one hand rubbing his sore loin and the other holding the steel watch. It had taken almost fifteen minutes to cross. They'd wait for five minutes, as the state prescribed, then they'd go back. "It'll be better going back," consoled Tony, "the wind's blowing directly at the island so we'll go with the current."

Mietemoei didn't answer. She sat shivering in the rain and let events take their course.

"Time!" said Tony, and they sailed back. It was easier now. Wind and current drove the ferry to the other side and they hardly had to pull. They were drenched when they entered the shack where the rebels sat smoking with expressionless faces. But there was shame behind their silence because they'd left the oldsters to their fate. And the stubbornness . . .

Mietemoei, too miserable to talk and too tired to get dry clothes, sat by the window and had a crying spell. This made the louts uncomfortable, for they knew Mietemoei was crying because of them and they were too stubborn to admit it. They got up and went outside, heads drawn into their shoulders that were hunched against the rain and wind.

"Stay here, salamanders," Tony yelled after them, "in half an hour we sail again!" But the brothers grinned and sauntered off into the polder without uttering another word. Tony was too tired and too disheartened to go after them. In dull resignation, as if broken on the wheel, he stayed in his chair. He paid no attention to the rain that was pattering against the windows, nor to Mietemoei who was sniffling in her apron.

He sat quietly and waited. Waited—for what? The clock. The broken-down little clock that he'd kept so carefully all these years, and polished and listened to, that now had become a brutal executioner, an arrogant tyrant. The voice of the state. It struck four times and Tony did not protest. His loin aching, he slowly got up and grabbed his cap.

"You stay here!" he growled to Mietemoei, who was blowing her nose. Mietemoei didn't say a word but stood up trembling, and together they went outside and crawled up the dike in the pouring rain, and when Mietemoei slid back Tony went to get her and helped her over the dike, giving her a boost on the behind. They slid down the other side like playing children, but as they were old people it seemed dreadfully serious, something that bore a resemblance to fate and that could only make one cry. . . .

Three more times Tony and Mietemoei crossed over that afternoon, stubborn as old animals who obey their instincts until they fall down. Then they did fall down. Mietemoei was no longer able to crawl up the dike from the ferry. She lay alongside the Dirty Hole, hollow-eyed, her pale face distorted. She didn't seem to be breathing, and Tony thought she had given up the ghost. With a last effort he grasped his old little wife under her arms and dragged her along the cinder path to the top of the dike. And he carried her inside to the bedstead. . . . And undressed her . . . And gathered all the covers in the dirty cottage and piled them on top of her skinny body. . . . Then he stoked the cannon stove till it glowed, and cried all by himself for a spell because the clock struck and he couldn't make the crossing again. . . . Mietemoei opened her eyes as a cough racked her. She sweated like a navvy and looked pityingly at her man who sat next to the stove in his steaming clothes.

"Come here, old duffer," said Mietemoei. Her voice was as

tender as a lovesick maiden's. Tony came to her. The crabbed little Tony sat himself down next to the bedstead and had no words in his misery. Then Mietemoei stuck her hand out from beneath the covers and stroked Tony's gray hair with infinite fondness.

"You are my fine fellow," said Mietemoei, and coughed.

"It's the first time in forty years!" sniffled Tony.

"That you're my fine fellow?" smiled Mietemoei.

"That the state doesn't find me on the job!" said Tony.

Then he undressed and crawled next to Mietemoei under the pile of covers. It grew very quiet in the cottage as dusk fell and the cannon stove glowed in the small room like a warning signal.

Now and then a coughing spell would tear Mietemoei's throat.

Then there was only the rain in the stillness. Outside the night came.

And the ferry bobbed up and down in the Dirty Hole.

10

Dr. de Geus didn't have the slightest idea that a little drama had developed around his extraordinary adventure at the ferry. Singing loudly and not completely Simon pure, he returned from the city where he had been courting a girl, a lovely sweet girl he knew from former years who'd been waiting patiently for the hairy barbarian. He'd visited the gentry all day and night, fashionable people who wondered why Dr. de Geus, that strange clown, suddenly appeared in their midst like one risen from the dead. There had been laughter and talk and drinking that evening. Much had happened that day, because they had a lot to say to each other, those important people who were all well educated and remembered the parties of yore and the crazy antics of Tom de Geus.

But beneath all the gaiety and among those happy people there was one who, with deep emotion, knew why he had come and what had driven him to the city. A woman is such a wonderful creature. She feels intuitively what is going on within a man behind all this noisy display of merriment and rousing fun. A surreptitious glance, a change in his happy countenance when he looks at her, those are the things that tell her: I am here just for your sake and I don't give a damn about the rest. She feels it by her quickening heartbeat as she sits next to him at the table in the midst of the boisterous guests. And with the falling night, when Tom de Geus says good-bye to his friends with the excuse that it's on account of his heavy practice on the island, she comes along with him, because she is going in the same direction. Then they sit together in the shiny car, while the rain pelts on its roof and the friends wave farewell and act as if nobody has the slightest idea of what is going through their heads. That's how modern city people are. Laughing and talking and being surprised about nothing, not even about a lovely woman who refused to marry anybody and now sits in the car with that rough de Geus to drive with him for awhile.

They drive away in the dusk, those two, and at once they can find no more words. They think their silent thoughts behind the pool of light made by the two headlights, and through it they see the rain tumble down on the shiny street. The doctor is aware of the woman beside him who is lovely and desirable. He knows she still wants him, even though he's almost ten years older than she, that she has waited for this night—for this hour. But now they are silent as they drive through the busy city. And later on they come to the deserted roads and still they are silent. Until the woman suddenly starts to laugh; a clear, youthful laugh with something of heaven in it and something of hell. "Damn!" says Dr. de Geus, and stops his car at the edge of the road beneath a mighty tree from which heavy drops of rain trickle down.

"Why don't you take me home?" she asks, and her eyes burn with a dark light and her throat is white and her red mouth provocative. He turns to her abruptly.

"Because you don't want to go home yet!"

They look at each other and explore the territory. They almost drown in each other's eyes, and their hearts beat hard and violently. Now they know how far they can go with each other, and it is infinitely far; there are no longer any limits. She bows her head: "Why did you let me wait such a long time, Tom?"

"I'm not free, you know that."

He looks at the dimple in her throat, and its sweetness makes him weak and passionate and infinitely sad. Then an image haunts him of an early-graying, silent woman who was once young and beautiful herself. But he pushes the thought back and now he only wants to see how lovely and provocative this one is, sitting there smiling at him. Now her dark eyes are closed and she rests against his shoulder and has her game with him. Her hair is in the curve of his arm and her slightly open mouth is lifted temptingly toward his face. Now he must swear or do crazy things. He does nothing. And she waits. She keeps her eyes closed, for she knows that otherwise he'll turn his glance away from everything that is lovely and sweet about her. She starts to talk anew, softly and melodiously, because she feels silence is dangerous at this moment. "And now?" she says. "Tom, are you free now?"

"No, but I don't care any more!"

She rejoices within but her face remains serious, her red mouth does not smile, she is careful, this woman. "Then what are you waiting for, Tom—Tommy? . . ."

It was after midnight when Dr. de Geus, singing loudly and reckless in his solitude, returned to the island. The rain had stopped but the sky was pitch dark and the headlights fiercely threw their brightness over the wet roads. The rough de Geus was returning triumphant from the city, and he didn't realize he was beaten by a girl, a kittenishly beautiful girl. He sang about Sir Halewyn, his voice resounding over the night-darkened fields, and later about the two royal children who loved each other so much, and also about the sly little fisherman. When he started on Landru, the woman killer, the Dirty Hole loomed like a slippery eel before his headlights, and the car came to a halt on the jetty with screeching tires. "Ho there!" shouted the gay doctor. "That was almost too far! If my ferry weren't here . . ."

But when he got out of his car he observed unhappily that the ferry was indeed not there, that he had driven his front wheels to the utmost edge of the jetty under which the Dirty Hole lapped darkly. He was so taken aback that he forgot to curse, and thoughtfully scratched his bare head. Had he drunk too much in the city? The front wheels of his car, dangerously close to the dark water, seemed to reproach him: "You did a lot of foolish things today; this could have been your last trick, old man! That business with the beautiful girl, that was no good either, and the Dirty Hole is mighty deep!"

"Don't rave!" the doctor said to himself. "The ferry's gone; a dirty trick! Here I am like a damn fool and the whole polder will laugh at me tomorrow because Tony the Ferry pulled a fast one on me!"

He peered to the other side but he couldn't make out the shore in the pitch dark. True, he did see that the window beneath the roof of Tony's cottage was feebly lighted. Barely visible above the dike, it was the yellow eye of a candle in the attic. It reminded Dr. de Geus of the candle of the king's two children. "My dear son swims across it," he hummed, taking off his city coat. "That's what the king's sons did!" he sang loudly as he slung his rumpled dress shirt and trousers in the car. He didn't want to think about the part of the song where the water was much too deep and the witch took away the candle so that the king's son drowned pitifully, because the wind slapped greedily at his hairy legs and nipped venomously at his naked body when a bit later he dove from the jetty as bare as old Adam. There was a loud splash in the silent night, and a moment later he came up snorting out of the water. He had to admit the Dirty Hole was colder than he'd expected and there was more current

than he cared for. The bright lights of his faithful vehicle threw
a milky path over the lapping waves, and in front of him—but it
looked damn far—he saw yellowish light in the attic window of
Tony the Ferry's cottage.

"Hold on, old boy!" he said to himself in encouragement,
and with forceful strokes he started swimming to the other side.
The sky hung low over his head and seemed to want to thrust
him down in the Dirty Hole that was sucking greedily at its victim. But the doctor swam with the quiet regularity of a man
confident in his own powers. His strokes were broad. The foam
danced around his ears and ice-cold water almost closed his eyes,
but he made steady progress. It was in vain that the current
sucked at his muscular wet body, and the wind held its breath
in order to follow the struggle of the lone man against the furious stream. The whole world lay wide and black all around him,
but it didn't worry the reckless doctor. He had already covered
half the distance and could now vaguely distinguish the jetty
and the lumbersome ferry bobbing safely up and down on its
double straps alongside the dike. With a grin of satisfaction on
his face he swam forcefully on; victory was his; the witch now
could take the candle away, as far as he was concerned, for the
king's son would find the way himself. The villagers would laugh
again, but not at that crazy doctor!

He performed his strokes and spat out the brackish water and
laughed on account of his thundering victory. Now the wind began to blow again and the Dirty Hole growled ominously and
the sky hung even lower to watch one of Adam's sons who, wet
and shining like an ugly mermaid, shot up out of the stream
and hoisted himself aboard Tony's ferry. From pure pleasure
Dr. de Geus slapped his own buttocks, but it made such a loud
report that he stopped startled. His plan shouldn't fail at the last
moment and he didn't need any spectators, either, as he jumped
up and down on the ferry to keep warm.

It was a weird sight, the way de Geus was carrying on in the
middle of the night. He unfastened the rope that moored the

ferry to the jetty and then grabbed for the steel cable to pull the ferry to the other side, where his car was waiting behind the pool of light of the headlights. He laid the line across his broad shoulders and started walking patiently with small steps from the front to the back, from the back to the front, seven steps one way and seven steps the other way, like an accomplished sailor. The wind was blowing icily around his wet body, but the crazy doctor had lots of fun, and he was singing loudly again, about a girl on the loose who wanted to go sailing.

When the song was finished the ferry banged against the jetty and Dr. de Geus was visible in his full glory in the naked light of the headlights. But only the dear Lord saw him from the low sky, and He had made him that way Himself. The wind had blown the bad boy dry, and whistling he put on his clothes again; his underwear, his socks, his trousers. He even put on his rumpled shirt and didn't forget to tie his fine tie, because he was returning to the polder a victor, and victors are well dressed, as a rule. He drove his car onto the ferry very carefully, for he was completely sober now, and his skidding down to the ferry had given him some worry.

Now he was sailing back to the island; the ferry almost moved by itself, with the strong wind behind, and the clothes that now hung so warmly on his body seemed to infuse him with renewed strength. He sang no longer about the clever girl and the clever fisherman and the children of the king who also remained in bed, but over the quiet water resounded his song about the little ship under Jesus' care, bobbing up and down on the ocean! And he meant it, as he pulled along, sounding off with a serious face. Perhaps in the glow of his headlights he had become aware for a moment of the weirdly blessed fact that only the dear Lord could see him now in the embracing darkness, only He could hear him in the stillness of the night. Who can tell what was going on in the head of that jolly doctor? He'd been a strange person, a foolish fellow, but one who knew what he wanted and would let nobody stand in his way. A man of whom you might

expect anything, but who couldn't be caught napping. Just try
to fool such a fellow; he's wise to you in no time at all. Driek of
Christ-in-the-Wilderness knew all about it. He'd found out that
you couldn't fool around with the doctor. Now the louts of
Tony the Ferry were finding out. Christ, how the polder would
laugh the next day!

And they did laugh when morning came! The louts had come
home late, and awakened later with the happy feeling that something funny was going to happen. The crazy doctor! In their
bare feet they ran downstairs, where Mietemoei was coughing
out her lungs from her scrawny throat and Tony met them with
a warning. "Mother is very ill," said Tony. "She's got a fever
like a horse."

Bang! That was the first disillusion. Somewhat taken aback,
the two gawked first at each other and then at Tony. Then they
avoided his glance, because there was something in it that made
them feel miserable. Tony didn't need to express it in words;
they knew quite well they were responsible for Mietemoei's high
fever. "Then she ought to stay in bed," mumbled Jochum.
"Keep her good and warm, and she'll be over it tomorrow."

"You're telling me what to do!" sneered Tony. "If Mother's
not very sick she won't stay in bed, and if she stays in bed she's
very sick and won't get better soon. You're no-good wastrels, because it's your fault!"

How could the louts counter the logic of small, venomous
Tony? He was right, they knew only too well. Without another
word they went outside.

"Where are you going in your bare feet?" the oldster yapped
at them.

"To see if that crazy doctor is waiting on the other side with
his car," Aai shouted, looking around, and like cats they
climbed up the slippery wet dike.

Tony stood in the doorway. "As if he didn't know as he stands
there that we'll sail him across right away!"

"Then do it yourself!" growled Aai. "We'll be damned if we will!"

Jochum said nothing; he just peered with his unwashed face over the dike and saw there was nothing to damn. The ferry lay quietly at the jetty, and there wasn't a human being to be seen on the other side.

That was the second disappointment, and the third came right afterwards when Aai discovered with a shout that somebody had tampered with their ferry! The rope was fastened in an awkward manner to the wrong pole, and the deep tracks in the muddy slope proved without a doubt that Dr. de Geus had returned to the island the night before. Now how was it God-possible that the ruffian de Geus had crossed on their ferry when there was nobody there to fetch him! Suspiciously they eyed Tony, who had joined them in alarm.

"Did you go sailing last night, old man?"

"Sailing? Sweating!" barked Tony. "I've been coughing my guts out and your mother too! Sailing? But who in God's name would sail at night?"

"But he's back!" roared Aai furiously. "God damn it all, he used our ferry!"

Yes, Tony saw it as well. After all, there was only one automobile on the island and the tire tracks were fresh. There was no doubt about it.

"It's the devil's work!" yapped Tony. "That it is, for sure!"

But Jochum was moodily silent; he didn't believe in the devil's tricks and he suspected that Dr. de Geus had an accomplice.

"Then we'll track down the devil," he growled. "Come on, Aai. Only Noltie Damhuus has a boat, and only Noltie Damhuus knew we didn't want de Geus on the island any more."

Aai growled like a wild animal. They'd teach Noltie Damhuus to connive with a city slicker and betray his own polder mates! They ran into the cottage and up to the attic. They put on their socks and their other clothes, and flew like the devil to Noltie Damhuus' cottage.

If they hadn't done it, those stupid louts, perhaps nobody would have been the wiser. Then that same day the whole polder wouldn't have known that Dr. de Geus had taken the ferry people for a ride. But now they came glowing with anger to Noltie Damhuus to complain, and Noltie said, "Go to hell! I didn't touch your ferry and I've slept like an ox! If you let yourselves be taken in by Dr. de Geus it's your own stupidity, but it ain't none of my affair! And now get the hell out of my yard, because you're just a pair of turds!" And with that he banged the door in their faces. Then all they could do was to beat it in shame. And that's what they did. . . .

But it created quite a stir in the polder, the trick Dr. de Geus had played on those ferry folk. That same morning the news spread over the island, for Noltie didn't keep a secret but told about it immediately, in no time whatever.

They laughed about clever de Geus, and they kidded the louts of Tony the Ferry, who thought they could make a fool out of the crazy doctor and had fallen into the trap themselves. There was one consolation for the ferry fellows; they were neither the first nor the last to be taken in by Dr. de Geus. There was Driek of Christ-in-the-Wilderness, and Siem of Geert de Molenaar, and Sebus Lens and a whole bunch of fellows who thought they were stronger or more clever than de Geus. They all lost out. There was no fooling with that hairy barbarian, they were convinced of it now. But how he got on the island again, how he took possession of the ferry on the other side, completely baffled the peasants. All right, it was a fact and they accepted it, as they would gradually accept everything about the crazy doctor, to whom absolutely nothing seemed impossible. There was more fun anyway when that crazy fellow, that learned Escul-ape, brought some life into the brewery. . . .

And life there was! During the next few weeks, more life than any of the polder boys had ever dared dream about.

It started with Tony's ferry and probably would have ended with the beautiful woman, you know whom, if it hadn't been for the pastor and the dominie and Driek of Christ-in-the-Wilderness.

It happened this way. After that rainy night, and the beautiful woman in his car, Dr. de Geus probably got a taste for it, because now he went to the city once a week. It was always on Friday. In the afternoon, after he'd finished his sick calls and eaten codfish and potatoes at the priest's, de Geus drove in his car to Tony the Ferry. Then he entered the cottage where the louts greeted him with embarrassed growls and Tony brought him reverently to the bedstead. There lay Mietemoei, almost ready to depart from this world, but the doctor wouldn't let her go. He kept her alive by the sheer might of his brains, and spent all his knowledge on the emaciated little woman. For deep in his heart he felt guilty toward Mietemoei, who had fallen ill when he stole the ferry. Certainly he hadn't asked her to sail and pull in the rain and the stiff wind over the Dirty Hole. But if he hadn't stolen the ferry and the louts hadn't walked out and Mietemoei hadn't jumped in the breach and . . . Thus Dr. de Geus argued with himself, and now he worked with might and main to pump some life into the emaciated Mietemoei. It was almost hopeless, for the little woman now looked nearly black from skinniness and grew worse every day. Soon she would depart for the beyond, the dominie had said. That good man also came daily now, when he knew for sure the doctor was gone, and he explained to her how it was over there. Mietemoei couldn't tell, because she had never been there.

When Dr. de Geus was finished he washed his hands again, and put on his city coat. He straightened his tie, looked in a broken mirror at his smoothly shaven face that he couldn't get accustomed to, and advanced the hand of the clock until it struck, then shouted, "All right, boys, it's time to go!"

And they left, for the boys of the ferry were men who went by the clock. Without grumbling they brought him to the other side, and when he drove his car from the ferry to the jetty, Tony stood with cap in hand and asked humbly when the doctor would be back.

"Tonight around eight o'clock," the doctor promised generously. "I'll whistle." And about one o'clock in the morning, when the whole polder was in a deep sleep, de Geus sounded his shrill whistle as he stuck two fingers in his mouth and blew out his breath with all his might. At the first sound of his whistle that trembled thinly across the water, Tony woke up moaning; at the second signal he stood yawning beside his bedstead, and before the doctor whistled again, small, venomous Tony yapped at the foot of the attic stairs, "He's there, boys, we're off!" There was some racket beneath the roof tiles, and a moment later the three ferrymen climbed over the dike in the pitch dark to fetch the doctor who was returning to the island from the outside world. Sometimes he was a bit tipsy and sometimes pretty sober, but he was always in a good mood. His first question was always about Mietemoei.

"Well, Charon, how's your wife?"

"All right." Tony wouldn't have dared say anything else.

"I'll get her well, my boy."

"The dominie says no."

"The dominie is crazy!"

"Let's hope so, Doctor."

"Tony, you'll see!"

Then the four of them lit their cigars from the doctor's case, and silently they pulled the ferry back to the island. When they had gotten the car across, the brothers climbed the dike behind their cigars, but Tony tarried a moment at the ferry. Then he would get a guilder, which he'd secretly been waiting for.

"Here, Tony, this is for you."

"That ain't necessary, Doctor, the ferry ride is only ten cents!" And gratefully he pocketed the guilder.

"Sleep well, Charon, and the best with your wife."

"She won't last much longer, Doctor."

"She'll last as long as I want her to!"

"If the dear Lord weren't there!"

"He doesn't exist, Tony, don't be afraid."

"The doctor doesn't know what he's talking about!"

"G'night, Tony!"

"G'night, Doctor!"

Then he drove off into the night, singing loudly, and Tony stared after him shaking his head until the red tail light melted away in the dark. From afar the horn sounded, at the foot of the dike a cow coughed, and on the other side the Dirty Hole was splashing.

But every Friday when the doctor put on his city clothes again and was ferried across, every Friday when he was fashionably decked out and walked around with a smooth face, of course there was gossip. How was it? One knows this and the other knows that and they all suspected the game was about a woman. A woman . . .

On Friday the priest's Bertha stands in the hallway and smells de Geus' overcoat as she fixes the codfish and potatoes. She establishes that his coat lapels stink with perfume.

So a woman it must be.

And one Friday night Jochum of Tony the Ferry saw a silken something on the back seat of the car. It may have been a woman's shawl, a thing the not-too-bright Jochum has no knowledge of. But in any case a woman.

Pretty Mieke became furiously jealous; just why, she didn't know herself. But she itches from spite when she thinks of the woman she's never seen but who certainly must exist. She gives her fantasy free rein, and in the evening under the linden tree behind the little church, where the young folk gather, she tells spicy tales of what might very well have happened: One night she lay at the bottom of the dike alongside the ferry, all by herself. The doctor came ashore in his car with the foolish wife who was dead drunk and cursing something awful. And the doctor said to Tony the Ferry and his louts that he'd knock their brains out if they said anything about the woman. So they shut up like clams, and now they don't tell how they sailed that female across again toward morning. But pretty Mieke saw it all. And the boys believe it implicitly. They believe everything that pretty Mieke tells them, if it's funny and spicy. Well, spicy it is; she saw even more, and it has to be told in a whisper so Simon Sas won't hear it, because sometimes the constable has the peculiar habit of riding his bicycle closely alongside the young folk and giving his eyes and ears the benefit of their conversations. Simon Sas, the representative of the state, doesn't want any part of Mieke's stories; he doesn't appreciate humor. But the young fellows snicker and listen, faces red and eyes shining, to the spicy stories of pretty Mieke.

Such a foolish Mieke, such a strange and fiery thing! She should have known she'd be exposed some day and nobody would believe her any more. For a few weeks later all the villagers had a chance to get a look at the doctor's "ugly female," and the young fellows gaped at her when she drove by with the doctor in his car.

It happened one morning in early spring when all the green burst forth tenderly from the soil. The sun hung brightly in a clear blue sky, and the pear tree was parading a wealth of white blossoms. It was the right kind of weather for the festive entry of Dr. de Geus' ugly female. Ugly female? Who said that again? Not pretty Mieke, was it? . . .

No; pretty Mieke, disconsolate and alone, was sobbing so hard behind Melis Eilers' haystack that her whole young body shook. "The old tart!" sniveled Mieke. "The damn ugly old tart! Why did she have to come to the polder? Why is she driving our fellows crazy?" And Mieke sobbed more violently. But the old tart was triumphantly driven through the village, and uncouth de Geus sat grinning beside her. And the fellows of the polder—their eyes popped out of their heads!

11

That poor pretty Mieke, how badly she had played her cards! None of the fellows believed her stories any more, now that they'd seen the doctor's ugly female. She was neither old nor ugly, and she wasn't a drunkard. She upset the young lads with her large, mocking eyes which looked straight through their clothes, and that wasn't so astonishing either.

Driek of Christ-in-the-Wilderness was one of the first who experienced the strange charm of her passionate being and her dark eyes and mysteriously smiling mouth, moist and red like a child's mouth, but still not quite that either. Driek couldn't resist it. It made him feel disturbed and unsure. It made him do foolish things. This seemed to be the fate of the Bladders, to end up by being taken in. Aai Bladder himself, Christ-in-the-Wilderness, had experienced it with the old broken-down horse of Dr. Walrave. With the fury of a tortured bull he'd beaten the old animal to death because it wouldn't make way for his Satan.

It was an easy victory, little changed by the fact that he had perhaps saved the lives of the little Briools. Aai Bladder had been exposed to the view of the villagers, in spite of all his bravery. And later Driek, his giant son, was felled by the sledge-hammer blow of the little doctor, right before the eyes of pretty Mieke. The villagers also knew about the fight in the middle of the night, when those three powerful young fellows hadn't been able to floor that one little doctor.

But now something else was going to happen in the polder. Now a little child was coming. This, of course, means nothing; such things happen every day and you can be glad about it. The polder is a fertile region. The beets shoot from the soil like mushrooms, and the potatoes, the turnips, the cabbage, the rye are all flourishing. And it's no different with the calves and the colts and the little pigs. Should the farm hands lag behind? Of course not. With small purple heads like nervous little oldsters, they take possession of the island and announce their presence with a bit of crying and tiny, wide-open gullets. All that doesn't matter. There is nothing strange in it.

But Geerte of Christ-in-the-Wilderness was going to have a baby, and this was really remarkable. Aai Bladder didn't know himself how it had happened, because his youngest was almost sixteen and Geerte was deep in her fifties. You can't gainsay that. The whole polder knew about it, about Geerte of Christ-in-the-Wilderness, and all of them lived with it intensely, knew almost to the day when it was to happen. But when it was about to happen, that great and mighty miracle, nobody was prepared. Then those two big tough men were pacing at their wits' end through the house, Christ-in-the-Wilderness and Driek, his giant son; two men with hands like shovels, but when it came to having babies, they knew nothing. "To Janne!" shouted Aai to his oldest. "Go right away to Janne of Nol de Biek and tell her to hurry over! Tell her the baby's coming! Tell her that Mother's about to peg off!" Now Driek actually thought so, for poor Geerte with her yellowish drawn face was lying there in her bedstead moaning something awful. Driek shot into his wooden shoes and clumped over the dike to the midwife, Janne of Nol de Biek. In his great anxiety he didn't even notice that his wooden shoes took in water and the sweeping rain was drenching him through and through. He ran as fast as he could, that mighty Driek, and he felt a lump in his throat, because in spite of all his bravado he was crazy about his mother, and now she lay in her bed like a person in death's agony. He ran breathlessly over the deserted dike and prayed that Geerte wouldn't die, that the good Lord wouldn't abandon her! Driek's anxiety was not exaggerated, for Janne of Nol de Biek had said it wasn't an easy matter for somebody Geerte's age to have a child and Geerte Bladder was in a bad way. That's why Driek was running all the way, praying that Geerte wouldn't breathe her last in the meantime. When he came to Janne's cottage, which leaned against the dike a little way beyond the village, he knocked on the shutters and Nol de Biek met him gaily in the narrow hallway with an oil lamp.

"She said you must go and fetch the doctor; go right away to de Geus, because she's just been called to Femme of Kees Kranebil who's having her seventh, and your mother's is a special case and Dr. de Geus should handle it."

Black Driek cursed in disappointment, but he realized it wouldn't help Geerte even if he knocked everything to smithereens in his fury. It wasn't the fault of Janne nor Nol de Biek that Femme of Kees Kranebil was also lying *in extremis.* So Driek ran back over the dike to the doctor's house. As he clumped into the bare carriage drive he was suddenly struck with fear, remembering the last time he'd been there, almost a year ago, when they'd planned to beat up the crazy doctor. Now he was all by himself, and he could only hope that de Geus wouldn't avenge himself by refusing to help his mother in her hour of need. . . . Driek was trembling with anxiety as he rang the bell and waited in the drenching rain.

At first nothing happened; all was quiet for a moment behind the wide door after the bell sounded, and Driek cursed through his Hail Marys for fear the doctor mightn't be home. But when once again he nearly tore the bell from its chain, a window was opened above, the same window de Geus had called from almost a year ago. But that had been a clear, frosty night, and now the night was filled with squalls of rain. Then the crazy doctor had hung out the window in his undershirt, and now . . . Whatever it was it didn't sound very friendly up there.

"You see," thought Driek, "now there'll be some Goddamn trouble! He's still furious at me, since that night!" But when he stuttered that the baby was coming and that Janne de Biek wasn't home, something changed in the forbidding features of Dr. de Geus.

"One moment, my friend! I'll be down in a minute." "My friend," he had said, "my friend," as if they hadn't wanted to skin each other alive, those two ruffians! Driek thought about it with a queasy feeling in his stomach, and for all he possessed he wished he'd never fought with the doctor. The case of Mother Geerte proved conclusively that you should never lift your hand to your superior, because today or tomorrow you might need him just the same. It was a damned shame he'd behaved so badly. Now his mother was delivered to the mercy of de Geus. . . . With mounting anxiety he suddenly heard someone fussing with the chain inside the door. Now it would happen, he thought. Now de Geus would laugh at him and kick him away from the door. Now he'd have to beg on his knees for mercy for Mother Geerte, who had nothing to do with that brawl. . . .

But the door swung open slowly, and it wasn't out of fear that Driek's eyes bulged from their sockets when the light in the hallway was lit. What he saw was so unbelievable and unexpected that Driek lost his breath in astonishment. It wasn't the crazy doctor who stood there in his hastily donned coat and trousers, but someone quite different who had hurriedly put on a wrap. She smiled so sweetly at him, and she had such a moist red mouth and deep dark eyes in her beautiful face, that Driek in his wonder didn't hear what she said and just stood staring in disbelief at that pretty face and smiling mouth and deep white throat. He looked at her silk kimono and her partially bare feet that were stuck in red mules. Then Black Driek said, "Damn, it ain't God-possible!"

And she: "Come in, friend, everything's possible here. Don't stand there in the rain; the doctor will be down in a minute."

Driek followed her through the marble hall, dazed as a beaten schoolboy. "Friend," she'd said to him, she too! But of course she didn't know he had fought with the doctor the previous year. . . . He followed the pretty woman into the living room where she motioned him to a chair with a slight gesture of her white hand. "I'm soaked through," he mumbled, "I'll wait outside." But he remained standing on the rug in his soaking wet socks and looked at her, wondering how it was God-possible that the beautiful creature belonged with that hirsute Geus upstairs.

But it must be so, because from upstairs came the stentorian voice of de Geus: "Corrie! Get my bag ready! I'll be down in a moment. And tell the black one to wait; he can come along with me in the car!"

So her name was Corrie. It gave him a vague feeling of displeasure that this beautiful, proud creature who moved through the silent room like an Eastern princess had to obey the shouting voice of the uncouth de Geus. So she must belong to him, for zealously she began packing his things. Then she put the big leather satchel on the table and smiled again at Black Driek, who couldn't keep from looking at her.

"Sit down," she said, and Driek sank to a chair, weak-kneed. "Have a cigarette," she said. "The doctor will be ready soon."

She took a lovely box from the smoking table, and still smiling her mysterious coquettish smile, she floated toward him and bent over him. Driek bowed his head and tremblingly took a cigarette. He was aware of the disturbing perfume or whatever it was—he didn't know—and as she stood before him he was shocked by the whiteness of this beautiful creature. How delicate and strange she was. Now he was even more disturbed. He didn't dare look up when she remained there a moment. He knew she was looking down at him with a mocking smile, her eyes glowing with a deep dark fire.

He grumbled "thanksmerci" and searched his pockets for matches, his head still bowed. He didn't find any, but the strange woman tripped out of the room, turning around to say there were matches on the smoking table. Suddenly the tone of her voice was oddly different, cold, and the black one looked up in surprise, afraid he'd done something wrong and made her angry. But she was out of the room, and he heard the doctor growl upstairs, and after that he heard her cooing laughter and the noise of boots. Driek stared into emptiness. How was it God-possible that there were such beautiful women, who walk around in a whatyoumacallum like that and come to live with the crazy doctor! Black Driek was nonplussed. He forgot his cigarette, he forgot the matches on the smoking table and Mother Geerte who was having a baby. Driek stared at the open door through which the beautiful woman had disappeared, and listened sharply to all the noises that reached him from upstairs. Then resounding footsteps came down the stairs and de Geus appeared in person, hastily dressed and good-humored as always.

"Well, my friend, so it's on the way? Has she been laboring a long time, or did you fly out the door at the first sign? Then you could've let me rest for a few hours, black one! But of course you don't know about such things. Light your cigarette, before it's a soggy quid!"

Driek agreed that he didn't know a thing about it, but nevertheless Mother Geerte was shrieking with pain, and then he accepted a light from the revolver that de Geus had frightened him with so badly that other time. They looked at each other above the small flame, and pinpoints of mockery sparkled in de Geus' eyes. Driek smiled shyly back at him; they both thought about their first meeting, almost a year ago. Then the doctor went quickly to the door. "Corrie, I'm going, you hear?" he shouted.

"Yoohoo!" was the reply from upstairs.

Dr. de Geus furrowed his brows, but immediately his face looked gay again. "I'll drive the car to the front of the house," he growled. "Just wait here a minute."

Driek waited. He sucked nervously at his cigarette and thought about Mother Geerte in her bedstead and then about the beautiful woman, and then, with flaring anger, about pretty Mieke who had told so many ugly lies about this creature. Dr. de Geus drove up and entered the hallway.

"She's insane!" growled Black Driek. "She said it all because she was jealous!"

"Who are you talking about?" said de Geus, standing before him suspiciously.

"Aw, nothing," mumbled Driek confusedly, "I was thinking of pretty Mieke."

Dr. de Geus smiled subtly; he understood the connection. He preceded Driek outside as he hummed.

He would have to get accustomed to many things; to a woman who's beautiful, a woman who's sweet, a woman who keeps you waiting while she dresses . . .

Finally she came down. Black Driek meanwhile was struck with the frightening thought that the baby could have been born three times over, and with a sickly feeling he reflected on Mother Geerte again as he sat down in the car beside Dr. de Geus. Things would be in a mess at the farm of Christ-in-the-Wilderness; the neighbors had all said the child could never be born in the customary way and Geerte was much to old for such an adventure. . . .

They raced over the dike. The rain stippled the windshield with oval drops and the cobblestones shone dark gray in the glare of the headlights. After a neck-breaking trip they swung into the yard of Christ-in-the-Wilderness. Driving past the broken-down pigsty, they stopped at the back door under the leaky drainpipe. They had no sooner crossed the threshing floor when they were met by the shrieking of Mother Geerte in her labor. "Go and find some chore, Black'un," said de Geus. "There's nothing you can do inside."

Driek nodded curtly and walked around the house in the pouring rain. He didn't want to be inside, but neither did he want to go to the village. He walked through the wet grass. For a moment it would be quiet inside the house, then the shrieking would start again and Driek would stop in horror. Alternately he swore and said little prayers until it became quiet again, then he resumed his walk in the wet darkness.

The lower part of the door squeaked, and Christ-in-the-Wilderness bent under the low drainpipe. There he stood, large and powerful in the flickering light of the stable lantern, but his fierce eyes stared in fright into the darkness and his mouth trembled as if he were going to cry.

"She'll die from it!" he growled to Black Driek. "She'll never make it, and we can't even help! They sent me away." Driek nodded feebly, and together the two big frightened men began walking around the broken-down house. Silently they made their rounds, bowed by the worry that rested heavily on their shoulders, indifferent to the rain. They listened intently and stood still in horror when Geerte's shrieks, no longer resembling anything human, tore through the silence again.

How long did they pace and stand and listen? The darkness grew heavier and the rain kept up. The night hung thick and impenetrable over the polder and the little dwelling. They felt their knees shake and went to sit in the pigsty where Tienus, the mighty boar, was grunting contentedly.

"She'll die of it for sure!" Christ-in-the-Wilderness moaned again, and a little later: "I sent the kids to Aunt Jannegie. They can't do anything here. . . . There's three of them in there busy with it. . . . Janne of Nol de Biek came too, and a little later Truike Pothuis. . . . So they sent me outside, because there were women galore. . . ."

"It's a Goddamn shame," growled Black Driek, "but we can't help it, old man, everything has to go on just the same."

"He had forceps in his bag like this," muttered Christ-in-the-Wilderness, and he indicated in the dark how big they were.

"Forceps?" Driek said, shocked.

"It has to be taken with forceps," sniffled Aai. "That's the worst that can happen to a woman, with the forceps, God damn it!"

Driek couldn't stand it in the close pigsty. The sweat poured from his wet back, and Geerte started to cry out louder than before. The two fellows jumped up and made their rounds again in the night, shivering with wetness and misery. Then a small figure came walking over the muddy yard. They nearly walked over him at the corner of the house.

"Good evening to you," said Nol de Biek.

"Damn it!" said Christ-in-the-Wilderness with a start. "What are you doing here?"

"I came to fetch Janne. They've called for her. It's very busy tonight. And how are things here?" asked Nol. "Why are you outside with Driek? It ain't that . . ."

The three men were silent. It had been disturbingly quiet inside the house for quite a long time now, much too long, according to the two men, who had only half listened to Nol de Biek. Until now they had paid undivided attention to the goings-on inside the house, and the sounds that should be coming from there had stopped. Christ-in-the-Wilderness sweated; the silence was oppressive after all those raw shrieks in the night. Questioningly he looked at Black Driek and Driek at him. The three of them stood there and the rain rustled down endlessly, and they heard the water gurgling in the drainpipe. They listened. . . .

Then Driek couldn't bear it any longer. "Damn!" he said, and Nol de Biek was shocked, not by the curse word but the suddenness of it. Aai Bladder, the bony giant, almost collapsed, and felt himself shrinking with a throttling fear.

"She's not making a sound any more!" he whispered; and then violently: "If it's true, that she—that she . . ." And suddenly more violently to Nol de Biek: "Why do you stand there? Must I call that wife of yours?" Nol de Biek didn't say a word. He'd been accustomed to so much during his life, he gently laid a thin moist hand on the giant's shoulder and Aai calmed down. His resistance was broken in a hoarse sob.

"She suffered from poverty and misery all her life, and if she doesn't pull through now . . ."

"She'll pull through!" Biek soothed him, as if he had something to say about it. "You must pray, Aai, trust in our good Lord. . . ."

"What else do you think I've been walking around all night for?" growled Aai. And rebelliously again: "Now I want to see what's happened!" He didn't want to, but he couldn't wait any longer. He climbed to the door and bent beneath the leaking drainpipe. Hesitatingly Nol de Biek and Black Driek, big scared Driek, followed him, and then—look, how funny—he turned around howling and went in the pigsty to sit next to Tienus. Tienus opened one eye and grunted with satisfaction; then the boar rubbed against the straw and went to sleep again, unconscious of the miracle that was happening nearby. But Christ-in-the-Wilderness, despite his wetness, clumped into the low-ceilinged room, where Geerte was paying a high price for the new and tender life. There was a haze in the room and a sickly odor, and the womenfolk moved whispering around the doctor who grumblingly gave short orders. The lamplight shone dimly through the haze and the people looked ghostlike, exercising their functions in a weird manner. But Christ-in-the-Wilderness saw none of this. His ears caught a small sound, a wee cry, and in the lamplight his wild glance caught a squirming red doll that was being hurriedly washed by Janne of Nol de Biek. His joy at the sight was at once tempered by the mysterious actions of the others near the bed, and by Geerte's drawn gray face and her strangely upturned eyes.

"How's she doing?" he cried in uncontrolled anguish. "What's happening here, for God's sake! Geerte, girl, how are you!"

"Get the hell out of here!" growled de Geus over his shoulder, all tense himself. "There's another one on the way!"

The powerful Christ-in-the-Wilderness was too dazed to get mad; he permitted Truike Pothuis to lead him outside.

"We don't need men," she whispered in his ear. "You mustn't be so upset; the doctor's here, isn't he?"

"Yes," whined the farmer in his great anguish. "I guess so, but, but . . ." For a few moments they were lost in thought, then Christ-in-the-Wilderness broke the weighty silence.

"This—this I never meant!" he complained. "It—it can't be true!"

Nol de Biek, who also was pushed aside without being able to deliver his message, smiled in the darkness. "The good Lord wanted it this way!" he whispered. "He is so good and wise—He always gives us more than we ask for!"

"But I didn't ask for any of it," moaned Aai. "I only want to keep Geerte! We can't do without mothers, don't you understand?"

Nol de Biek understood. He understood that Geerte Bladder had to go on living, that she had to bring her hard job to a good end and must be spared for her family.

Christ-in-the-Wilderness couldn't stand it outside the door through which he heard no sound but the child's crying. He clumped across the yard. He cursed and he prayed and he gathered his big hands into fists and beat them on the pigsty to calm his nerves and his anguish. He almost beat his huge fists to blood, and it echoed so loudly through the night that Tienus sprang to his feet with a grunt and Black Driek flew outside with his heart sunk to his wooden shoes.

"What happened?" he cried in terror. "How's Mother and everything?" He stood trembling before his father and paid no attention to Nol de Biek who stood nearby nor to the rain that poured in buckets from the gray sky.

"The first one came!" growled Christ-in-the-Wilderness. "Only the first!"

Black Driek looked at him as though seeing water afire. He grew dizzy. "Only the first? . . . But how many? . . ."

This was enough for Nol de Biek. The rain had drenched him to the skin and he was shivering from the cold.

"Don't stand there shouting like a couple of idiots!" he said, in a more unfriendly tone than he intended. "Have some faith in our good Lord, Who rules everything for the best. Let's go in the barn; at least we'll be dry, and you better pray, for all blessing comes from above."

They followed him hesitatingly into the barn, where Satan turned his head a moment and pawed the stones as they entered. Christ-in-the-Wilderness, that huge scared fellow, really believed that blessings came from above. He fell on his knees next to Satan in the stable, folded his hands and prayed with tightly closed eyes. And Black Driek wouldn't do less, so he started saying Hail Marys loudly, and he beat his chest and promised he'd never do anything bad any more. Nol de Biek, who was childless, watched the two powerful men. He listened to them and thought that with all their violence and passion and bravado they were only big children. Of praying and the good Lord and all the rest he had little notion, for Biek wasn't such a fine fellow, either. But when he saw the two men kneel he did the same, so that Geerte's ordeal wouldn't last much longer and the next Bladder would come soon. Moreover, Janne had to make another call.

Then the last little Bladder was born. A little girl of five pounds! Aai Bladder gave a yell when Janne de Biek came to tell him. And he yelled again when Dr. de Geus told him that Geerte was asleep. Asleep, and she didn't die! That was too much for the rough giant. He cried like a stuck pig and laughed through his tears and said that he couldn't believe it, he had to see it first, and he'd gone through such a hard night!

Then the fellows laughed so much in the dark barn that Satan grew restless. They laughed about Aai Bladder, who had spent such a hard night, and about the two new little Bladders and about life that was so beautiful again for a poor manure farmer. He wasn't allowed to see Geerte, whose night had been somewhat harder; she needed rest now to get back her strength. This the fellows believed. But they were allowed to see the two newly born in the room upstairs, two delicate rosy dolls, a boy and a girl. A girl was something Aai Bladder hadn't expected at all.

"What'll we call the thing?" he asked nonplussed. Up till now they were always boys. Then they all burst into laughter again and resoundingly slapped each other's shoulders.

12

The priest had been bitterly disappointed in his friend since the first time he and one of his parishioners had come face to face with the beautiful woman who lived at the crazy doctor's house. Why did he have to hear everything from outsiders? Until just lately, hadn't de Geus been coming to his parsonage every Friday to eat fish and potatoes, and hadn't they sat together many long nights in the haunted house and talked about things that interested both of them? A fine friendship had developed between the priest and the rugged doctor. They had told each other all their secrets, except this one. Sure, the priest knew that Dr. de Geus had gone to the city every Friday the last few months all dressed up like a gentleman. He'd also heard rumors here and there, for the villagers gossiped a lot. One rumor was that the doctor went to the city because of a woman, and this the priest understood quite well himself.

But what the villagers didn't know about was de Geus' own wife, how he had left her and how she was patiently waiting for him. It was a secret between the two friends. It was buried deep since the evening when de Geus had made a clean breast of it. They never mentioned it again, and when de Geus started to dress up and go to the city once a week, never telling his old friend what he did there . . . Yes, perhaps it was a hasty conclusion on the priest's part, for he liked to believe the best of everyone; he happily noticed the change in the crazy doctor, and doubled his prayers for him. He implored the dear Lord fervently to let it be true, to please let it be true that de Geus was finding his way back to his own wife. Gradually his hope became a conviction, when one Friday afternoon during the meal, after Bertha had been unusually harsh with the doctor, de Geus had joked, "Bertha, my daughter, save me from your charm, or soon I won't be able to face my wife!"

"My wife," he said; there was no question about it.

The priest laughed heartily and Bertha closed the door violently behind her, and afterward de Geus looked so serious that the priest no longer had any doubts. He didn't dare to ask, nor did he want to, but as he prayed even more ardently for his good friend his certainty increased about the doctor returning to his wife.

Now he was suddenly disillusioned. Now the priest was confronted by the beautiful woman called Corrie Bergmans, who had looked at him mockingly with her dark eyes when he met her for the first time. It had happened the afternoon before the twins were born at the farm of Christ-in-the-Wilderness. Bertha had heard about it. The priest reflected on these things in his silent room. He had said nine o'clock mass and eaten two thin slices of bread with cheese, and Bertha had cleared the table in an evil mood.

The priest sighed. "Bertha, my daughter, you and I are getting old. . . . Shouldn't we start judging our fellow human

beings with more compassion?" he said, after a venomous remark by Bertha about the doctor and his "concubine."

"She drinks like a fish, and—she shouldn't live with him.
She's disgracing the village. And you too!"

"Me, Bertha?"

"Yes, you, and our parsonage! You receive the heathen here
in your home and visit him in his robber's den, where the
devil lives and the dead notary's spooking around, and now
he's brought a witch from the city! It's a shame!"

"You dare say a great deal to your old parson today, Bertha! Come on, my daughter, drink a cup of coffee and rinse
your mouth."

"Shame!" Bertha repeated stubbornly. "The whole village
is ashamed of the way that creature lives, and you're together
almost every night."

The priest grew impatient. After all, there were limits. "I
have my reasons for visiting Dr. de Geus, Bertha. And now
leave me alone. I've still got a lot to do."

Bertha hesitated. She knew she had gone too far this time.
But she meant well for the priest, who after all was entrusted
to her motherly care.

"I'm saying it for your own good," she whimpered. "I'm
saying it just because I don't want the villagers to soil your
reputation."

"I know you mean well, Bertha, but your tongue is too
sharp, and you're not gentle enough in your judgment. People
love to gossip, Bertha. Nearly all the villagers owe a lot to
Dr. de Geus, but when they can blacken him they love it.
That's how people are. They don't mean much harm, but
they crave sensation."

Bertha blew her nose hard and left the room. You couldn't
talk reasonably to the priest anyway. That man let himself be
fooled by the doctor with his eyes wide open. He smiled a bit
when they said bad things about him and raked him over the
coals, he prayed for that heathenish barbarian who didn't want

to mend his ways, and he agreed with the villagers when they called him an innocent old fool. These things irritated Bertha every day and burdened her life.

The priest thought about the joy of Aai Bladder, who had come to church that morning to have his two urchins christened. Truike Pothuis had hobbled along with a tiny creature on each arm, as proud as if they were her own. The little girl had a name now; she was named Geerte after her mother, and the little fellow's name was Tony. After the nine o'clock mass they were baptized, and afterward Christ-in-the-Wilderness had downed a pint with his oldest in the Silver Swan. They deserved it, after a night that had taxed their nerves so heavily.

The priest's thoughts wandered from the Bladders to Dr. de Geus again and the strange woman who was living with him. It was a great shame that de Geus hadn't told him about it before. He would have spoken seriously to him and shown him his duty as a married man and a Christian. Yes, as a Christian, for in spite of all his bravado and rebelliousness toward our dear Lord, the doctor couldn't convince himself there was no God. The doctor would have been furious at the priest's exhortations, but subsequently he would have agreed with him. Subsequently the priest was always right. Subsequently, that's what made it so bitter. Thus the priest thought in the loneliness of his room, as he searched for a way to make everything turn out all right for his friend. He prayed to the Holy Ghost, Who sometimes seemed to find so little pleasure in him. He prayed for enlightenment of his mind to find the right solution in this desperately difficult dilemma.

Then he went out, without having drawn up a definite plan. On his way he convinced himself that his mind was barely sufficient for a simple village priest. He walked with bowed head, deeply aware of his incompetence and convinced of his unworthiness to protect God's lambs. Hadn't he always and everywhere come too late? Hadn't he always found the right word and gesture too late? Now again. Now with lead in his shoes he was on his way to the house of his good friend. Now he would try to mend the damage he should have prevented. And he didn't even know how to begin, or what to tell those two in the haunted house. The priest was afraid— and he felt so old and tired. . . .

He had to stop awhile along the dike, leaning on his black cane. He shivered. Perhaps it was from the cold he'd caught late the night before. Perhaps too it was worry about the difficult job ahead, where he must mend what he should have prevented. He didn't know. He only felt sick and miserable, and tears sprang into his eyes when he thought of his impotence.

Bertha's words weighed heavily on his shoulders: "The whole village is ashamed of the way that creature lives. . . ." Yes, the whole village. The priest knew how de Geus' conduct was the center of attention. The whole village. And now there was even much more material for gossip, and he couldn't deny that the villagers were right. A man can't take a woman he hasn't married to his house. . . .

Sighing, the priest continued his way along the foggy dike, and now and then a peasant's cart drove toward him, with a rattling of milk cans and a curt greeting from the farmer. "Hoi!" the farmer would say, raising his whip a bit. It meant the same as "Good morning." The distraught priest returned the greeting with a short wave of his hand. He didn't notice who was passing. He was much too immersed in his worries and bowed by his burden.

He reached the doctor's house. It was nearly noon, and de Geus would be there now with the strange woman. He would find them together and wouldn't know how to begin nor what to say.

"*Emitte Spiritum tuum,*" prayed the priest, but his head remained empty, though his heart brimmed with love and sadness. Then he pulled the bell. It was too late now for retreat.

The good Lord had sent him; from now on he must handle it himself. He coughed behind his pale hands and waited. The strange woman opened the door.

"Good morning, eh . . ." he said. "I'm the priest."

The woman looked at him mockingly, then preceded him inside silently, and the priest followed her with hesitance. He hung up his overcoat and cane on the clothes tree in the hall, as he always did. He entered the large room where the woman waited for him, all by herself.

"My friend the doctor, isn't he home?" he said uncertainly.

"If you mean my husband, he went to see a patient."

"Your husband? . . . I didn't know . . ."

"No, we're not married," she interrupted, "but that's no-body's business. Won't you sit down?"

There'd been hostility and fear in her voice, but she controlled herself, offered him a chair and, when he sat down, a cigar.

"Shall we have coffee first, or do you want to start your sermon right now?"

The priest preferred coffee first. This way he would gain time, and then maybe his rapidly beating heart would calm down.

"I'd love a cup of coffee," he said, smiling weakly, and with trembling fingers he plucked at the tip of his cigar. She gave him a light, lit a cigarette herself and poured the coffee. Then she sat opposite him in a deep easy chair, crossed her legs nonchalantly and smoked in silence. Through the smoke rings that she blew from her mouth in the shape of an O, her dark eyes were fixed on the priest. He was stirring his coffee steadily and fervently beseeching the Holy Ghost to help him go on. He felt her cold gaze directed at him, and perspiration appeared on his brow from his strenuous thinking.

Veni Sancte Spiritus! How could he reach this woman without destroying all he'd built up during those long evenings with his good friend? She was so strange—so completely different from any of the village women. She knew beforehand why he came, and her defense was well prepared. She had no intention of giving up to the old village priest all she had gained with so much effort. . . . The ticking of the clock was disagreeably loud, and the cup trembled in his thin hand as he brought it to his mouth. The coffee warmed him inside, but he was uncomfortable under her steady gaze and defiant silence. The clock's slow ticking was stealing seconds from eternity. Now he had to say something. He looked up and gazed into her cold eyes. A discouraged smile spread over his old face. He sighed. His cigar had gone out, and he trembled as he searched his pockets for matches. Then she got up and offered him a light again, like an obedient child. She shouldn't have done it, that delicate white woman, for when she stood beside him in the quiet room, meekly bending over him with the light in her small hands, the priest's heart went out to her. He could have cried for this human child, one of God's lambs, who yearned for a bit of happiness, a bit of love, and now had to defend herself against the man who wouldn't allow her that stolen happiness.

She sat down again, small and pale in the big easy chair, and waited for the sentence he was about to pronounce. The gray light of the autumnlike morning entered the window behind her and fell on her blonde hair and along her cheeks. There was something touchingly sweet about her, and when she closed her dark eyes a moment the proud mocking expression she'd greeted him with had disappeared. The little priest swallowed, sought desperately for the right phrase, and began.

"Do you love him so much that you must make him unhappy, my child?"

Perhaps it was a foolish question, but she suddenly looked at him with big, frightened eyes and for a moment her lips moved nervously as if she were going to cry.

"Do you realize you can never make him happy this way? Don't you know someone else has a right to his love, and that God doesn't offer His finest gift to be bargained with?"

She sat up stiffly and there was honest indignation in her voice.

"I don't bargain with love! You know better than that. I'm attached to him because I can't help it! Because I love him! What do you know about it? Do you know how much a man and woman can love each other?"

She gave him a hostile look.

"Do you know, my child? And have you no pity for the other, the only one with a right to his love?" The little priest felt his arguments were poor, but he clung desperately to this one point, that it was unjust to steal the love that belonged to someone else.

"She has no right to it!" the woman defended herself furiously. "Their love wasn't mutual! She didn't know how to love a man! She couldn't make him happy, so she has no right to his love! I have a right because I love him and he loves me! But what do you priests know about it? All you care about is everybody hypocritically following the right and narrow path, and above all, nobody must be shocked! You preach righteousness and love, and meanwhile your heart stays cold! There are rich farmers and their wives on this island who crawl in bed together to heap money upon money, but there's no love between them. Still, you marry them off and call this hypocritical alliance holy because it was made in church. But you point your finger at two people who just love one another and live together in one house! That happiness must be destroyed because the church wasn't involved! You want to deprive me of that happiness, don't you?"

She jumped up furiously before the little priest was able to interrupt her flood of words. She was no longer the delicate little woman the priest had felt compassion for a little while ago; as she confronted him with outstretched arm, she was an angel of vengeance with an angry red face.

"But I won't put up with it, do you get that? I won't let

you smash my happiness with pharisaical talk. Get out, and don't you ever dare show your hypocritical face here again!"

Trembling with rage she went to the door and held it wide open for him. "Get out! You, get out! . . ."

And what else could the little priest do but leave with a sigh? He was completely discouraged and unsure of himself. He would go. He had worked himself into a daze trying to find the right word, the right tone for this strange, hysterical woman. But she talked so fast and passionately, and the Holy Ghost allowed him to muddle along by himself today, and he found no words to correct her or defend his point. He only knew he was a stupid old man who couldn't face the problem. With bowed head he walked through the hall to the clothes tree.

She suddenly gained control of herself, though she was breathing hard with anger. She helped him on with his coat, gave him his hat and cane. She opened the front door for him.

"I'm sorry," she said calmly. "I'm sorry it had to happen this way, but it's your own fault. You came to take away the happiness I've found, after I yearned for it for years. You don't understand what he means to me or you would have left us alone!"

The priest hesitated at the door. He thought about the other woman he didn't know. Was she yearning for her husband? Hadn't she been robbed? That thought wouldn't leave him alone; it had become an obsession to him all during her short and angry talk. That's why he didn't need any other argument, only this one, the worst. Now he had to tell her, even if it was on the threshold of the house she was chasing him from. He looked in her angry eyes. He leaned against the doorpost, so weak and discouraged did he feel.

"But the other one—" he began uncertainly. . . . "She has the first right. . . ."

"For my part, the other one can—!" shouted the lady. She

didn't complete the sentence and slammed the door furiously behind him.

The little priest shrank. His hand slid slowly along the doorpost, and leaning on his cane he stepped down the flight of stairs. He bowed his head and trudged slowly along the driveway toward the dike. A haze trembled before his old eyes. He attempted to take a few more steps. He was so tired. . . . The doctor's car came to a halt with shrieking tires right in front of him at the turn to the dike.

"Damn!" said de Geus, frightened. "I just missed you by a hair's breadth, old fellow! Where are you bound for? Won't you stay for lunch?"

The priest looked up, and the crazy doctor was shocked by his terribly sad face. In no time at all he was out of the car and laid a heavy hand on the priest's shoulder. "Come on, old man, what's the trouble now? Not any difficulties?" He smiled broadly.

The priest nodded seriously. "Yes, friend, difficulties—and you know why. . . ."

Suddenly the doctor knew. The sweet smile disappeared from his face and he looked at his old friend, touched. "Of course—it's on account of her, eh?"

The priest nodded. "It's a shame you didn't tell me about it before, my friend. . . . We had no secrets from each other, did we?"

De Geus was silent. This was the break, he knew. It hurt him that now he'd have to choose between him and her. He could have told him before, months ago, when it first started. But what did the old priest know about it? Of his struggle, his loneliness and his yearning for a woman? What could this spiritual old man know about the longing and passion that gripped a vital young fellow like de Geus? What did he know about beautiful women, who smiled at you and tempted, tempted . . . ?

"You shouldn't have done it," said the little priest feebly.

"You shouldn't do this, my friend. You must undo it and—and think of your own wife."

"And send her away, eh?" de Geus suddenly snapped at him.

"And send her away," answered the priest.

De Geus offered him his large hand. The small, frail hand of the priest lay in it. That meant adieu. It was the end of a beautiful friendship.

"I'm sorry," said the doctor. "I'm sorrier than I can say, but it isn't possible. The other thing is stronger than I am myself, stronger than your good Lord and everything."

The priest looked deep into his eyes.

"I'll pray for you," he whispered; then his voice broke in a sob, and he turned away so he wouldn't stand there and cry in the middle of the road.

He trudged up the dike, bowed down and feeling his way with the cane, because he couldn't see the cobblestones. . . .

Behind him the car door slammed loudly and the motor buzzed louder. But Dr. de Geus, what did he do? He looked around once more at the small black figure on the dike, and cursed regretfully. Why was happiness so fickle? Why must a man sacrifice one thing to gain another? . . . He drove his car up to the house and turned sharply around the lawn with the rhododendrons. Then he drove down the driveway onto the dike. He pulled up and stopped by the priest and opened the door.

"I'll bring you home—you have such trouble walking. . . ."

"Thanks, friend . . ."

"I'm no longer your friend! I can't give her up!"

"And still you are my friend . . ."

The priest got into the car, where he'd sat so often beside his friend. Where he would ride again when one of his lambs was dying. Didn't de Geus also fetch the dominie when some-

body was *in extremis?* Thus they would sit next to each other
in the future, in silence—like strangers. They drove over the
dike; the fog had dissipated, and the gray day hung in the
melancholy mood of autumn, which is also an adieu. When
they reached the parsonage Dr. de Geus opened the car door
and rang the bell. Then, without looking any more at his
old friend, he got into his car and drove away. Further words
would only have made the split deeper. He couldn't deny it
had upset him deeply. Only now he knew how attached he'd
become to the old man and what a high price he had to pay
for a fickle and beautiful woman. . . . It was a bitter pill to
swallow. . . .

"Did you go to that man again, and that when she's living
with him?" Bertha greeted him sulkily in the hallway "It's a
crying shame to the village, that's what it is!"

"Be still, Bertha," sighed the priest. "Please let me alone today." He unbuttoned his overcoat slowly.

"The people will talk about your disgrace," Bertha said venomously. "They'll point their fingers at you!"

"People can't act otherwise," said the priest bitterly. "They
love to sour each other's lives."

He went inside and sank into his tall chair beside the stove.
He closed his eyes and rested his face in his hands. God, how
tired and defeated he felt! Life had become very hard lately.
Bertha stood beside him, stiffly clean in her white apron and
severely moral in her black silk dress. Her cold eyes looked
down at him sternly and her bony finger rapped on the
table.

"The dominie was here. He wanted to talk to you about the
shame on the village, and what steps you're going to take to
stop it!"

Bertha lied till she was blue in the face, for the dominie was much too important a person to tell a servant the purpose of his visit. But Bertha had guessed at the purpose, and concocted the rest herself.

"And he also said . . ."

"The dominie is a very righteous man, Bertha, almost as just as you. Only I think he judges his fellow man with more compassion."

Bertha grew angry. She rushed out of the room but turned at the door to shoot her last poisonous barb. "I told him you had a nice cup of coffee at the home of the village's shame, and the two of you . . ."

The priest straightened up. The last bit of energy flamed in his gray eyes.

"Shut up, Bertha! Go to the kitchen! Go and sit there ashamed and don't let me see you again today! You're a bad woman! Our good Lord knows you're lying and that you have mighty little love for your fellow man!"

Bertha was stunned. With eyes as big as saucers she stared at the priest. Never had he talked to her like this! The doorknob trembled in her bony hand. Her rebelliousness broke, and she went weeping to the kitchen to be ashamed of herself. . . .

And Dr. de Geus left his car standing in front of the house. He entered the room in a bad mood, and his wife met him with great excitement.

"I showed that priest the door! Who does he think he is? He came here to torture me! Can I help it that I'm not a Catholic?"

Dr. de Geus sat by the window and gazed at the chilly autumnal garden. He was silent, nervously smoking one cigarette after another, as the stream of her indignation passed over his head. And the woman talked and talked, until it began to bore him.

"Let's not talk about it any more," he said calmly. "The old priest was my best friend, the only wise person I've met here. I'll miss him."

He peered outside reflectively.

It became very quiet behind him. The woman went upstairs silently, suddenly aware of her shaky position.

"He's the only wise person I've met here. . . ."

She knew she wasn't wise, that she couldn't argue profoundly nor talk about the things that were close to Tom's heart. But she had other gifts, and of these she was aware. And so she stood long before the mirror upstairs and made herself beautiful and pulled something here and there, fixed something elsewhere and accentuated something in another place, and looked in the mirror again and saw that she was beautiful and seductive. Then she slid softly, softly and smiling, downstairs again, where de Geus was still sitting in front of the window and staring outside moodily. She came up behind him. She put her white arms around his head and her hair was silken soft against his cheek.

"Tom," she whispered, "Tom. . . . Boy . . . !"

He turned around. He took her in from head to foot. He saw how red her lips were, and how brilliant her dark eyes. How she smiled and gave amorous glances. But his eyes remained sad, and it was as if the chill of fall were around him.

"Get dinner ready," he said softly. "I'm hungry."

"Tom!" she cried, shocked and insulted. "Tom!"

"Teun Briool is dying," he said. "I have to go in a minute. It'll be all over with him today." And then, when he saw the tears welling in her eyes: "My patients before anything else, child. . . . You don't become a doctor for your pleasure."

Crying with disillusionment, she went upstairs. She looked at her tear-stained face in the mirror. She saw that she was beautiful. "My patients before anything else," she said scornfully. She dried her tears and nervously dabbed some powder on her cheeks.

"My patients before anything else. . . . Get dinner ready.

. . . I'm hungry . . . !" She fell face forward on the bed sobbing violently.

She cried long and emphatically.

Downstairs she heard de Geus rattling the dishes.

Later on the door banged shut.

Then there was silence around the beautiful, strange
woman. . . .

13

When Dr. de Geus went to Teun Briool that afternoon he saw that now he really was dying. It wasn't so unexpected, for Black Nick had been hanging around the twin brothers' cottage for a long time with his scythe, and some day he was bound to slip in. And he did, on the sad fall day when de Geus had to prepare his own lunch and the beautiful woman had wet the pillows of his bed with her tears.

That's how it goes in life, always saying good-bye and taking leave of one another and dying. The fall is the time for it. But it can happen just as well in spring.

The crazy doctor had scarcely won his great victory and gotten his feline beauty of a woman into his bachelor's abode when he had to pay the price for his stolen happiness. He had to say good-bye to his old friend, with a lump in his throat but too proud to admit to himself the price was too high. And hardly had he bartered the little old priest for the beautiful woman when he no longer found her so beautiful or sweet or desirable. . . . A good-bye? At any rate a separation, a shadow cast over his stolen happiness, and a chill, a lessening of his ardent passion. "Every evil finds its own punishment," he admitted to himself grimly as he drove from home over the desolate dike, but the next moment his rebelliousness was roused anew.

"Be damned with your punishment!" he raged. "I'll make my own life and take what's been held from me. Corrie is sweet and beautiful—and good! She's worth more to me than that old priest and more than the respect of those gossiping, talky villagers! Corrie's a damned beautiful girl, and all the fellows are jealous of me because of her!"

De Geus mumbled thus to himself as he drove to the village, trying to convince himself that he was really happy now and that the village and priest and their opinions left him cold. But he didn't laugh or whistle as usual. No, he sat in his car and couldn't help thinking about the old priest walking over the dike toward his house, his shoulders sadly hunched.

When he drove past the parsonage he didn't even have the courage to glance sideways as before. He was afraid he'd see the small white face of the priest and read the sadness that filled those old eyes. He stared straight ahead as he passed it, and when he saw Teun Briool in his death agony, he was really glad the little fellow wasn't a Catholic and he wouldn't have to fetch the priest.

"He's going," he said to Kris, who was trembling beside the bedstead and plaintively calling "Teun, Teun" softly, like one who doesn't believe he's heard. Old Kris looked at him with small watery eyes and grinned emptily. "It ain't so," said Kris, "by jiminee it ain't!" And stubbornly he kept repeating "Teun . . . Teun . . ." as if his twin brother would find consolation therein.

"It ain't so," repeated Kris, and grasped the skinny hand of Teun, which lay weakly in his own.

"All our lives we were twins together—always we sat together on the bench and trudged along the polder. . . . It ain't so!"

But the emaciated Teun gasped for breath like a fish on dry land; he opened his mouth wide and his small eyes stared straight up.

"I can do no more," growled de Geus. "I'll fetch the dominie."

"Is he dying?" fussed Kris like a whimpering child. "It ain't possible, no it ain't."

Dr. de Geus tapped his shoulder encouragingly and left the cottage where all their lives the little Briools had patched shoes and drunk their Schiedams and said jiminee in turn.

He drove to the dominie's house to fetch the righteous man.

"Tell your husband to come along!"

The dominie wasn't insulted; he came and sat down in the back of the car. He knew where they were going. The doctor was silent as always when he drove with the dominie. But the dominie began to talk, contrary to his usual custom. He said things that were dictated by his heart, and he meant well. He addressed the back of the crazy doctor, who sat stiffly behind the wheel and didn't say a word.

"My friend," said the dominie, "my friend, I'm greatly worried about you."

The doctor kept a grim silence and drove faster.

"Old Teun Briool will soon see the eternal light and enter into blessedness like all those who die in the Lord. He'll go through the gate where all of us must pass sooner or later. You too, my friend. And that's why I worry about you, because you do not walk the small and narrow path. . . ."

"I never walk," growled de Geus, and like a streak his car entered the village street.

"You walk the broad road that leads to damnation," retorted the dominie. "You walk in darkness, and the woman you took into your house . . ."

"We're here," snarled the crazy doctor as the car stopped

with shrieking tires in front of the Briools' cottage. He held the car door open for the dominie and looked furiously into his face.

"That woman of mine is none of your concern, and whether I walk on small or broad roads is my affair!"

The dominie looked at him gravely a moment with deep pity in his eyes. Then he bowed his head and they entered together, two gentlemen who had nothing in common. A righteous man and a sinner. They entered the cottage of the Briools where death blew its cold breath over an exhausted little fellow.

"He ain't said another word," whimpered old Kris. "It ain't possible! All our lives we've been twins together. . . ."

Dr. de Geus bent over the shrunken body of old Teun and closed his eyes.

"He's gone," he growled, and he didn't know why it hurt him so to say it.

"It ain't possible," whined Kris. "He ain't said another word, but it ain't so!"

Then the dominie began praying beside the little man who had toiled and moiled all his life for a dry crust of bread, whose greatest curse had been jiminee and his only joy a swallow of clear gin. . . . And de Geus left, furious at Black Nick, who had no compassion for a worn-out soul like Teun Briool, and angry at the dominie who wanted to keep him away from the broad road.

"Teun Briool will go through the gate we'll all have to pass through sooner or later," the dominie had said, and this irritated de Geus profoundly. Never had he denied its truth, for he knew better than almost anyone how quickly the end of life comes. But in his great fear of the hereafter he had always tried to push back the thought of it. He always tried to convince himself that in his own case the broad road was still very long, and that at the end he would find some hidden path that would bring him to the small right road. Deep in his heart the rough de Geus was a believing soul, scared to death of God, on Whom he'd declared war with a bad boy's bravado. Deep in his heart he believed everything would turn out well between him and his great enemy, that God would someday stretch out His hand to him and say: "Come on, old plodder, I've tortured you in life a bit too much. Now let's smoke the pipe of peace and don't let's plague each other any more."

That's the way Dr. de Geus imagined the end of the conflict, convinced that after all he was right and that God had a lot to make up to him. But now the good dominie came and without further ado told de Geus his path led straight to damnation! Look here, he shouldn't have said that. He had touched the doctor in a sore spot: damnation, which he never wanted to think about and didn't believe in. The path that leads to damnation . . .

"To hell with damnation!" raged the doctor, pressing the accelerator to the floor. But a moment later the words echoed again in his ears, and he was confronted with the death of Teun Briool and the gate we all have to pass through and the eternity behind it. Damnation?

"It ain't possible!" he said, with Kris Briool, but deep in his heart he felt the dominie was right, that behind the unavoidable gate there were only two extremes, the eternal light and damnation. . . . He could think the dominie a fool, he could laugh about it like a bold bad boy and tell the dominie he never took a walk, neither on a narrow nor a wide path, but in the endless polder and alone on the long silent dike where the grayness of autumn hung, it started to gnaw at him. Notwithstanding all his crude indifference, he was too honest to fool himself.

"You've spoiled it with the big chief above," he growled to himself. "You declared war on Him because He didn't give you a son. . . . You abandoned the woman He sent you because she couldn't give you what she didn't receive. . . . Perhaps it's all your own fault. . . . To barter the little old priest for a

beautiful woman's body . . . Will she be able to give you
what Janette couldn't? . . . He thought about Corrie and
how she had disappointed him that very afternoon. How she'd
gone upstairs to make herself pretty and seductive, when he
had other needs . . . "A beautiful body!" he growled, "but
only body; no mind, no heart, no . . ." But hadn't he
wanted her that way himself?

He couldn't avoid it. Deep in his heart he had to admit he'd
started on the wrong foot and that he alone was at fault.
And this made him melancholy and furious at the same time.
Anyone who crossed his path now to frustrate him was a lost
creature, for de Geus was in one of his rare, black moods.

But who was crossing his path? Black Driek! The big, awkward oaf, the giant son of Christ-in-the-Wilderness, was un-
wittingly approaching. That same afternoon, when the doctor was busy with Teun Briool, Driek drove to the doctor's
house with his cart and horse. What did he have in his gig?
A pig, an imposing-looking boar. Tienus, enthroned in all
his fat portliness, his small stinging eyes darting venomously about as he sought a victim for his fury. And fat Tienus
had good reason to be furious. Hadn't his master just swapped
him for two crying urchins?

"I'm so glad," Geerte had said when the two newly christened babies were laid in her arms. "We must pay de Geus.
If it weren't for him I would've breathed my last." And
Christ-in-the-Wilderness had sucked at his pipe and agreed,
looking thoughtfully at the two urchins who lay next to
Geerte in the bedstead like happy little animals. "How pretty
they are," sighed Geerte, "how sweet they are . . . ! We must
pay de Geus. The fellow's earned it. Next to the good Lord,
we owe him everything."

And they talked no more about it that morning, but
when Aai Bladder went to work he wondered how he could

pay the doctor for saving Geerte's life and the twins, when he didn't even have a guilder in his pocket that day. He mulled over the terrible anguish he'd been through and the great happiness he felt when Geerte appeared to be saved and the babies were sound of life and limb. These things cannot be paid for, certainly not by a poor peasant. And as he worked a plan ripened in his mind, a plan that shocked him at first but gradually gave him a cruel pleasure. He had received great gifts from de Geus, second only to the Lord's. He would return great gifts! A gift fit for a king . . . !

And that's why Driek of Christ-in-the-Wilderness drove to the doctor's house that melancholy afternoon. The royal gift lay in the back of the gig grunting in indignation, and on the box sat Black Driek holding the reins. They drove around the house with a loud rattle and grinding on the cinder path. Then they came to the kitchen door and Driek called out "Ho!" in his deep voice. The noise drifted upstairs where the bored, beautiful woman had just dried her tears and made up her doll's face again with powder. She dropped her little compact in surprise and continued to look at herself in the mirror a second before she walked to the open window to see who had broken the stillness of the polder with his racket. She looked down at Black Driek, who tethered Satan to a pear tree and rattled the kitchen door gently.

"Hello, black one," she smiled.

Startled, Black Driek looked to the right and left, then looked up and bashfully took off his cap.

"Here I am with the boar!"

"Are you coming for the doctor, or . . ."

"For the doctor."

"He isn't here. Can I take the message?"

"It's too heavy," answered Driek, with a sideward glance at Tienus. "I came, uh—to . . ."

"A moment, boy; I'll be right down!"

Driek waited three minutes, five minutes. . . . Then the

doctor's wife stood in the kitchen door with her smiling face and disturbing dark eyes that looked at him mockingly.

"So, boy, tell me now what that important message is."

Driek crumpled his cap and stared at the woman who aroused intense admiration and fear within him, both at the same time. He was silent.

"Is it so bad?" she smiled. "Am I allowed to know it?"

"Oh yes," grumbled Driek good-naturedly. "It's about the boar." And he looked at Tienus, who pushed his wet nose grimly over the backboard of the gig. Now he could talk better because he didn't have to look at her and wasn't upset by her eyes. "It's Tienus. I brought him for the doctor. Father said two chilluns and a woman are worth more than a boar, so we both loaded her on the gig because we're so happy about the chilluns. Can I unload him?"

Now it was the woman's turn to look nonplussed. She didn't understand the connection between the chilluns and the grisly boar in the cart. She had no inkling what the big fellow was talking about.

"Unload him? What do you mean?"

"Well him, of course!" Driek nodded in the direction of the cart. "Or maybe you don't want him?" he added hopefully. "In the whole polder there's no boar to equal him, and father's only giving him away because he's so terribly glad about the chilluns."

With a feeble cry of fright she grasped the situation and stared anxiously at Tienus, who began to make threatening noises and actually gave her a hostile look. "Jesus! What a filthy animal! What would we do with it?"

Black Driek looked at her indignantly.

"Filthy animal? It's the best boar in the whole polder! Even Arend de Gripert hasn't got one like it!"

"And you wanted to give it to us?"

"On account of the chilluns and mother."

Her laughter rang clearly through the day. "Funny fellow!

What would we do with such a beast? I'm scared to death of animals and the doctor doesn't know anything about them, either. Now listen, take that monster back right away. It's all right!"

Driek was perplexed. He didn't understand this new turn of events. With heavy hearts they had agreed to sacrifice the magnificent porker to thank the doctor for his help; with tears of regret they had hoisted the gift into the gig, knowing they were offering this precious possession in exchange for two small pink children there in the bedstead. But the woman, instead of rejoicing, instead of stammering her thanks for this too great gift . . .

"Ain't you really wanting it?" He still hesitated. She laughed straight at him. "You don't think we intend to go in for farming?" she roared with laughter. "I can see myself running around in wooden shoes and a dirty apron. Listen, just take that pig right home again and tell your father he doesn't have to pay Dr. de Geus."

"As you please," mumbled Black Driek. "You ought to know yourself. . . . Well, I guess I'll be going then." And embarrassedly he shuffled back to the gig, glad and disappointed at the same time. She followed him, serious now. Perhaps she was beginning to understand a little of what this great sacrifice had meant to these people. She saw him hesitate as he loosened the rope from the pear tree.

"Say, black one . . ."

He looked up, unsure, confused. She was touched, and suddenly she felt a great pity for the big, awkward boy. She felt that in some way she had hurt him deeply by refusing his gift. What did she know about the people on this island? Silent and surly at anything that was strange to them. This fellow in particular, whom she admired for the strength of his muscular body, whom she'd mocked for his awkward manners, with whom she'd unconsciously played a provocative game, and was still playing . . .

"Say, Blackie, tether the horse again and we'll have a cup

of tea together, yes? It's no fun by one's self, and you must want one too."

Driek obeyed silently. Of course he didn't care for any tea. They never drank it at home, and he would have preferred to hurry home and give his father the glad tidings; besides, he actually was somewhat afraid of this woman with her mocking eyes. But she had called him back; he couldn't refuse her this small favor. So he tethered Satan firmly to the pear tree again, patted the fiery animal affectionately on his shiny black neck, checked the gig to make sure Tienus couldn't fall out, and when he could think of no further delay he went in his stocking feet through the kitchen into the beautiful room where the woman was humming as she waited for him. She offered him a cigarette and lit one herself from the light he gave her with his trembling hand. For a moment her face was close to his and the flame sparkled in her black eyes as she looked warmly at him over her cigarette and said "Merci." Then Driek sat for a long time looking at the pattern of the rug and smoking silently while she wandered about the house busying herself. She brewed tea in a funny little pot that gleamed primly in her small hands. She put sugar in the little cups, so fragile that Driek almost didn't dare touch them. Then she sat down facing him and smiled. Driek smiled bashfully in return and wiped the sweat from his brow with his large red handkerchief. He took a cup of tea and held it carefully in the hollow of his calloused hands. He was given a small cake on a glass plate; he didn't know what to do with it, and now he no longer had his hand free to wipe off the new sweat.

But the woman didn't seem to notice his embarrassment. She leaned back nonchalantly in her easy chair and smoked in comfort, sipping her tea and talking about the city and the doctor and many other things that Driek immediately forgot, because in his confusion he wasn't able to pay much attention. He gulped the tea from the little cup in the palm of his hand, and

then he was happy to have his hand free again for his handkerchief.

"It's hot," he brought forth at last. Then he received another small cup of the stuff, and he had to tell how Geerte
was doing and how many little brothers and sisters he had and
whether he was the oldest. He answered dutifully and heard his
own deep voice echo strangely through the beautiful room, but
the silence was as fragile as the china thing in his peasant fist
and as delicate as the strange beautiful creature opposite him,
whom he didn't dare look at during the conversation. But gradually he was more at ease. She smiled so encouragingly and
listened so intently that gradually the surly boy loosened up. He
talked about home and his work and the boys and girls from the
village. And later on, about the first time he met de Geus and
how he'd floored him with one blow while pretty Mieke was
looking on. He laughed a bit sourly about this, and was immediately sorry he told her. After all, it was shameful enough for
a big fellow like him to be floored by the small doctor. But the
woman didn't believe him. Why, he was almost two feet taller
than Dr. de Geus, and he was floored? Come, come, Blackie
shouldn't tell such fairy tales! She had noticed a long time ago
that he was strong as an ox.

"And de Geus then!" said Driek, warming up to his subject.
"Did you ever see him in his shirt? That feller has muscles
like . . ." Eh, why did she suddenly laugh so hard? Driek was
abashed and got red as a beet when he suddenly realized what
a crazy question he'd asked her in his enthusiasm. He lost his
speech and sat with a glowing face looking at the floor. But the
laughter died on her lips, for there in the doorway stood a grim-
faced Dr. de Geus. . . .

How long had he been standing there . . . ? It was proved by
his angry eyes and the effort he made to keep quiet. Driek,
astonished by her sudden silence, looked up into the gaze of Dr.
de Geus. In a flash he read the hatred and senseless jealousy

there. What did Black Driek know of a bachelor's possessiveness with his hard-to-get prize? Could he surmise that de Geus, in an unpleasant mood, had sneaked in in his stocking feet and listened suspiciously when he heard a man's voice and the cooing laughter of the beautiful woman?

What was about to happen in that silent room? . . .

The woman stood up immediately, uttering a small cry, and the men suddenly faced each other with hot heads and flaming eyes. Why did this murderous silence last so long? Why didn't they say or do something . . . ? Yes, de Geus was going to say something. One word. "Outside!"

And Black Driek, like a beaten dog, bowed his head and went. Shamefully he walked out of the room and through the kitchen to the outside. He jerked the rope loose from the pear tree, jumped on the box like a savage and walloped Satan's black coat mercilessly with his whip. The animal took off, whinnying furiously, and Tienus, not expecting such violence, shrieked as he toppled in the gig that disappeared creaking around the house.

The woman saw everything happen, and in her nervous state she burst into laughter at the funny sight and the foolish misunderstanding. This only made matters worse.

Now de Geus thought she was laughing at him, and a renewed fury gripped him. Trembling with rage, he grasped the edge of the table to keep from shouting aloud. Then she was suddenly calm, and looked boldly into his eyes.

"Stupid, jealous boy," she laughed mockingly, "what do you think? Don't be so upset."

"What do I think?" said de Geus, breathing hard. "What do I think? That you—that you . . ."

No, what was the use of talking now? To knock to smithereens what you built up with so much trouble? Rather bite your tongue off, Tom de Geus! Slap your own suspicious face, but don't say things that will upset your own insecure happiness. He was profoundly aware how critical this moment was, for him, for her, for everything that had grown so precious to him in such a short time. He felt that something had to be smashed or broken, but not their relationship, in God's name not the tie that bound them together! He boiled and seethed inside with an insane fury he couldn't control, that would result, if it burst forth, in the sad end of their infatuation. So he fled from her; he ran from the destructive words. He stamped out of the room in a purple fog, breathing hard, through the kitchen, outside, to smash what he tried in vain to save. The red haze disappeared from his eyes in one indivisible moment when, as he had that time before with Black Driek, he vented his fury on an inanimate thing, a dead piece of stone.

In the garden near the small pond stood Eros, a nude little marble boy on a freestone pedestal. In his fury he tore it from its pedestal and smashed it in two, three resounding blows against the coach house, not because it was the little god of love but simply because it was the first thing he could lay his trembling fists on. The little boy was destroyed with a cry and the pieces of stone flew around like bomb fragments. The empty freestone pedestal was senselessly reflected in the small pond. The red haze had disappeared, the joke was gone and his fury was abated. It had spent itself in aimless destruction. He looked at the stone fragments, he looked at his hands no longer clenched in their fury, then he looked up at the window and saw her. Pale as death, she had watched his insane rage and her dark eyes were wide with fright. With that little Cupid she had seen something else knocked to smithereens.

At the sight of the raving maniac she suddenly knew that everything had been as nothing. As nothing . . . Her long wait for him, her intrigues, her conquest, her coming to this endlessly desolate island, where only he could have filled her life. He? That senselessly jealous fool? That uncouth barbarian who stood there in the gray daylight? He who was looking at his hairy fists that had destroyed the first thing his eyes lighted on? Was he the man she had waited for so desperately all these years, idealizing him like a demigod? Was this the man? Sadly she turned from the window, unable to bear the sight of him in his smallness as he stood in his stocking feet on the wet grass, a ridiculously small caricature of the hero she used to dream about. . . .

Later on he came uncertainly into the room, and they sat together, silent with the humiliation and shame of it all. He grimly smoked cigarette after cigarette, and they listened surreptitiously to the loud ticking of the clock, both too stubborn to utter the first soft word. She found him ridiculous with the smallness of his bad little boy's jealousy. Unbearable he found her with her pose of insulted innocence. And at the same time both were filled with despair that this spelled the unavoidable end, that with the little god of love, the only fine thing between them had died. . . . When he was finally ready to speak, hoarse with shame and haltingly seeking for words, she got up and walked out of the room with uplifted head. Then he cursed. He couldn't do anything else. He was a puny human being. Stillness hung in the room, and it was a bitter stillness. . . .

14

On the day that Teun Briool was to be buried, Dr. de Geus awoke with an anguished feeling. There was a weight on his chest that sent shooting pains into the region of his stomach. He got up, threw open his bedroom door and saw that the door of the room across the hall stood ajar. The bed had not been slept in and he found a note on the pillow informing him laconically that everything was all over, that she had left for the city for good. De Geus didn't swear or dramatize the situation; he had seen it coming for days and for weeks. The house built on such weak foundations had toppled. He went back to his bedroom and sat on the edge of his bed. He stared dumbly at the words written in a woman's trembling hand. Slowly the protest welled in his heart, a savage protest against God, Who wouldn't allow him to arrange his life according to his own choice. A protest against God Who wanted him to return to the crossway of life where he had rejected his wife and wilfully left her. But what man retraces his steps so long as he is fit and strong enough to fight the handicaps and the contrary winds and his blood is roused by an urge for adventure?

"I won't give in and I won't retrace my steps!" he growled, knowing it was strange that he should think out loud. "And I'll make it clear to that little priest that he needn't foster new hopes now the beautiful woman is gone." He stretched, and a feeling of undiminished strength ran through his taut muscles. Strong as an ox, he would meet God and life, they would never get him down, and to nobody, neither God nor the little priest nor anybody else, would he admit that his life had become almost senseless, a life without content or aim. For awhile he'd thought a charming woman could give meaning to his life; now he knew he was wrong, and wouldn't make the same mistake another time.

Humming without pleasure he went to the mirror to shave, but when he looked at his lather-covered face he was filled with disdain, threw the razor in a corner and started wiping the lather from his face with nervous gestures. Whom was he shaving for anyway, why was he acting like a small bourgeois? He no longer had to do it for her. She was gone. She had a charming little affair with him. Had been his love for a few months. Had enough of the affair when everything wasn't moonlight and roses. Went back to the milieu of the feeble, small bourgeois, and by now was enjoying the memory. No longer must he strike the pose of a bourgeois little fool, no longer must he dress like a fop. He washed himself and looked with grim pleasure at his black stubble that he could grow again in peace. He took the bourgeois costume and tore it into strips. Then he looked for his corduroy pants and blouse and wooden shoes.

He went out into the young day where the sun was shining and tried to convince himself that he was rid of a heavy burden and felt happier than before. But the pain in his heart gnawed deep within him, and his shrill whistle trembled through the garden like the cries of a wounded bird. He couldn't accept, or even admit, that henceforth he was alone again confronting God Who barred his way. God took him by the scruff of his neck and said, "This is the way you're going! This is the way I've laid out for you, Tom de Geus!" But he kicked around and said he'd make his own way, he'd go where he wished and do as he pleased. So he trampled the dewy grass and breathed God's clean air and convinced himself that he was bold and strong and gay.

He threw off his shirt and corduroy pants and dived into the cold pond that was still blanketed with the silvery morning dew. When he dove down, the water buzzed dully in his ears and there was an infinity pressing him under, but he surfaced with a snort at the freestone pedestal that was reflected in the water, gray and lonely because the little god of love was gone, crushed by his mighty fist, as his love had cracked, as God would if He barred his way again. Later he stood flushed and shiny in the newborn day and walked to the house to get dressed, the house that looked hollow in its dark emptiness and loneliness. The silence hung about him as it had before she came, as it would in the future, now and always. For the first time that morning he swore; sadness came sneaking up to him as he saw the little silken thing she had left behind, and his fury fought the emotion that threatened to be stronger than his will. But then he found his balance again and hummed as he prepared breakfast and did the daily tasks. Whistling a moment later to drown out the voice of his heart, he walked through the halls of the house, filled with memories of her that he wanted to forget at any price.

So again the rough de Geus began to make his own way and life, strong and bold in his hurt pride. He opened the front door wide for the patients and kept his consulting hours. He had a kindly word for everyone and a broad grin for pretty Mieke, who finally showed up hesitatingly, this time with a sore finger.

"Well, Mieke girl, how are you?"

"All right, Doctor, except for this finger."

"Let's see it! Oh, this is bad, sister! It'll have to come off!"

"Never on me!" Mieke smiled whitely. "You're still the same clown."

The clown took his big knife and behaved like a crazy fool. Mieke uttered a small cry of fear, but everything was fine when she saw the doctor was only joking. This encouraged her to put a question to him, a question she was burning to ask. "Is she gone? Forever?"

De Geus looked at her in astonishment. What did that jealous little thing know about it? Had the news spread that quickly through the village? Had they seen her? Of course, pretty Mieke lived close to Tony the Ferry. She knew all right.

Mieke smiled shrewdly. "The door's wide open, just like before she came. . . . Ouch! you hurt me! It was a splinter from a churning barrel; got in deep under my nail. Do you have to do it so hard? . . . I always thought she wouldn't stay, a city lady like her. Who'll cook for you now and fix things up? Everything will be getting dirty here, you'll see."

De Geus growled something incomprehensible and put a neat little bandage around Mieke's throbbing finger. "So, and in the future look out for the churning barrel, Mieke!"

"Shall I come to fix things up for you, Doctor? I can work much better than her, and I'm as fine a cook as you can find."

She looked at him hopefully. Just imagine, if she got the chance!

"Next patient!" roared de Geus, and Keetje Kranebil came into the room with a very long face.

"Well, I might as well be going," sighed pretty Mieke.

"So long," said the doctor, "and be careful with that churning barrel!"

"It's my varicose veins again," said Keetje Kranebil, and Mieke sighed as she slunk into the hall, disappointed and hopeful at the same time.

Later in the day he visited the seriously ill patients in the customary daily sequel. The last one he called on was Tony the Ferry. Nobody in the village had made any allusion to the hasty departure of the beautiful woman; they apparently didn't know about it yet. But Tony's loutish sons looked at him in an oddly mocking way, and Tony didn't know what attitude to strike; he felt a complicity, for he had helped the citified lady to escape from the island to the outside world. . . .

"Morning, Charon, how's the woman?"

Tony looked at de Geus with fright.

"I couldn't help it," he meant to say. "She paid me well to take her across last night." But then he understood that the doctor was simply inquiring after Mietemoei, and she shook his head sadly.

"So so, it's up and down, but she's gradually failing; she won't last much longer, Doctor."

"I'll get her well, Charon, mark my words!"

Tony sighed.

"The doctor's been saying that for a long time and the dominie thinks . . ."

"Ah well, the dominie!"

De Geus had almost flown into a temper again, but he thought better of it. He remembered that he'd resolved to be a strong human being, not a venomous, humiliated, little man who let himself be defeated by reverses. "The dominie's a fine fellow," he corrected himself, "he knows a lot about over yonder, but not so much of life on this side. Let everybody stick to his own last, Tony; let the dominie take care of Mietemoei's soul, and I'll tend to her body, then we'll both have our hands full."

Tony eagerly agreed. He thought everything was fine, he was ready to agree to everything if only the doctor wouldn't start talking about the beautiful woman, so long as he wasn't made responsible for what happened the night before. And he didn't have to worry. The doctor did his job the same as every other day. He bent over the shriveled little woman in the dark bedstead and had Tony hold the oil lamp so he could see better. He smiled at Mietemoei: "I'll get you well, old one," and when she turned her little potato head away silently, he said once more emphatically: "I'll get you well as sure as my name's de Geus."

Mietemoei didn't say a word and a bright tear ran along her shrunken cheek.

"If only the winter wasn't at hand," sighed Tony. "Then I could have some hope, but with the cursed cold and the dampness . . ."

The lamp trembled in his old hands, and Mietemoei shivered under the soiled blanket.

"Tell me what you need," growled de Geus almost gruffly. "Haven't you got enough covers? How about fuel and solid food?"

Tony said nothing. Wasn't he, after all, a government employee, and could he complain to such an Escul-ape? No, this he refused to do, but that very same night Kasper the messenger came with his dogcart carrying a pile of blankets and woolen underwear and linens, a collection such as Tony the Ferry and his sick little wife hadn't seen in all their living days. "From somebody who wants to remain unknown," said Kasper the messenger to the nonplussed Tony, and he clicked his tongue and drove away in his dogcart.

Look, see, a poor ferryman has a hard time swallowing such things, and tears burned in Tony's eyes as he dragged all his treasures up to Mietemoei.

"From somebody who wants to remain unknown!"

They both knew very well who this person was.

The louts sat there too and grinned about that so-called unknown person. They irritated Tony, and he scolded them through his tears. A little later Bram de Bolk came with cart and horse and filled the whole small shed with coal: "From somebody who wants to remain unknown!" He hadn't been gone but a minute when Tys of Giel de Tuut brought a sack filled with potatoes.

"From somebody who wants to remain unknown," grinned the two louts before Tys was able to say anything, and Tys agreed gruffly that they were right.

So gladness came to Tony the Ferry's little shack, the small, pathetic joy of poor folk who have to get things from charity. They slept that night under warm blankets that still smelled new, and thought about the crazy doctor who must be powerfully rich and who with all his foolishness had a warm heart for the poor. The louts rubbed pleasantly against each other and pulled the new blankets warmly around their unwashed bodies.

"That fellow's balmy," they told each other. "He's simple-minded."

But downstairs in the shack, Tony the Ferry kneels before a chair in his woolen underpants and prays for the strange fellow who wants to remain unknown. He prays for the crazy doctor who doesn't believe in God but who, with all his wickedness, does more good than the pious people who have God on their lips and greed in their eyes.

Meanwhile de Geus is walking all by himself through the rooms and hallways of his somber abode. All day he has tried to convince himself that he's enjoying his bachelor's existence and is glad the beautiful woman fled. But now the silence hangs so teasingly over him, and the furniture stares at him so dumbly and hostilely that he jumps up and begins to go through the house, from the front to the back and from downstairs to upstairs, to look, to hunt for something of her whom he wants to forget. In search of whom? Of what? . . . And when he finds a coat and a coquettish little hat, and the dresses she left behind, what then? Will the clothes console him in the stillness of the big house? Has he become an effete fool with a bunch of clothes in his arms who dreams about the happiness that could have been, that was destroyed by his own anger and suspicion? Happiness? So what! Is he the sort of man who can ever be happy? Hasn't he fought God all his life long, because he thought God thwarted him as soon as he got hold of some happiness? And God! Always God again, Who wouldn't let Himself be considered dead, Who knew how to find him everywhere and never let him alone.

De Geus was tired of fighting. He no longer wanted to delude himself that he was gay and happy, or contented in his loneliness. He was too discouraged now to despise God and too embittered to reconcile himself with Him. Growling like a tortured animal he threw himself on the bed completely dressed, and after lying awake staring began to annoy him, he poured himself a large glass of gin to forget everything and keep the illusion of gladness. But he wasn't cowardly enough for that. The villagers might need him during the night. They might want to fetch him for a confinement or a serious patient, and they mustn't find a senile drunkard, a trembling old fool sodden with gin and sobbing in his drunken sorrow. He nipped at the gin, two, three small swallows that coursed warmly through him and even gave him back some of his bravado. Then he went to the kitchen and emptied the glass in the kitchen sink, quiet now and controlled. And he brought the bottle back to the cellar as a sad smile played around his lips.

He went for a walk in the night, his head high and a forced quiet expression on his face. How long did he walk there on the dark dike, through the silent polder? Surely it was many hours. His wooden shoes clattered over the cobblestones and the noise died in the gray fog on either side of the dike, where occasionally a cow coughed. Not a star was visible overhead and the darkness closed in on him like a thick black curtain.

Thus de Geus went his way in the small dark world under a low black sky beneath God's almighty hands. God, Who was enthroned up there above him, Who had the power to blow rebellious men from this earth. But God didn't do it. De Geus went into the darkness and the endless stillness and gradually —he didn't want it but couldn't prevent it—from the encircling darkness a deep peace descended upon him like the undisturbed surface of a pool. His soul was open to God, Who could read it and understand all the troubles of little man. God breathed over the crazy doctor, who felt himself shriveling to nothing and helpless as a lonely child. The stillness was all around him and within him and he was gripped with the fear that he might have to go through life always alone. Something gnawed at his heart, but he refused to recognize it as remorse. He didn't want to think now, to think about her whose life was equally lonely, the woman who had voluntarily left him so alone. He rejected the thought completely, and dreading the voice of his conscience he began to hum, and a moment later when that didn't help, to whistle shrilly. It trembled through the night across the emptiness of the sleeping fields. But God was somewhere over him and silenced his song to make the stillness last, wherein He would speak. De Geus sat down at the edge of the gully in the dewy grass, and no sound reached him but the voice deep within himself of the God he'd wanted to consider dead. "I'm here," said God. "I'm here over you, and about you and in you. I'm everywhere and you can't avoid Me, anywhere."

"Go to hell!" said de Geus, and started to walk again, a grim expression on his face now, deliberately making a great noise with his wooden shoes.

But God didn't let him go; He pursued him; he couldn't avoid Him, because He was in him and about him and everywhere.

De Geus walked in the direction of the sleeping village and

felt in his pocket for cigarettes. He didn't find them and growled as he clattered on. God was next to him, he felt it now, and he'd be ridiculous to deny it any longer.

"Hallucinations!" he sneered in feeble retort, and trying to shut his mind to it, he accelerated his pace to reach home, but he was still hours away from the house. And God spoke in the silence.

"Here am I, God. And here you walk, puny little being. You think you can make your own way and go wherever you like. You won't succeed, Geus! I'll teach you to go My way and listen to My voice."

De Geus listened. He didn't give in yet, but he wanted to know what God meant to tell him. Later he'd still be able to laugh at God. It was no longer possible to declare Him dead, for God's presence had now been recognized and experienced.

"Just say what You want to say," growled de Geus. "Or rather no, say nothing; I know what You mean anyway. I left my wife because she couldn't give what she hadn't received. That's why I'm being punished now. I tried to forget in the loneliness of this accursed island, but life has its rights and I needed a woman. I offended love by taking a woman I shouldn't have. Now I'm punished for that too: You took the woman and her love away from me, because I kicked out my own wife and her love. I tried to delcare You dead and as a punishment You're haunting me now with Your actual presence. Isn't that so?"

But God was silent. When people talk as hard as that, they can't understand God. Perhaps the crazy doctor permitted the great grace to pass him by. He wanted to hear God talk, and yet he talked himself, as though he were trying to take things into his own hands again and solve his own problems. He saw God only as the avenger Who stood ready with punishment for all sins. Perhaps God might have told him much finer things if he'd only wanted to listen. But now the rebellious Geus walked along saying bitter things and didn't give God a chance to talk. Now he was going farther away from God's grace all the time, while in his deeply hurt heart he yearned for it. With a grim expression on his face, embittered toward God and humanity, he dragged himself along. De Geus was tired of worrying and fighting God and wandering through the sleeping polder.

He reached his home at the break of day, his limbs tired from the night-long walk. The first cock was crowing in the distance and the cry sounded over the fields like a shout of distress. A faint daylight appeared in the east, and the fog floated silver gray over the polder.

Then out of the grayness and the mist a figure came toward him. A large, dark man who looked like a threatening giant in the first shimmer of light. Broad and stocky, black and silent, he stood at last confronting the small tired Geus, and the two looked seachingly at each other for several seconds. There was something lugubrious and threatening about it, that silent meeting of the two dark figures in the sober dawn.

What was about to happen between the two ruffians? Each measured the other's taunting and threatening mien. They kept a haughty silence and approached each other slowly, step by step in the middle of the driveway, until they nearly touched, every thread taut in their powerful bodies, each ready to smash the other if he dared utter an uncontrolled word.

The wind seemed to hold its breath in rapt attention, and the hoarse shriek of a small steamer in the Dirty Hole shattered the silence. They stood chest to chest now, the embittered doctor and Driek of Christ-in-the-Wilderness, whose hot temper was rising about the way de Geus had insulted him before the beautiful woman.

Silence—threateningly gauging each other's strength. Then a furious growl deep in de Geus' throat. "Get going, yokel! Get out of my yard! She's not here any more, so you needn't look for anything!"

And Black Driek, with all the fury of the humiliation he had suffered, gave vent to his pent-up emotions as he snorted: "Away, dungfly! Jealous old fool! Ridiculous fop!"

The next moment the two powerful fellows were fighting silently and breathing hard in the chill of the newborn day, throwing short punches on one another's overheated, furious bodies. Hatred shone out of their eyes as they keenly measured each hard blow and prepared themselves for a new punch. The black one fought with all the strength of his muscular young body, thrashing about with his long arms and taking advantage of every chance. Little de Geus put the whole energy of his embittered and jealous soul behind every blow, parrying the wild thrusts and coolly figuring out the next one. Telling, dull-sounding blows, heaving bodies, overheated heads, a scene of savage hatred in the dawning light. Thus two men fought out their pent-up fury, a young, strong fellow who had found his master in this embittered, tired man who reacted more slowly than before and needed all his skill not to be beaten this time. De Geus felt exhaustion like a heavy burden on his limbs after his night of wandering and worry. He was even more eager to give harder blows, and he tried to suppress the panic that rose up out of his heart as he attacked the thrashing giant violently. Driek suddenly lunged to the side and gave the doctor in passing a resounding punch on his temple. De Geus wobbled. Bloody fury lit his eyes. His ears were buzzing, as they did when he was diving into the pond and felt the world was weighing upon him. With a last remnant of upsurging energy he re-established himself and got ready for a terrible blow. But he reacted too slowly to Black Driek's triumphant knockout punch. The buzzing in his ears got worse, the violent haze became more dense and the last thing that flashed through his mind was, "Now I must try to keep standing! Not on my knees! Not on my . . ." Then something cracked and the whole black world was like a dome falling over him.

Black Driek looked on, trembling and incredulous, when de Geus went down on his knees and lay dead to the world. The young giant hadn't counted on this, nor had he hoped for it. He had thrown himself on his attacker with the fury of a teased animal and defended himself valiantly against the telling blows of de Geus. Now he was astonished to see the doctor didn't get up, and the motionless body on the ground inspired him with greater fear than the panting, fighting de Geus of a short while before. He licked his bruised fists and looked about him, uncomprehending. The ghostly morning haze hung over them and enveloped the scene of battle. From beyond the dike the shriek of a small steamer sounded again, and the wind came running over the field to drive away the shreds of mist. A gig rattled over the dike and the noise brought him to his senses.

Did it react that way on the doctor too? He shivered a bit and sat up with a surprised grin on his face. He sat in the middle of the driveway looking around senselessly. Then he got up slowly and looked somewhat hesitatingly into Black Driek's eyes. Driek felt his pulse beat in his throat, for now that his fury had spent itself he was again very much afraid of this learned man. He suddenly remembered why he had run to the doctor's house in the middle of the night, and how they needed the Escul-ape. Good Lord, why had he fought with such a man? Weren't the farm hands dependent on him body and soul? But rough de Geus, what kind of crazy clown was he anyway? He began to grin broadly and offered Driek his hand.

"*Proficiat*," said de Geus. "You're improving." And with a painful gesture he rubbed his throbbing cranium.

"Come along, black one, we'll have to have a drink on that."

"I'll be damned if we will," said Driek. "Serious patients come first!" And he explained to de Geus why he had come so early to the haunted house. "Satan can't stand on his legs any longer, and we can't do without the animal. The veterinary has to come way from Middelharnis, and besides he doesn't want to come because we still owe him a bill from last year. and Mother thought that you—with your American pills . . . Of course, she didn't know we'd come to blows. . . ."

"All right, all right!" laughed de Geus, who saw the humor of the situation. "Let's have some fun that way too! Come on, black one, we'll have a look at Satan! I've never treated a horse before."

They walked through the dawn together, two rough, strong fellows. One of them walked a bit unsteadily and felt his bald pate from time to time. The other occasionally licked his fist, and was silent. The red sun threw shafts of bloody light over the dike and clad the whole polder in festive colors. Shreds of fog dissolved in a silvery glow, and all around the grass pearled the shiny dew. Straight ahead the bells of the little church began to ring and golden sounds frolicked over the dike, over the polder, and lost themselves in the distance.

"I'll be Goddamned if I understand you," said Black Driek. The crazy doctor looked at him and laughed broadly.

Bosom friends now, they clumped toward the horizon. One of them carefully felt the back of his head, the other licked his fist. And in the barn of Christ-in-the-Wilderness, beside the horse, they waited impatiently for the doctor. . . .

15

It probably did de Geus a lot of good, fighting God during the night and Black Driek the following dawn, because for a few weeks he was tame as a lamb. He hadn't allowed God to speak, although he no longer fooled himself that God was dead. But Black Driek, like an avenging angel, had done well. He had boxed the doctor, and there was no small merit in that. He himself was somewhat embarrassed about it, and for a tenspot he would have liked to see it undone, but when de Geus took it so lightly the black one wasn't a little proud of his resounding victory. Not that he broadcast it to everybody. He was too smart for that! Nobody would believe him any-way, for the villagers had woven a terrible legend around the doctor. They were more afraid of him than of his Uncle Bib-ber in his ghostly garb, despite the fact that de Geus always had a kind word for every poor bumpkin and free consultation and often a royal tip.

But how does it go in a village? The lugubrious and creepy things are believed much more readily than the good. They had schemed and gossiped so much about the doctor that falsehood and truth could no longer be told apart. The beautiful woman hadn't helped either, and when she suddenly disappeared from polder life, people looked for an evil meaning behind this too. . . . The crazy doctor, that barbarian, had perhaps mistreated her terribly. She had fled in the middle of the night, as the louts of Tony the Ferry related, and when they ferried her across the Dirty Hole she had looked behind her continuously, as though afraid de Geus would come after her to lock her up again in his house. But for weeks now de Geus had calmly made his visits throughout the polder just as if there'd never been a beautiful woman in his life. Suddenly—and nobody understood how it happened—he'd become bosom friends with Driek of Christ-in-the-Wilderness. He bought a big hunting rifle, and together the two went day after day into the osier beds to shoot ducks. And how that doctor could shoot! Dirk de Krotekoker, who had just gotten over an attack of floating kidneys, saw himself how the doctor shot three ducks with one shot! But Dirk, that awful liar, is cross-eyed; he probably saw one duck twice, and the other he probably imagined. You can only believe half of what Dirk de Krotekoker says; he hangs together by ailments and lies.

Nevertheless Black Driek and the doctor became fast friends after that night (which the villagers knew nothing about), and as soon as de Geus had finished his calls, the two friends would be off to the osier beds. Then the sky soon resounded with shots that echoed far and wide, and in the evening they could be seen returning like tramps with their magnificent booty slung from their shoulders on ropes. So everything went its way and nobody found fault, for when the two fellows returned to the village they would open the little doors of Tony van de Brant and Dirk de Krotekoker and the Houtermans and Daantje de Bietser and a few others and throw a dead duck inside, uttering not a single word. And then the two foolish ones would laugh and go on to the next address until all the ducks were distributed. At Kris Briool's, old Kris who was living all by himself now, they sometimes tied a little crock of Schiedam to the duck's neck. That was to make him feel better on account of the loss of Teun; poor old Kris couldn't get accustomed to the death of his twin, he grew paler every day, and he needed that drink very much to keep believing in the goodness of life. Life—what a strange thing it is. Look at Dr. de Geus. Life had dealt him many blows lately, but it seemed he was too stubborn to be defeated, for the harder the blows the stronger his resistance grew, and the gayer and rougher he lived. At least the villagers thought he acted crazier all the time, and if he hadn't been such an able physician and so good to the poor farm workers they would have thrown him out long ago. But no, let nobody say anything bad about the crazy doctor in public, for the farm workers would go through fire for him. And still they gossiped about him—in an underhanded way. And they still believed for sure he was a bad man and a convinced atheist— yet nowhere in the land was a better doctor to be found. . . .

The case of the crazy doctor is a curious one. You can never make him out. He's a walking problem . . . He is never seen at the priest's any more, and the dominie greets him pleasantly when he meets him on the street. How does that jibe, you will say!

The patients walked in and out all morning long during his consultation hours, and the front door remained wide open, as there was nobody to let them in any more, and the beautiful marble hallway was soiled again by mud. Once more Geerte of Gillis Bietebouw wanted to clean up the doctor's house, but just in time she bethought herself of her experience a year ago and decided to let the ungrateful de Geus' house get filthy again if it pleased him that way.

And pretty Mieke showed up at the doctor's house. Her

sore finger was cured and she had no other mishaps, but now she came on a business matter. She got quite a reception; the doctor was in a bad mood. How could Mieke know he'd been worrying and growling the past few nights? That he was battling again with God, Who never let him alone for long?

"Well, Mieke, what's the trouble?"

"Nothing, Doctor, nothing at all, but . . ."

"Get the hell out then!"

He said it quietly and almost in a friendly way. Mieke glared at him with her beautiful eyes grown large with fear, but it didn't make the slightest impression on de Geus, who looked tired and done in.

"Next patient!" roared the crazy doctor.

"But, Doctor, I came . . ."

"Are you sick? Something wrong with you? Sick in the *permetatie?*"

"No, uh—nothing really, I just wanted to help you, Doctor."

"Help me? Why? What for?"

"With your housekeeping," said Mieke timidly.

"My housekeeping is none of your concern," he barked unreasonably. "Well, Jochum, what ails you, friend?"

"Your house is getting filthy!" Mieke shouted furiously.

De Geus took her by the arm and pushed her roughly into the hallway in sight of all who waited there. The door slammed shut behind her and the young people in the waiting room snickered. Mieke cried from anger and shame and humiliation.

"He'd rather perish in the filth than let me clean it up," she sobbed. "He'd rather perish in the dirt, the ass!"

"He'd rather perish in the dirt." Those words still resounded in the doctor's ears more than an hour later when he closed the door behind the last patient and went to the kitchen to prepare a haphazard breakfast.

He looked around the room with dissatisfaction. Pretty Mieke was right, it was a mess, just like before.

"But is it any of that girl's business!" he thought angrily. "If I need a cleaning woman I'll get her myself."

He gathered the stuff together for his breakfast and thought about Mieke. What was the matter with the child that she came to force herself on him every time? . . . Still, a nice girl, but a wild one . . . No, he wasn't going to burn his fingers. Some girl would have to come, but not a flirt! Bah! The tea tasted like gutter water and his cup was sticky.

"He'd rather perish in the dirt!" Mieke's words stuck provocatively in his ears.

After ten minutes of desultory chewing he gathered the breakfast stuff and put it all in the kitchen next to a pile of dirty plates, crusted cups and dirty pans, and he didn't have the courage to clean them after his daily tasks.

"What a filthy mess!" he cursed. "It'll have to change."

The bell rang. He went in his stocking feet to the front room and the cold tiles felt disagreeable to his feet.

"Socks with holes in them," he growled, "dirty dishes, filthy rooms: good morning, you're late for a consultation!"

"I know, my friend," said the priest humbly, "but I couldn't walk fast."

De Geus opened the door wide for him and closed it with a bang.

"Who said you had to walk so far? You could've sent the old girl with a message and I would have come."

"Bertha's so busy," the priest excused himself, "and I can still walk that distance."

"So I notice!" growled de Geus mildly. "You're puffing like an old locomotive! Sit down and I'll brew you a cup of coffee."

He helped the priest off with his coat, pushed an easy chair next to the hearth and went to work in the kitchen with a lot of noise. The priest looked around happily. It was more than half a year since he had sat here. Much had happened in the meantime. . . . With difficulty he got up and shuffled to the kitchen where de Geus was fussing with the dirty cups.

"Sit down, old man, you're dead tired. It's a mess here since she left. Everything's dirty and I can't find anything. Now where did I put the coffee? Oh, here. Hell, the milk is sour. Shall I drive to Melis Eilers' or shall we have a schnapps?"

"Don't put yourself out, my friend," smiled the priest. "I've had my coffee, and a schnapps so early in the morning . . ."

"A cigar then?"

"With pleasure!"

They smoked. They were silent for a long time and stared into the fire. Then the priest started to talk.

"You'll perish here with dirt like this."

The doctor looked at him surprised.

"Did you talk to pretty Mieke?"

"Pretty Mieke?" The priest smiled.

"She said the same thing to me this morning."

"And do you want to argue that she isn't right?" smiled the priest.

"When she was here there was no mess," de Geus said grimly.

"Admitted, but she didn't belong here."

"Nor does pretty Mieke, and if she dares show up again I'll kick her right onto the dike! I don't want any of the polder people in the house; they gossip enough about me as it is!"

"So I've found another solution."

De Geus was surprised. "You've found a solution? But . . ."

"I've thought a lot about you the last few months. I knew how things were going here and that a man can't keep a house clean and wash dishes and so on. Especially not a doctor who has his hands full with his patients. And I understood you didn't want any help from the village; it's better the villagers don't go any further than the consulting room."

"Except the black one; he comes here often."

"Black Driek's as taciturn as his father; he won't talk your ears off. But the female element, they love to talk. I've known these people almost forty years. No, I thought to myself, I have a cousin living in Slikgat with about half a dozen girls, and one of them certainly wouldn't be missed. Yes, I think I ought to make a trip to Slikgat."

For awhile the doctor stared ahead in thought. He was moved by the devotion of the little old priest whom he'd given up and set aside, and who in the meantime had worried about the welfare of the godless dog who'd rejected his own wife and taken another woman into his house.

"You're a damn fine fellow," he said finally and shook hands with the priest. "If I can ever do you a favor . . ."

"Maybe you can," the priest smiled happily. "I really came for my rheumatism."

"Come and show me your rheumatic legs!" said the crazy doctor jovially, and arm in arm they went into the consulting room, these two men, these two happy people, warmed by their renewed friendship.

The priest made his trip to Slikgat, and when he had settled the matter with his niece, he went on to settle still another problem. The problem was about to be solved although Dr. de Geus didn't allow the outside to know how much trouble it caused him. The priest spoke to nobody about the second problem of his journey, but when he returned to the village everyone could see he felt happy. Happy and contented.

A week later she arrived, little Christine. From Slikgat she went by Klundert and Willemstad to the island, where Kasper the messenger met her at Tony the Ferry's and brought her by dogcart to the parsonage.

It was quite an event for Christine. During her twenty springs she had never left Slikgat, and now suddenly she had made this long trip on two autobusses, a tram, a ferry and a dogcart. She arrived tired and hungry at the parsonage as the winter sun shone palely in the bitter cold.

"Here's where your reverend uncle lives," said Kasper the messenger as he almost pulled the bell out of the wall.

Christine smiled, but the smile died on her lips when Bertha appeared at the door like a jack-in-the-box and asked sourly what all the noise was about.

"I just came to deliver her," smiled Kasper, "and the fee is twenty-five cents, please."

"I'm Christine," she said bashfully, "and my uncle said . . ."

"I know all about it," snapped Bertha, looking at the girl with barely concealed disdain. "You can come in!"

Christine took her straw bag from the broadly grinning Kasper and stepped into the dark hallway as Bertha searched furiously in her apron pocket for twenty-five cents.

"I've got it here," said Christine.

"There you are," said Bertha, ignoring Christine's gesture, "and in the future don't pull the bell out of the wall, understand?"

Kasper understood, and he drove away whistling in his dogcart. Bertha closed the door with a deep sigh.

"You can hang your coat on the clothes tree over there. The priest was called to Keetje Trul, and when he gets back he'll take you to that crazy clown."

"Crazy clown?" Christine's eyes sparkled with pleasure, but Bertha made no further comment till they reached the parlor.

"Sit down here and I'll set the table for you. Though it's bothersome enough to come an hour after mealtime."

Christine blushed. "Don't trouble yourself, Juffrouw; I ate a sandwich on the way, and I'm not a bit hungry," she said pluckily.

Bertha snorted disdainfully and shuffled out of the room. Christine sat on the edge of a chair and looked around with great curiosity. Gosh! What a lot of books! She had never seen so many in one place. And what beautiful pictures on the wall! . . . Otherwise an awfully chilly reception. She had thought it would be quite different. Her uncle was supposed to meet her at the ferry, and then they were to go together to the doctor. Instead the ferryman put her on a dogcart because her uncle didn't show up, and here she was, received by a sour-faced maid who called the doctor a "strange clown" . . . No, Christine was very disappointed.

She was startled out of her thoughts as Bertha came in with the tableware and began setting the table noisily.

"You can wash up upstairs; one flight up, first door to the right."

Obediently Christine went up and entered the first door to the right. Obediently she washed up and went downstairs again and sat down like a good child at the table where Bertha had set her place and served the soup.

"Now say your prayers and start eating!"

The good child prayed, but she couldn't help bursting into laughter in the middle of a Hail Mary at the ridiculousness of the situation: she, Christine van de Mortel, who passed for a marriageable young girl in her hamlet, was treated here like a schoolchild and naughty girl by an old sourpuss.

"Amen!" she said and looked triumphantly into Bertha's eyes; naturally she expected a sermon about disrespectful pray-ing, and she wasn't going to let the old maid call her down any longer. But Bertha didn't say a word; she just looked at her with sharp eyes and waited until Christine, still unsure of herself, carefully started to eat the hot soup. Then she fired her first shaft.

"I can't understand how a self-respecting girl would dare to live under the same roof with that crazy clown!"

Christine looked at her questioningly.

"Or don't you know all that's happened here?"

Christine shook her head in denial.

"Uncle came to our house a week ago and asked Mother if

she could spare one of us to serve at the doctor's. Otherwise I don't know a thing, but I suppose it's all right, or Uncle wouldn't have asked me, would he?"

Bertha was uncertain for a moment.

"The priest's getting old! That man hardly knows what's going on in the world, and he only wants to hear good things about people; whatever's bad he doesn't believe! Do you want some more soup, eh? . . ."

"No, thank you, it was fine!"

Bertha walked out, leaving Christine in uncertainty. A moment later she came back with a dish of steaming potatoes, vegetables, meat and other products of her culinary skill. She was very busy with awkward, unfriendly gestures. But Christine soon understood her bark was worse than her bite.

"Now eat heartily, Sientje."

"Christine . . . At home they call me Stiene."

"Well that's all right with me, but take a warning from someone who knows; that crazy doctor, he's a bad one, and I think it's a great pity that the priest lets a young thing like you go into the house of such a beastly wicked man. How old are you?"

"Twenty, Juffrouw."

"You don't need to call me Juffrouw; just call me Bertha. But the priest should know better. I tell him so often, but do you think he listens? He smiles and says the crazy doctor is a good man, that's what he says!"

"Then it must be true," smiled Christine reassured, but now Bertha became really angry.

"Must be true? Must be true? What do you know about it? Do you know what the barbarian did with that—with that trollop who came to live with him? Do you know he abandoned his own wife and he never goes to church and he's a confirmed atheist? Do you know all that? Hey?"

Christine was staring at her with eyes enlarged by fear. It had never occurred to the simple farm girl to imagine the life of such people, and even less had she expected that her uncle would put her in such bad company. Her appetite disappeared completely and tears sprang in her large blue eyes.

"Is—is all that really true? Is that doctor I was going to work for . . ."

"How could I say so otherwise?"

Christine got up resolutely. She had grown pale, but an inflexible expression appeared on her fresh girl's face.

"What are you going to do?" Bertha asked a bit worriedly.

Christine shook her blond hair energetically and stood proudly before Bertha. "I'm going back right away! Mother told me to take good care of myself, and if it didn't suit me to come back immediately. I don't want to serve a bad man."

"Oh well," said Bertha pacifyingly, for she was somewhat taken aback, "it's not as bad as all that. You look like somebody who can take care of herself and . . ."

"Yes, I can!" said Christine proudly, "and that's why I'm going back!"

Then the priest came into the room, small and shivering in his ample greatcoat. For a moment he stood on the threshold in surprise, and approached his niece with wide open arms. "Hello, Christine!"

"Hello, Uncle . . ."

Heavy-hearted, Bertha took her refuge in the kitchen and Christine started to cry.

"I'm going away again," she sobbed. "I don't want to serve such a bad man! . . . Mother said I must take care of myself, and he's such a very bad man!"

The priest knew that Bertha had spilled her gall. With a deep sigh he took off his coat and walked to the fire, rubbing his hands.

"Come sit next to me, Christine, won't you?"

The girl obeyed and dried her tears on the sleeve of her peasant dress. For awhile they sat together silently, and then the priest began talking softly and friendlily.

"Now, Christine, listen carefully to an old man who has seen and experienced much of life, who has a hard time saying things that come to his mind. . . ."

Christine listened, completely quiet as she sat next to the old priest who, choosing his words with difficulty, told about a good, confused man who needed to be helped to believe in our good Lord, and about the villagers here whose tongues wagged so quickly, how ungrateful they were to the doctor who did everything for them but was still a strange sort of person. . . .

"Really, Christine, he's no barbarian, the way they picture him. He's a good man who lost his way on one of many small paths that lead away from God but will finally lead to Him again. He's an embittered human being whom our good Lord has punished often and heavily; perhaps he's too learned to understand the simplest things of life. Dr. de Geus—they call him the crazy doctor here because he doesn't follow the same rules of life the others do—Dr. de Geus is really a big, rebellious, mischievous boy who thinks he can play a game with our good Lord, but he's a plaything in God's almighty hands.

"I'll tell it more simply, Christine, straight out, because you have a right to know everything. Dr. de Geus had a difficult childhood and he wasn't any too sure of himself when he married in the church. Still, he tried to be good and devout, but he exaggerated things, as he exaggerates everything, and gradually became a caricature of what he had intended to be, a man filled with contradictions. When after all his praying and begging our good Lord didn't give him a child, he turned his back upon God. He shouldn't have done it, but an embittered human being, Christine, is so unreasonable. He does things he never wanted to do; in his despair he begins to blame the good Lord for letting him muddle along and placing him at a disadvantage compared to other people. Dr. de Geus delcared war on our good Lord and went from bad to worse. In a crazy mood he left his wife, and was too stub-

born later on to go back to her. He came here to the polder to
escape the scandal of family and acquaintances, perhaps to bury
himself in the loneliness of the polder to escape from our good
Lord. But man always finds again what he is most anxious to
avoid. There is more gossip about him here in the polder than
there ever would have been in the city, the good Lord Whom
he couldn't escape in the city doesn't leave him alone here
either. He's been punished heavily here for the love he trampled on over there. . . ."

Her uncle was silent, sighing deeply, and for a long time
the room was still.

Christine stared at the fire with her large clear eyes; despite
her horror at all the bad things she'd heard, she felt almost
pity now for the lonely barbarian and rebellious man. She
couldn't understand where the man got his courage to rebel
against the good Lord, and much of what her uncle had said
still wasn't clear to her, but she felt with fine feminine instinct
that at the base of the doctor's misbehavior there was a great
tragedy, and there must have been something wrong with the
woman from the city too, before he had reached this stage.

"You must look at these things with tolerant eyes," pursued
her uncle almost imploringly, "as our good Lord probably
looks at them too. Our dear Lord is so good and wise, Christine. He often smiles at the little human beings who think
they can solve the deepest problems themselves. Dr. de Geus
asserts he is an atheist. That's just a big word, Christine, and
typical of Dr. de Geus' bad boy's bravado, for in spite of his
stout-heartedness his fear of God is greater than in any of us.
The doctor distrusts God; he thinks God is always scheming
to beat him down and belittle him in his smallness. The
doctor declared war on our good Lord and in the meantime he
spends his money to repair my little church and help the poor
farm hands. He does crazy things, but always to defend himself against God's grace that pursues him everywhere. And

that's why someday our good Lord will win. The good Lord always wins, Christine. . . ."

Christine nodded. She was a bit dizzy. She had always looked at life in an uncomplicated manner, and her belief in the good Lord was the simplest thing in the world. She couldn't understand a man like the crazy doctor; he filled her with horror, despite the pity she felt for him. It was easy for her uncle to talk, but a man who rebelled against God . . .

"I know all this is difficult for you to digest," sighed the priest. "I'm not able to put these things into the right words and phrases, but above all, Christine, you must believe that this doctor isn't as bad as people make him out. . . ."

"But he fights against our good Lord!" she hesitated.

"From fear! Self-defense, Christine, and hurt pride. But someday his resistance will break, and he'll fall on his knees and reconcile himself with the good Lord."

Christine sighed. It was all so strange, so confusing. A man who dared fight God and still was a good human being. A man who did many bad things and still helped repair her uncle's little church and helped the poor people of the village . . . The priest got up.

"Come," he smiled, "you mustn't worry about all these things, Christine. I told you about them so you'd understand the talk of Bertha and the villagers a bit—and so you'd say a few prayers for that crazy doctor, who has an extra special place in my heart. Now I'll take you to him, and I hope you'll look after him well."

They went into the polder in the wintry cold, and their steps sounded clearly in the frosty air and over the dike.

Christine, a little pale, walked in silence beside her uncle, who was bowed in his heavy coat.

The fields lay desolate all around and a cow lowed in a stable as they passed by. Over the broad white polder hung a pale little winter sun like a nostalgic smile. Christine sighed. She was afraid. Life was such a strange thing. . . .

16

Christine had been going her way for months now through the house of Dr. de Geus, and she was singing her highest song. She scrubbed and polished and cooked and did everything a good housekeeper should do. She knew every nook and cranny of the big house, and everything shone with cleanliness. When de Geus came home in the afternoon from his sick calls or the visits with his old friend the priest, he always found the table set and was greeted by the aromas of a simple meal wafted across a bunch of spring flowers. And there, behind a steaming pan, laughed Christine's light blue eyes in a cloud of golden blond hair. Then the lines of worry disappeared from the doctor's face and he grinned expansively.

"Krissie, you're a jewel!"

"That's possible," smiled Christine, and happily she went to work. She was glad when the doctor looked contented and the creases disappeared from his wide brow.

In the kitchen she thought about him; what worries the man must have, when after the exultant and somewhat artificial jolliness of the day he could sit so absorbed in deep thought at night when he thought she wasn't paying attention to him.

In the beginning the doctor's behavior seemed very strange to her. His peasant clothing and eternal stubbly beard, even though he was supposed to be a very learned and proper gentleman. His noisy boisterousness during the day when he received his patients or raced through the polder in his beautiful car. His rough hunting parties with Black Driek. And later his melancholy reflections when the house was quiet and the evening spread a sad stillness over all things.

Then she would sit facing him by the fireplace and darn his thick blue socks with woolen yarn. She did this very neatly, bending over her work with devotion, and the lamplight was reflected in her needle shuttling back and forth and gleamed in her gold hair that framed her calm face like a halo. He looked at her over his glasses, sharing her serenity. Surreptitiously he regarded her quiet bowed head and the fine outline of her red mouth. Sometimes she would look up and smile, somewhat confused as she met his gaze. Then everything would be as before, her pervading calm, her attentiveness to her work, the melancholy associated with a thing that is beautiful and good but too delicate to shatter with noise.

Sometimes on a long evening, after they had sat facing each other quietly and listening to the wind humming in the chimney, he would suddenly jump up and pace the big room agitatedly. Christine would be startled out of her peaceful thoughts, not daring to look up at him. Then she would bend deeper over her work, knowing the worried line was on his forehead again, and he was looking at her from beneath knitted brows. His unrest would make her restless too, and she'd get up sooner than usual to brew coffee or do some superfluous work in the kitchen.

On other evenings everything would be peaceful and quiet. The doctor would smoke silently and read from learned books that filled Christine with vague shivers. She had looked into one of these books as she was dusting the bookcase, but she couldn't understand the language and the illustrations were so confusing and weird that she never felt the urge again to look into them.

Sometimes she would spend long evenings alone. Then the doctor was either at her uncle's or had gone to someone who was struggling with death. She would do her work in the loneliness of the somber house, as contented as a child. She never went to bed until the doctor returned because he might need her for something.

He found her very late one night, sleeping at the table, her head resting on her arms and the lamplight gleaming on her golden hair. He stood still in surprise for a moment, smiling with pleasure at the sight. She was sleeping quietly in the circle of her hair, and her face, resting sideways on her arms, had all the peace of complete innocence. She was breathing noiselessly, and the low hiss of the gas was the only sound in the night. He stood there almost withdrawn, looking at the young girl until resentment appeared on his face at the thought of . . .

"No, you idiot!" he upbraided himself.

And softly he went outside, opened the door with a loud rattling of his keys and banged it shut. Then he entered the room where Christine stared at him, her face flushed, her eyes large with fright.

"Did I—I think I fell asleep, Doctor!"

He stroked her hair from behind, smiling broadly.

"I think I made a late night of it, Krissie! From now on you mustn't wait up for me after ten. And now quick! Upstairs with you!"

"Doesn't the doctor want something to drink? I kept the coffee warm!"

And busily she walked to the kitchen while she surreptitiously rubbed the sleep from her eyes.

What should a fellow do in a case like that? He was really very eager for a cup of coffee, so they drank it together in the middle of the night, the tired doctor and the sleepy young girl who tried valiantly to keep her eyes open. He found her so sweet with the blush of sleep on her cheeks and the tousled blond hair hanging to her shoulders and shining in the yellow lamplight that he couldn't help looking at her time and again over the steaming coffee.

"Tomorrow you must come along with me to the city."

"Why, Doctor?" She looked at him, startled. She had never been to the city, and she hadn't the slightest desire to go.

"I want to buy you a few nice dresses."

"But Doctor, I . . ." She lowered her eyes timidly.

"Red velvet would go well with your blond curls."

"But I don't need clothes at all, Doctor! This dress is all right, isn't it? And upstairs I still . . ."

"Bordeaux red," he said, looking at the small dimple in her white throat. "That'll be fine on you, Krissie. And I'd like you to . . ."

Christine got up suddenly. She was completely confused and her cheeks flamed.

"Doctor, I—I think . . ."

"That you should go right to bed," smiled de Geus. "It's past two, damn it all."

With a bashful "G'night, Doctor," Christine fled upstairs. On the steps she fought back her tears; she didn't know why, but suddenly she felt terribly sad and confused. Why? The city—a velvet dress—and her woolen dress was still all right . . .

She undressed and stood thoughtfully before the mirror a moment, her gray dress in her hands. She didn't notice the reflection of her white body in the mirror. She stared ahead seeing nothing, suddenly filled with a lonely, frightening feeling of abandonment. She sat on the edge of the bed with the dress over her knees and thoughtlessly stroked the strong rough material. She had worn this dress for a long time. It was still fine. Why did the doctor have to buy her a new one? . . . The doctor . . . He was such a good man. She smiled at the thought. The people of the village and the polder were very ungrateful to say such bad things about him. She herself knew how much good he did for the poorest among them, and the villagers knew it too, and they were always experiencing how he was ready for them day and night. But some of them took advantage of this kindness. They besmirched him behind his back.

She heard the door being locked downstairs. The doctor was going to bed too. She heard him climbing the stairs softly in his stocking feet, almost sneaking; he probably thought she was asleep. But the third step creaked and she knew exactly when he was upstairs, no matter how careful he was. She heard him opening the door across the hall and then noticed the temporary dimming and flaring up of her gas lamp when he lit his light. She shivered. She hadn't even put on her nightgown. Funny girl! She must have mulled things over for half an hour, and it was so late at night.

She kneeled by the bed, and as she said her rosary she couldn't help thinking of the doctor who was so good, but who went happily through life without our dear Lord, without saying a prayer before he crawled into bed at night, without a prayer before he took his meals. That was very bad! That was . . . Her head nodded forward over her nightgown which was still neatly folded on the counterpane, and she fell asleep with the rosary between her fingers. She slept soundly, and above her the gas lamp hissed and all around her reigned the stillness of the large somber house. Outside the polder was asleep in the early spring under a cover of thick fog. Under the high heavens stood the cattle, lost in the fog. A few stars twinkled in the purple. Silence and rest. Peace over the wide vast polder . . .

De Geus had sent Christine upstairs and had drunk a few schnapps. He was thinking about the girl and what a neat thing she was and how well she did her job. Life was so much more pleasant with a lively young thing in the house to take care of the place. A lively thing—a sweet thing. He smiled as he remembered finding her asleep and how he'd felt the urge to kiss the nape of her neck and startle her awake. Afterward he was glad he hadn't done it, that he'd repressed that urge. She had been beautiful, too, as she sat opposite him, her cheeks rosy, drinking coffee late into the night. She was beautiful in a different way from the city's vaunted beauties. "Country beauty," he smiled, "a country beauty." Ah well! he mustn't have foolish thoughts. This child was tender as the spring and beautiful by the very fact of her innocence. It was something unreal to him, something his rough nature couldn't grasp. He had to keep his distance and leave that beauty untouched.

He swallowed his schnapps and turned off the light. Then he locked the front door.

As he went up the stairs he thought about Krissie. Here was a simple woman, still almost a child, a girl without problems who went along straight paths and never hesitated at the crossroads.

Involuntarily de Geus drew the comparison with his own wife. He sat quietly on the edge of his bed. She too was simple by nature, and the difficulties he'd created in his own head hadn't existed for her. He thought back to that evening when for the first time he burst into fury because their marriage wasn't blessed with children. His whole attitude had been reproachful, blaming her, though he pretended it was God's intention.

Funny, how Dr. de Geus thought back so calmly and clearly, for the first time in many years, to that evening. It was because Krissie reminded him of his wife in many small ways. It was because Krissie affected him like a tender, dew-drenched

May morning, after the depressing thunder-and-lightning tensions the beautiful city woman had aroused in him.

For the first time he felt that a woman of simplicity was really the focal point for a quiet atmosphere which a man expects to find in his home before anything else; that a woman should bring rest, not unrest, into a man's life, satisfaction, not a never-to-be-stilled hunger. Dr. de Geus, the barbarian, had hoped to find that rest by chasing everything desirable and attractive that danced before his eyes; he had wilfully chased away the rest and quietude because he didn't dare to admit what he now recognized for the first time. He had acted stupidly; he had stressed the unimportant things that had little or no reference to his conflict. Instead of giving in, he had become rebellious; he had made demands where there should have been none. As a physician he should have known better all along.

The peace which Krissie brought to his home was like the peace he had tasted before, during the first years of his marriage, before he reproached his wife for being too simple and plain, in feature as well as spirit.

The doctor toyed a moment longer with these thoughts, then blew out the lamp without the usual cursing, and noticed some light beneath Christine's door. "Much too late," he growled in displeasure. "The lamb should've gone to bed long ago. Tomorrow I'll get home earlier, or else send her to bed before I go."

De Geus lay down. He closed his eyes, but the thoughts that flew like birds through his head wouldn't let him rest, and when he opened his eyes a while later he still saw the yellowish streak of light coming from Christine's room. "The child probably has a lot to pray for," he mumbled. "They must have taught her at home. What innocence to believe so implicitly in the good Father at that age. I thought differently about it at her age, though I didn't want to admit it to myself."

He yawned and threw himself on his other side, turning away

from the light, and his thoughts wandered to the other girls he had known. To the young women who at Christine's age had already enjoyed life so much that they were "more knowing" than the village women would ever be. And not ashamed to speak about it. He compared them to Christine, and her with his wife again. And then the little priest came peeking around the corner, the little priest who had brought this innocent child to his house.

He turned again in bed and the yellow streak of light was still there. He looked at his watch. Half-past four! Had Christine fallen asleep and forgotten to turn out the light? Would he—but no, what did he care if the light burned all night? Or had she—no, why should the child pack her trunk and flee the house in the middle of the night like that other one?

He fought for sleep, but his unrest became so great that he got up to find out whether the child was quietly asleep or if she had secretly left, in fear of the barbarian she felt unprotected against.

He put on his corduroy pants and walked softly out of the room, up the hall to Christine's door. He listened, holding his breath. Everything was deathly quiet but the light shone feebly across the threshold. He peeked through the keyhole but could see little else than the corner of the bed and the counterpane that still neatly covered it.

So that was it! Christine had fled! Why did his heart beat in his throat? Why had disaster and misfortune attacked him again on a peaceful night? He knocked softly on the door and slowly turned the knob.

He looked around in surprise and smiled at what he saw: Christine on her bare knees beside the bed, sleeping peacefully, the rosary between her fingers.

Should he let her sleep? He called her name and Christine awoke with a cry of fear.

"Oh, Doctor! Did I fall asleep?"

"You did, and it's better done in bed. Come on! Quick! It's half-past four. Turn off your light and sleep well."

"G'night, Doctor," sounded a small, trembling voice.

De Geus heaved a deep sigh as he fell on his bed. What he had feared for a moment hadn't happened; Christine hadn't fled from his house. The peace he'd found wouldn't be cruelly broken again.

And in the darkness Christine was sobbing.

Sobbing because this had happened to her, because the doctor saw her kneeling by the bed this way. The doctor who was such a good person, but—but about whom the villagers said such weird things . . .

Oh, tomorrow she wouldn't dare meet his eyes after what happened! And still she couldn't help it. She fell asleep as she was saying her rosary. If only she had locked her door before . . . She put the rosary on her night table and pulled the covers closer around her. She shivered. How nasty everything had become! All day long she was so glad and contented and now this happened. . . . She cried quietly in her pillow. . . . A little later she fell asleep.

But de Geus couldn't get to sleep, and he turned in his bed with a jerk. The blue reflection of a starlit night dripped through the windows. A bird uttered a raucous cry as it flew past the roof. He lay on his back and lit a cigarette. He stared thoughtfully at the fiery end that glowed red from time to time in the pervading blackness.

Greedily he inhaled the prickly cigarette smoke and impatiently crushed the red spark to extinction in the ash tray.

He threw himself around in the bed and closed his eyes, but he knew only too well that sleep was still far away. He lay very quiet and gradually became more calm. Now he lay still for a long time, almost without a thought. A mouse gnawed somewhere in a corner of the house. This awoke him from his half slumber, and the thoughts began again as he lay wide-eyed, staring at a twinkling star through the window.

"That's the eye of God the Father. He is looking through the window. He sees everything. He sees Krissie lying in her bed. And my wife, whom I left . . . He sees me too. *Bonjour*, God the Father! Here lies Tom de Geus in all his smallness stretched out under Your high heaven, an abortion of all that should have been good and noble, malformed because he never wanted the good. No, I'm lying, and You know I'm lying. Let's play an open game of cards. Aren't You bored that I'm blabbing this way to You? I'm doing it to get through the night, You see, to distract my thoughts from—from the things I don't want, that I don't want for purely sound reasons, You understand? Not because I'm afraid, but only because You put a heart in my *corpus*, and accidentally it's still beating warmly for . . . No, that's talk, God, You know that. I love the little thing sleeping next door a bit. That's the way things are. And since I care so much for her I want her to remain happy with her dear God . . . Do you know there was a time when I felt the same way she does? I must've been pretty nice in those days. I said my rosary just as devoutly as she, I had plans to become a brave and noble *pater familias*. *Pater familias!* If You'd given me that chance I wouldn't be laughing at You now! But no, You only gave me a wife and no children! I was just a tough human animal. You probably had enough respectable family men. . . . Damned idiot that I was, to think that I too had a right to happiness! Now I am wandering over Your good world beneath Your almighty hands. You can floor me with one blow, for eternity. Still I'm not afraid of the blow that will come someday. I live my little life and I greatly enjoy the devout little people You have surrounded me with. I practice a little robbery, God, and try to pluck from Your world whatever is left. I abandoned the woman You gave me. That was one of my worst tricks, and

You'll get me for it later. I took another woman, but it didn't make me happy, for You don't allow me even the smallest pleasure. Stolen goods don't last, do they? Now this child has come into my life, and I could pluck this flower if I cared to. But now I don't want to. I'm almost begging You to spare her from all the rottenness of Your beautiful world, because her happiness is worth more than my own and it comes from a spiritual peace that radiates from her. . . . Don't You think I'm a sentimental fool, God? A rascal really ought to take what's coming to him; that's his right. But I'm still a little too tender-hearted for that. . . . I'll confess to You, when I see a child like that in her innocence, her pure life, I could whimper with jealousy, yearning for that peace that I too used to know. . . . If I told that to Father Conings he'd say that the urge in my soul is toward God. But I know better. It's nothing but selfishness. I always want to go back to the thing I've destroyed. So I yearn for happiness that I threw away myself. . . ."

Suddenly his face stiffened. He stared sadly at the star and closed his eyes a moment in weariness. "Why should I ask anything from God for myself?" he mumbled dejectedly. "Why should I—from Him? . . . He won't grant me a bit of happiness. . . ."

His soliloquy seemed to end in a dry sob. He lay very quiet now, his eyes closed, his face turned from the window with the star. Was rough de Geus, with all his bravado and pride, still so small that he took God for a bogeyman and didn't dare believe in His eternal love? It was sad the way he was stretched out beneath God's heaven. Infinity was domed above him, and the star paled gradually as the firmament grew blue. The little man slept in the first dawn of morning. A tired man, a worried creature in the shadow of God's being.

But high above him God in His wisdom knew the things that the little human couldn't express in words, and His infinite love took pity on the sleeping Geus, who perhaps was not as bad as he thought himself to be. "Let's come to an understanding," de Geus had said, just before he fell asleep discouraged and tired. "An understanding from man to man." God smiled at the presumption of such an insignificant creature, but He approved of his good intentions. He would keep his understanding with de Geus. The wild animal would be tamed, and then . . .

De Geus slept in the new day that God gave him. And Christine slept, tired from her late vigil, with a dried-up tear on her cheek. Two human children slept. God saw them both, as He sees us all. And God smiled on the earth and spread his blessing over human joy and human suffering. . . .

17

The next day, faithful to his agreement, de Geus started to squelch the beast in him, not because he was afraid of God but solely because he was beginning to love Christine. He had discovered in her a source of restfulness that he'd looked for everywhere else in vain. She was his only connection to a happy past.

"Let's get this straight," he said to himself as he sat on the edge of the bed pulling on his socks, "it's a purely platonic love and nothing else. I want to see Krissie happy, and I can only do it by excluding myself. *Fiat!*" He looked out the window. The eye of God the Father had disappeared. The sun blazed splendidly in the blue sky and the polder sparkled with a pearly dew. The grass was freshly green and heavy with moisture and the buttercups sucked greedily at the young light.

He threw the windows wide open to let the daylight in.

Downstairs in the kitchen he heard Christine pumping water. She wasn't singing as she usually did. De Geus shook his head and smiled. "She's still upset about last night," he said.

He rubbed his chin.

"Shall I shave or not?"

He went ahead and shaved himself carefully and decided he didn't look much better after the treatment.

"You really need an unctuous face now," he said to his image in the mirror. "Fellows who follow the straight and narrow path can't walk around with a week-old beard."

He whistled as he continued his toilet and even hummed as he went downstairs. The fine aroma of coffee and frying bacon met him at the stairs.

Christine was dawdling in the kitchen. At other times she was the first to wish a good morning; now she seemed to be hiding. His face showed irritation for a moment as he sat at the table and she remained in the kitchen. What the hell! Didn't she hear him come downstairs? But he thought about his agreement and smiled. He wouldn't make it more difficult for Krissie than was necessary. The child would have quite a job already to strike an attitude.

"Moooorning, Krissie!" he called gaily. Christine was startled with fright.

"Gosh, Doctor! Are you downstairs already?"

"As you see," he grinned amiably.

"Good morning, Doctor."

She lowered her eyes and stood motionless for a moment. She wanted to say something, but quickly went back to the kitchen for the coffee.

He looked smilingly after her.

"Did you sleep well, Krissie?"

"So-so, Doctor. . . ."

She was blushing violently. She had heavy circles under her eyes and he knew she hadn't slept much the night before.

"Listen to me, Krissie," he began a moment later when they

sat facing each other at the table. She looked at him with a kind of fear in her eyes. "You're a good child and our dear Lord must like you damn well, because I'm convinced you live the way He wants people to live. But you mustn't take this childish attitude, Krissie!"

"Do I, Doctor?"

Her cheeks were a fiery red and he saw she was struggling to keep her tears back.

"Let's call things by their name, Krissie. You're no bigot, and no prude, no, on the contrary you're a fine lively girl, and it's done me a lot of good these past months to watch you going through life singing and gay. But I want to talk about last night. . . ."

She lowered her eyes, and her eyelids trembled.

"It's my fault that I came home last night at two o'clock. It's my fault that you didn't go upstairs till a quarter after three, dizzy with sleep, and fell asleep during your evening prayer or whatever else you were doing. It's all my fault and you couldn't help it one little bit, understand? But isn't it reasonable that I thought it rather strange when I saw your light burning more than an hour later? What does a normal person do under those circumstances? He goes to find out if maybe you've fallen asleep. Well, when I knocked on the door and got no answer, I opened the door and woke you up."

"Doctor, I think it's horrible."

"What do you think is so horrible?"

"Well, that I stayed up so late and then fell asleep by my bed and—and you came to look."

"Your uncle would have done the same thing."

Yes, her uncle would. But her uncle was quite different from the doctor they told all those stories about. No, it was impossible to explain to Dr. de Geus, and even though nothing much had happened, she wished that nothing at all had happened.

It was painfully quiet, and the longer the stillness lasted

the less Christine felt at ease. She realized she was exaggerating the incident, but de Geus, who viewed her difficulties from quite a different angle, couldn't possibly find the words or attitude to reduce the disagreeable tension.

Come, it was best to forget the whole thing. Then, to break the silence and maintain his stature as an older man who knows better, he remarked airily, "Well, the next time you stay up so late I'd advise you to skip the rosary, or whatever your prayer may be."

Suddenly Christine lost her timidity. She looked at him squarely and her eyes were very serious.

"A dog goes to sleep without praying, Doctor!" she sallied. "But a thinking human being does no such thing."

The doctor blinked.

"I never pray either," he said, outwardly calm. "Not in the evening and not in the morning and not in the afternoon."

He didn't mention the fact that deep within himself he was at odds with God and often held very emotional monologues with Him.

"That's even worse than the animals, Doctor. At least they pay homage to God with their voices. But as long as I've been here I've prayed every night for both of us. Even when I was tired."

Dr. de Geus was ill at ease as Christine straightened him out in her quiet manner. His wife had done it too, quietly, but deeply convinced. Damnation, how alike those two were in many respects. Still—he put Christine and his wife above the beautiful vision he had brought from the city. His wife too? . . .

"I suppose you're thinking 'Let the child talk. What does she know?' But in your heart, Dr. de Geus, you'll have to agree with me. You're much too good and too learned a person not to know things that I myself know so well. The good Lord can't be overwhelmed by brilliant words, and you know very well you're as dependent on Him as everyone else."

"Sure I know!" de Geus asserted angrily. But then he saw her small, frightened face and controlled himself. "I know, Krissie," he repeated more amiably. "All these things you're telling me I've known for a long time. I'm only surprised that you express them so well. I know God exists, that He created everything and that I'm eating His bread and breathing His air and can't take a step unless He lets me. . . ."

"Well then," proffered Christine in astonishment, "how dare you eat His bread and breathe His air without thanking Him for all that?"

"I dare it, all right," answered de Geus. "I know as much about God as you do and perhaps a bit more, but I still dare to laugh right in His face!"

"Oh, Doctor!"

"And use His bounty without thanking Him for it."

"But, Doctor—why is that?"

"Because I've declared war on Him, even though I know that today or tomorrow He can take me in, Christine."

The girl smiled pityingly.

"My little brother was as silly as you are, but I could understand that, because he was only ten years old. One day he laughed at my father, also in his face, when Father forbade him to steal medlars. Father boxed his ears and little Kees kicked Father. Then he got a thorough thrashing that he'll remember ten years from now. A few days later a little friend taunted him to steal more medlars, and you know what little Kees said?"

De Geus looked at her laughingly.

"He said, I ain't crazy, Father's much stronger! That's how bright little Kees was, Doctor!"

There was a moment of silence. De Geus stared thoughtfully out the window. Christine traced figures with her hand on the tablecloth, not daring to look at him again. She suddenly felt she'd been much too bold, saying all those things to the doctor.

But his voice wasn't angry when he began to speak a moment later.

"And now you want to say, Krissie, that little Kees is more intelligent than I am because he won't fight somebody who's stronger than himself . . ."

Something like pain trembled in his voice, something that made Christine look up in surprise.

"But with me the question isn't quite as simple, Krissie. . . . Your little brother fought his father once because he was angry and forgot himself. Later on he didn't dare to. I fight God continuously and not because I'm angry. I fight Him because I hate Him!"

She shivered.

"You don't believe that yourself, Doctor!"

He looked into her honest blue eyes. For some time he regretted starting this conversation. It was radically opposed to his resolution to take good care of Christine and allow her to believe in God's great love. But now that it had taken this turn, he felt compelled to explain his point of view to her. What the hell, was he going to be beaten by this simple peasant child? Wasn't his outlook much better than hers?

"Look here, Krissie," he began again with less conviction, "what would you think if you'd been praying ardently for something for years, and God gave those things to others, but not to you?"

"I'd think they were all right for the others, but not for me, Doctor. And then I'd thank God for all the things that I had and the others didn't get."

"Yes, but what I asked God for was just as good for me as for the others," he maintained stubbornly.

"How do you know?" she asked simply.

"Well, because . . ."

Now he hesitated with his answer. Had that little kitten managed to drive him into a corner? That really would be too fantastic! She looked at him in friendly query. He couldn't evade it. He had to give her a satisfactory answer or all his convictions and his grim outlook on life would totter about him. He racked his brains. He moved restlessly on his chair. Hell and damnation! Didn't he know . . .

"Well, I'm sure it would have been fine for me to have children, because . . ."

He stared at her. Sweat broke out on his brow. Her friendly, questioning smile and her large, honest eyes were blurred to his gaze as he strained to keep the lead in this duel, to hold out against this peasant child; he couldn't give up his carefully built conviction, for if he accepted one premise all the rest would follow! He was too honest to lie, to dismiss the problem with a shrug of the shoulders. But facing him sat this simple child with her great wisdom that she hadn't acquired from book reading. There sat little Krissie for whom he'd felt a paternal affection and who now turned out to be a wise woman in her simple faith. The silence weighed between them. He groaned inwardly with impotence.

"May I tell you what I think, Doctor?" She asked this almost reverently and her cheeks grew red from excitement. He looked at her, too confused to speak, dismayed by the inexplicable fact that he knew of no solution, whereas she was about to speak with great ease.

"If I may put it this way . . . I don't think it would be right for you to have children, because you yourself haven't learned obedience. You can't even obey God, Who is far above all human beings. How could you expect your children to obey you? They'd see your bad example and they would become bad too and cause you nothing but sorrow. . . . Maybe that's why the good Lord wouldn't permit you to have any children. Of course I don't know, Doctor, but it might be the reason. And our dear Lord could have a thousand other reasons for not answering your prayer. If that's why you're angry with Him, then you're like the small boy who's angry with his father because he won't give him a knife to cut his fingers with. . . ." She looked up, surprised at the prolonged silence that followed her words. Dr. de Geus was facing her, resting his head on his strong hands. He sat motionless and the silence persisted.

"Are you angry with me now?" she asked anxiously. "Maybe I—I was too impertinent. . . ."

De Geus uttered a deep sigh and looked at her with a tired smile. "No, Krissie. I could never be angry with you. But you gave me a lot to think about. . . . You said things that—you couldn't know about all by yourself, and yet you said them. . . ." He got up and rubbed his forehead.

"It all sounds so simple, the way you tell it. But it's so hard for me to understand such simple things, Krissie—in order to believe them." He paced the room, nervous and upset. "For years I built up my conception of life. I began to hate God because I didn't get my way. If only I could see how you're right, that God inspires you with all this clever talk, to stretch out a hand to me—that I didn't get what I asked for, only because it wasn't good for me. If I could be convinced that God is right, then I think I could obey Him."

"We can't always see where Father is right, and still we must obey him," Christine said with a smile.

"As a child you have to obey, because your father knows better," he countered.

"And as a learned doctor you needn't obey, because the dear Lord doesn't know any better? Do human beings exist who are wiser than our dear Lord?"

He stared at the girl incredulously. Was this Christine putting these difficult questions to him? Were her questions to remain unanswered time and again? "It's almost eight o'clock," he said irritatedly. "Time for my consulting hour, but we'll continue our conversation later, Krissie. You've driven me into a corner for the time being, though I don't understand how."

"I'll pray that you stay in the corner," Christine promised

generously. "It seems that learned people need to learn things simple people know even before they're grown up."

De Geus kept a depressed silence and shuffled out of the room. He felt like a defeated schoolboy. He was distraught all day, plunged into deep thought.

He went out to call on his patients. He visited Kris Briool and Tony the Ferry and Dirk de Krotekoker and few other humble folk. He also called on Sebus Lens, the old miser who, to the great satisfaction of his prospective heirs, was now in fact about to die. The doctor had a kind word and a friendly smile for everyone. But he was so distraught and his glance so thoughtful that they all knew something unusual was happening to the doctor. This furnished new material for gossip. Later he drove by the priest's house. For the last few weeks the little priest had not been able to go any further than his church, for his life light was only a flicker. Bertha-my-daughter met the doctor in the hallway, but he scarcely noticed her sour face as he went directly to his friend's room.

The priest sat in his armchair in front of the window, a pillow behind his back and one behind his head. The spring sun shone on his fine face and the silver strands of his sparse hair. He held a breviary in his slender white hands and looked up in surprise when de Geus entered the room. He proffered his small, shaking hand, but de Geus didn't even see it and immediately sat down on a chair facing him.

"Now, tell me where that niece of yours gets all her wisdom from!" he began abruptly. "Did you incite her to attack me with her dear Lord, or did someone else teach her to bowl a fellow over with her palaver?"

The startled priest looked at him, and the doctor's serious mien worried him somewhat. De Geus didn't seem to expect an answer and gazed absent-mindedly out the window.

"You know the worst of it?" he began again. "Everything she tells me seems crystal clear; I can't contradict her arguments, but when I think it over it seems ridiculous that all this should apply to me. . . . The little witch says, something that's right for other people wouldn't be right for me, and if I had children they'd grow up as criminals because I haven't learned how to obey!"

The priest smiled subtly. That last trick had certainly worked, but he was careful not to say so. He allowed the excited de Geus to talk himself out, and it gradually became clear to him that in her very simplicity Christine had stirred the doctor's soul to the core. He thanked God silently, for he knew the doctor was sincere enough to bear the consequences once he saw that the girl was right.

"You must try to avoid such conversations with Christine," he warned him seriously. "Don't talk to her about religious matters!"

Nonplussed, de Geus stared at him.

"Why shouldn't we talk about them?"

"Because it's not good for your peace of soul," smiled the old man. "If you talk about God and religion and about conceited girls who think they're brighter and shrewder than God Himself, Christine will corner you with her simple faith. She'll utter truths a child can understand but you're too proud to accept. Then it's safer not to talk about it at all, Tom de Geus. When you've said *a* you must say *b*, and that you dare not do."

"That, damn it all, remains to be seen," said de Geus, getting very excited. "Do you think I'm not honest enough to recognize my error when I see I'm sitting next to it?"

"That's exactly what I mean," said the priest quietly. "You know Christine's right; she gave you the only possible reason why God didn't answer your prayers. But because that same God inspired a simple child and not the brilliant Tom de Geus, you won't bow your stubborn head. You're so conceited and self-opinionated, Tom, that you want to know better than God Himself. That's the cause of all your misery!"

"Go to hell!" said de Geus from the bottom of his heart, and without giving his old friend another look he walked out of the room and closed the front door with such a bang that Bertha came running out of the kitchen with a terrible shriek.

But when de Geus, purple with rage, jumped into his car, the priest opened the window with his last ounce of strength and called after him. "God's love is stronger than you, Tom de Geus; it will follow you wherever you go and God will win out. . . . God will win and drive you back to your wife. God . . ."

Startled by the strange, broken tone in the old voice, de Geus looked up. He jumped out of his car with a fearful curse when he saw the priest bent over the window sill with an ashen face while his bony white hands sought to support him on the back of his chair.

In two or three jumps de Geus was on the freestone stoop and tore the bell from the wall, but Bertha, beside herself with fright, stood shrieking by the motionless body of the priest and ignored the ringing bell.

"Open up, damn it all," roared de Geus, and as the maid continued to look at the old man with bulging eyes, he jerked the window open farther and climbed inside over the window sill. He shook the dazed Bertha until she ran crying out of the room and fell on her knees in terror, imploring God to let the disaster pass.

The disaster did not pass. De Geus realized it at first glance. The stout Geus, the imperturbable ruffian, trembled like a young girl as he lifted the priest's head very carefully and looked in the purple face and the lifeless eyes. The pupils, dull and strangely enlarged, seemed to stare in great anxiety toward something in the distance. The light was extinguished in them, lost beyond repair. "Good God!" de Geus cried silently as he sought the pulse that had ceased. "Great God! For the end to come this way!"

He looked into the broken eyes, he looked into the mouth.

He felt the pulse again, knowing it was in vain. "O God," he cried inwardly, "God, why did You do this! Why does my friend have to go like this, so disconsolate and so helpless!"

He supported the priest's tired old head with his strong hand and fussed carefully with the other until he had unfastened the collar at the neck. He opened the little priest's cassock and laid his hand on the stilled heart. The heart that had always beat for others, until it suddenly broke from emotion. He lifted the litle man in his strong arms. He carried him like a feather out of the room, moaning without a sound, crying to God, Who heard him.

"God! Why this too! If You have a reason for everything, if You only do what is good for us, what purpose can this serve?"

But God didn't give an answer. In his own soul the rough Geus would experience what was good for him, in his rebellious soul that now was only defeated and endlessly sad. In the hallway he met Bertha who looked up at him weeping. He merely nodded and Bertha understood. He went up the creaking stairs and opened the bedroom door with his knee. He laid the priest on the bed, under the ivory crucifix, and started taking off the worn-out cassock by which the villagers had known their shepherd for years.

Bertha stood crying in the hallway. She dared not come closer.

"Bertha-my-daughter," he said in a strange choked-up voice, "Bertha, God has taken our old friend away from life. Light the candles and do the customary things. Notify the sexton and ask Truike Pothuis to come and help you. Don't whimper, Bertha, because if your Catholicism is the right kind, you know there's one more saint in heaven now."

Bertha's Catholicism must have been sincere, but she couldn't help crying more violently. She put a candle on either side of the bed and de Geus lit them himself with his revolverlike lighter.

Bertha closed the curtains and went to Kobus the sexton. "The priest is dead!" she cried. "The priest is dead!"

And Kobus, his knees almost giving way, clumped to Truike Pothuis and told her the terrible news.

Truike shouted the news to Geertje of Giel Pik whom she met in the street, while Kobus the sexton knew nothing better to do than to ring the large bell as he blubbered. The sad news spread like wildfire through the village.

The priest is dead! The priest is dead! O God, O God, the priest is dead!

Heavy and somber the bell resounded over the fields. Over the wide polder the ringing echoed, and the farmers and field workers, the men and girls and all the young 'uns and oldsters looked up with fright, wondering what the ringing of the bell meant at this unusual hour. But they didn't remain in the dark for long; like one possessed, Christ-in-the-Wilderness rode through the fields on his shiny black horse. His rough beard flapped in the wind, and his face was transfixed with sorrow.

"Our priest is dead!" he shouted to all the houses as he passed at a stiff gallop. "Our priest is dead!"

He rode for two hours through the endless polder and brought the sad tidings to all, even to Tony the Ferry and Noltie Damhuus, who lived on the edge of the Dirty Hole. And wherever he went the people were shocked by the news. The few Catholics in the polder nearly wept as they told one another, repeating again and again, O God, O God! the priest is dead! And the many, many farmers and field workers who had never been inside the little Catholic church but knew the priest as a good and noble man, heard it all with the same deep emotion: the priest is dead!

But still the bell kept ringing, ringing and bemoaning in its bronze voice, for when Kobus the sexton tired of pulling and crying, Teunis Trul followed and after him Jochum Sloor and Giel de Tuut and Daantje de Bietser. With sorrow in their hearts the humble farm hands spelled each other and pulled the bell each in turn, all morning and afternoon until night fell, and they gave their old shepherd a fine and solemn exit with sounding bells that cried for mercy from God, not for the saintly little priest who was surely in heaven now, but for the tired, defeated folk who remained behind.

Later that evening, when a brown monk arrived from across the Dirty Hole, they all gathered in the small church that was filled to the bursting point with sad little people, and they said their rosaries and implored the holy priest to intercede for his poor flock that was left without a shepherd.

And night fell over the wide polder, and the wind whispered in the scarce trees. The little houses crouched disconsolately around the tower that pointed toward the heavens like a long black finger. No star winked reassuringly from the firmament now; heavy clouds had drawn a thick veil, and toward midnight when the wind stopped whispering, a heavy rain fell bleakly over the land.

The priest is dead . . .

Sadness among the peasants.

The priest is dead . . .

Remorse for de Geus.

The priest is dead . . .

Christine weeps in her bed.

And de Geus lies awake. He has much to reflect about. He has great remorse, and black despair is eating at his heart. The sound of the bell reverberates in his head, and his thoughts won't leave him alone. All morning and all afternoon he heard the dark chiming of the bell until his ears rang and he pressed his fists against his head to shut out the voice. But then another voice came to life in his soul. The dead priest began talking to him. "God is love," said the old man. "He won't leave you alone."

De Geus jumped up. He wanted to drown the voice with great activity. But when he took his fists away from his ears, the sounds of the bell tumbled about and over him and resounded in the depths of his soul. He shuddered and feared he was going mad with the incessant chiming. He stood all alone in his pharmacy and balled his fists, lifting them to the gray sky, to the resounding tower, perhaps even to God Himself. But the chiming continued, and he seemed to be standing in a large glass bell filled with sound. He shouted to heaven in rage and ever-increasing anguish. Then he threw down one of his finest receptacles, knocking it to smithereens, and burst into a noiseless and senseless laughter. The laugh turned into a grin, he looked at the fragments of the receptacle, and at the sky that was turning a threatening gray.

"God!" he shouted, "I'm going mad! I'm going mad!" But deep in his heart sounded a voice that was stronger than the ringing bell and yet as soft and quiet as the voice of his dead friend.

"You're not going mad," said the voice. "You're merely being molded in God's almighty hands. God's love pursues you wherever you go. You can't escape Him!"

De Geus trembled. Never before had he felt God's presence so powerfully within, around and above him. He closes his ears again to the noises outside. The voice became stronger within him. He closed both eyes firmly, but then he saw his old friend in the white light, as he had sat in his armchair, gentle and fragile, but with the spark of conviction in his tired eyes at last.

"Tom de Geus," said the priest, "you're only a speck of dust in the hand of God. What do you have against Him? For as long as I've known you I've loved you. But I was too weak to fight you and too stupid to talk to you about God. Now I'm strong, my friend. I won't leave you again, and all the wisdom I tried to win you with, all the knowledge I begged God for in vain, seems utterly simple now. It's contained in a few words. God is love. God follows you everywhere, and He will be triumphant."

The little priest smiled gently, sweetly, but his face was so awesome that de Geus opened his eyes and looked around. The bell reverberated in his smarting head. The bell, always the bell! God will win. You're molded in His hands until . . .

De Geus sank into his chair and wept. He was so tired, so tired. "Yes, yes," he cried, "I know . . . God must win. . . . I can't fight Him! I know what I have to do, but I can't! God, everything would be all right, but that one thing! I'll do everything for You, but don't kick me so deep into Your heaven that I have to humiliate myself to—to . . ."

He didn't dare pronounce her name. He didn't want to think he had to go back where he started. He wanted to retrace all the steps that had led him away from God; he would crawl back on his knees along all the ways of error, if God wished him to do so, if he only could skip the starting point. He was broken and crushed and he stumbled out the door like a beaten man. A dull resignation came over him, and it seemed as though God were allowing him to catch his breath, the better to attack him later. The voice was silent. The sounds around him didn't concern him any longer. They were only a dull echo in his tired head.

He walked in the dusk on the lonesome dike crying like a small scared child. The wind blew squalls of rain on his face. What did it matter? A lost human, a beaten child walked over the dike and nobody saw him but God Who sees all, and He smiled at His handiwork. God shook His wise head; He knew He had beaten the stubborn human child, crushed him, but had not yet completely conquered him, and the child must follow the road to the bitter end where his error had begun. De Geus was converted through the death of his friend, through the power of God's love. But he still groaned under the weight of his pride. "God!" he said. "You may win, but don't ask for this one thing! Everything, but not that one thing; even for You I can't do it."

Then he stumbled over a clump of grass by the side of the road and fell flat against the dark earth, as though God had dealt him a final blow for that small spark of pride. He lay prone under the gray sky in a dull stupor. A small, formless spot, lost in the broad silence of the polder. No more thought . . . No rebellion . . . No pain. . . .

Silence and darkness all around. And rain over the polder.

One quiet day in late summer Dr. de Geus left for the city to fetch a woman again. But this time it was his own wife, to whom he'd spoken a few times during the last months and sent long, serious letters.

Krissie would stay another month. Her mother could no longer spare her. The sun hung low on the horizon like an exotic Chinese lantern and hesitated a moment before it faded; the Dirty Hole and the polder caught the last purple glow, and the dreamlike silhouettes of the cattle stood out against the even sky. High overhead a skylark sang a farewell to the dying day, and a tired human being looked at the singing speck with a bitter smile. Dr. de Geus looked across the polder before he drove down the cinder path to the ferry. He had made his appearance here not so long ago as a daring bad boy. A tired man now, with the wisdom of the years and the stamp of disillusion on his face, he was returning to the spot where he had started his wandering. To the woman God had given him. To love her—to protect her—to share love and sorrow with her. He had enjoyed the love greedily in those restless years when they were still young and eager and faced life with beautiful ideals. The sorrow had made him bitter and rebellious, unreasonable with his patient wife and arrogant toward God. He left his wife, abandoned God and came to the island as a lonely wanderer to hide from God and men. God is patient. But finally He called a halt and sent him back. De Geus fought violently and stubbornly. Now he was conquered by God's love. Now he was fetching her. He looked thoughtfully over the fields. The village, ridiculously small, stood far from the world. The little tower pointed skyward like a black finger. Around it crouched the small gray houses where poverty and sorrow huddled together and the tiny joys were rare. A poor little village with small, humble folk he had learned to love.

Tony the Ferry and his louts saw the doctor off. Silently the men stepped onto the ferry, scarcely daring to look at the quiet man huddled in his car and gazing back at the polder where night was falling.

"Will you stay away for long, Doctor?" asked Tony the Ferry in an oddly hoarse voice, as if it were good-bye forever.

"For a fortnight, Tony. But my replacement's coming tonight."

"We'll miss you," said Tony.

"It's only for a short time," murmured de Geus, moved by the simple expression of the little man's emotion.

The sun had set in the Dirty Hole. Darkness descended on the wide, vast polder. Far away, somewhere in the darkness, the house waited for his return. His and his wife's. The single bright star twinkled again; the eye of God the Father. Dr. de Geus looked at it as he drove faster toward the city, to Janette.

"It'll be all right," he mumbled. "It'll be all right."

ABOUT THE AUTHOR

ARIE VAN DER LUGT was born in 1917 in Vlaar-dingen, a fishing village in The Netherlands. He began to write detective stories while still a student at the gymnasium, and then published a whole series of juveniles. After finishing his studies of languages and psychology, he settled down for a few years as a teacher of English. Then he toured all over Holland with a group of amateur actors, putting on his own plays; thus far he has written over seventy plays, many of which have been very successful.

Mr. van der Lugt is the author of six novels in addition to *The Crazy Doctor*, but it is the first to be published in the United States. In between his novels he lectures and continues to turn out juveniles and plays. Mr. van der Lugt is married and has four children. He is fond of red roses, pancakes and America. In his spare time he is studying Spanish and Italian—to add to the six languages he speaks already.